THE
ARABIAN
NIGHTS

THE ARABIAN NIGHTS

Tales from the Thousand
and One Nights

THE ARABIAN NIGHTS

THE ARABIAN NIGHTS, a collection of more than 250 tales are called in Arabic *"The Thousand and One Nights."* According to the fiction which binds the collection together, the stories are told by Scheherazade to prevent her husband, the sultan Schariar, from killing her. Each night Scheherazade postpones the climax of her narrative to the following night, thus postponing, and eventually escaping entirely, the fate of her predecessors as wife to the sultan—death the day following the bridal night.

Many of the Arabic tales have been traced to Indic, Persian, Grecian, and Egyptian sources, and some possibly may have come from China and Japan. A simple form of their framework existed in papyrus as early as 2000 B. C., but they were originally related and handed down by traveling storytellers. Later, around 1450, they were transcribed by Egyptian scholars. Between 1704 and 1717, a French translation by Antoine Galland appeared, and since that time the tales have been translated into every principal language in the world. The best-known English translation is that of Sir Richard Burton (1885-88). With the exception of the Bible, no other compilation has so circled the globe. The seven voyages of Sinbad the Sailor, Ali Baba's encounter with the forty thieves, and many other events have become familiar to readers throughout the world.

Abounding with imagination and spiced with lively incidents, the tales present picture after picture of luxurious Eastern material splendor. For the most part, however, they are grounded on a description of the manners and customs of the medieval Moslem middle and lower classes, and concern themselves chiefly with myth and magic. In addition to story patterns common to fairly tales, they utilize beast fables, folk tales, simple anecdotes, stories with morals, and accounts of strange adventure and Arabic chivalry, love, valor, and military achievement. Harun-er-Rashid, whose nocturnal excursions through Baghdad provide the starting point of many of the tales, was introduced as a hero in the eighth century because the entertainers at his court wished to flatter him.

Contents

THE ARABIAN NIGHTS

The history of Codadad & his Brothers & of the Princess Deryabar

In the city of Harran there once lived a King who had every happiness which life and fortune could bestow save that he lacked an heir. Although, according to royal custom, he had in his household fifty wives, fair to look upon and affectionate in disposition, and though he continually invoked on these unions the blessing of Heaven, still he remained childless; for which cause all his joy was turned to affliction, and his wealth and power and magnificence became as of no account.

Now one night as he slept there appeared before him an old man of venerable appearance who, addressing him in mild accents, spoke thus: "The prayer of the faithful among fifty has been heard. Arise, therefore, and go into the gardens of your palace and cause the gardener to bring you a pomegranate fully ripe. Eat as many of the seeds as you desire children, and your wish shall be fulfilled."

Immediately upon awaking the King remembered the dream, and going down into the gardens of the palace he took fifty pomegranate seeds, and counting them one by one ate them all. So in due course, according to the promise of his dream, each of his wives gave birth to a son all about the same time. To this, however, there was an exception, for one of the fifty, whose name was Pirouzè, the fairest and the most honourably born, she alone, as time went on, showed no sign of that which was expected of her. Then was the King's anger kindled against her because in her alone the promise of his dream was not fulfilled; and deeming such a one hateful in the eyes of Heaven he was minded to put her to death. His vizier, however, dissuaded him. "Time alone can show," said he, "whether her demerits are so great as you now suppose. Let her go back to her own people and remain in banishment until the will of Heaven shall declare itself, and if within due time she give birth to a son then can she return to you with all honour." So the King did as his vizier advised, and sent Pirouzè back to her own country to the court of the Prince of Samaria; and there before long she who had seemed barren had the joy of becoming a mother and gave birth to a son whom she named Codadad, that is to say, "the Gift of God." Nevertheless, because the King of Harran had put upon her so public a disgrace, the Prince of Samaria would send no word to him of the event; so the young Prince was brought up at his uncle's court, and there he learned to ride and to shoot and to perform such warlike feats as become a prince, and in all that country he had no equal for accomplishment or courage.

Now one day, when Codadad had reached the age of eighteen, word came to him that his father the King of Harran was engaged in war and surrounded by enemies; so the Prince said to his mother, "Now is it time that I should go and prove myself worthy of my birth and the equal of my brethren; for here in Samaria all is peace and indolence, but in Harran are hardship and dangers, and great deeds waiting to be done." And his mother said to him, "O my son, since it seems good to thee, go; but how wilt thou declare thyself to thy father, or cause him to believe thy word, seeing that he is ignorant of thy birth?" Codadad answered, "I will so declare myself by my deeds that before my father knows the truth he shall wish that it were true."

So he departed and came in princely arms to the city of Harran, and there offered his service to the King against all his enemies. Now, no sooner had the King looked upon the youth than his heart was drawn toward him because of his beauty and the secret ties of blood; but when he asked from what country he came, Codadad answered, "I am the son of an emir of Cairo, and wherever there is war I go to win fame, nor do I care in what cause I fight so long as I be proved worthy."

The Prince was not slow in making his valour known; before long he had risen to the command of the whole army, not only over the heads of his brethren but also of the more experienced officers. And thereafter, when peace was re-established, the King, finding Codadad as prudent as he was valiant, appointed him governor to the young Princes.

Now this act, though justified by merit, could not fail to increase the hatred and jealousy which Codadad's brethren had long felt towards him. "What?" they cried, "shall this stranger not only steal from us the first place in the King's favour, but must we also be in obedience to his ruling and judgment? Surely if we do so we are no sons of a King."

So they conspired together how best to be rid of him. One said, "Let us fall upon him with our swords." "No, no," said another, "for so doing we shall but bring punishment upon ourselves. But let us so arrange matters as to draw on him the weight of the King's anger; thus shall our vengeance be made both safe and complete."

To this the other Princes agreed; so, forming a design which seemed favourable to their end, they approached Codadad, and besought his permission to go forth together on a hunting expedition, promising to return the same day. Codadad, deeming the request reasonable, immediately granted it: the brothers departed, but they did not return.

On the third day the King made inquiry as to the reason of their absence. Codadad replied that they were gone on a hunting expedition but had promised to return much sooner. Another day passed and the King grew anxious; yet another, and he became furious; and all his wrath was directed against Codadad. "O traitor," he cried, "why hast thou neglected thy trust and allowed my sons to go anywhere unaccompanied by thee? Now go instantly and search for them, and if thou find them not, be assured that on thy head shall fall the penalty."

At these words the Prince was filled with sudden foreboding, for he knew that the brothers had no love for him, and well could he see now the danger into which he had fallen. All he could do, however, was to obey; so, furnishing himself with arms and a horse good for travelling, he set out in search of his brethren.

After some days employed in a fruitless quest he came to a desolate tract in the midst of which stood a castle of black marble. As he approached he beheld at an upper window a damsel of marvellous beauty, with torn garments, dishevelled hair, and a countenance expressive of the most lively affliction, who immediately that she set eyes on him wrung her hands and waved him away, crying, "Oh, fly, fly from this place of death and the monster which inhabits it! For here lives a black giant which feeds on human flesh, seizing all he can find. Even now in his dungeons you may hear the cries of those whom for his next meal he will devour."

"Madam," replied the Prince, "for my safety you need have no care. Only be good enough to inform me who you are and how you came to be in your present plight." "I come from Cairo," she replied, "where my birth gives me rank. And as I was travelling from thence on my road to Bagdad this monstrous negro suddenly fell upon us, and having slain my escort brought me hither a captive, to endure, if Heaven refuses me succour, things far worse than death. But though I know my own peril, I will not see others perish in a vain attempt to rescue me, therefore once more I entreat you to fly ere it be too late!"

But even as she spoke, the negro, a horrible and gigantic monster of loathsome appearance, came in sight moving rapidly toward the palace. No sooner had he caught sight of the Prince than he rushed upon him with growls of fury, and drawing his scimitar aimed at him a blow which, had it found him, must there and then have ended the fight. The Prince, however, swerved nimbly under the stroke, and reaching his farthest, wounded the giant in the knee; then wheeling his charger about before the negro could turn on his maimed limb he attacked him from the rear, and with one fortunate blow brought him to earth. Instantly, before the giant could gather up his huge length and regain his vantage, Codadad spurred forward and with a single sweep of his sword smote off his head.

Meanwhile, all breathless above, the lady had leaned watching the contest. Now, seeing that victory was secured, she gave free vent to her joy and gratitude. "O Prince of men!" she cried, "now is revealed to me the high rank to which thou wast born. Finish, then, thy work; take from the girdle of yonder wretch the keys of the castle, and come quickly to the release of me and my fellow prisoners."

The Prince did according to her directions; as he opened the gates and entered the forecourt the lady advanced to meet him, ready, had he permitted it, to throw herself in gratitude at his feet. And now, as he beheld near at hand the beauty which had charmed him from a distance, Codadad realised how great had been his fortune, and with his whole heart rejoiced at the deliverance of one in whose nature so much virtue and grace seemed blended.

But while he was thus lost in the contemplation of her loveliness there arose from the basement of the castle a dreadful sound of crying and lamentation. "What is that?" inquired the Prince. "It is the cry of the prisoners," replied the lady, "to whom, I doubt not, the opening of the gates has betokened the monster's return. Come, therefore, quickly and relieve them of their misery." And so saying she pointed to the door which led to the place of confinement.

Thither, accompanied by the lady, went Codadad with all speed. Descending by a dark stair he came upon a vast cavern dimly lighted, around the walls of which a hundred prisoners lay chained. Instantly he set to work to loose their bonds, informing them at the same time of the death of their captor and of their freedom from all further danger. At these unexpected tidings the captives raised a cry of joy and thanksgiving; but great as was their surprise at such unlooked-for deliverance, greater still was that of the Prince when, on bringing them to the light, he discovered that forty-nine of the hundred whom he had released were his own brethren.

The Princes received the cordial embraces of their deliverer with little embarrassment, for the disaster into which they had fallen had caused them almost entirely to forget their original intent. Satisfied with expressing in proper terms their obligation and gratitude toward Codadad, they now joined eagerly in his survey of the castle; there upon examination·they found an extraordinary variety and wealth of booty, consisting for the most part of merchandise which the negro had pillaged from passing caravans, some of it actually belonging to those whom Codadad had so recently rescued.

The Prince accordingly ordered the merchants each to take what he recognised as his own; and this being done he divided the rest equally between them. The question then arose how they should remove their plunder from a place so desolately situated, where it would seem impossible to procure means of conveyance; but on a further search they found not only the camels of the merchants, but also the horses on which the Princes of Harran had ridden; and as at their ap-

[7]

proach the black slaves who were in charge of the stables fell into headlong flight, Codadad and his companions found themselves left in undisputed possession. The merchants therefore loaded their camels, and with renewed protestations of gratitude departed on the several roads by which their avocations called them.

When they were gone Codadad's next care was to inquire of the lady in what direction she wished to travel, promising that he and the Princes would conduct her in safety to any place she might name. The lady replied, thanking him for his generous offer. "But wherever I go," said she, "it cannot be to my own country, for not only is it too far distant, but cruel misfortune has separated me from it for ever. And since you have put me under so great an obligation, let me now confess the truth which before I thought it prudent to conceal. My dignity of rank is far higher than that to which I recently laid claim; in me you behold a King's daughter, and if it will interest you to hear the story of my misfortunes, I shall be happy to recount it." Assured of the lively sympathy of her auditors she began as follows:—

"My father was the King of a city among the isles named Deryabar, and I was his only child; for, in spite of his many prayers directed to that end, Heaven had not granted him a son. And for this cause, though he bestowed upon my education all imaginable care, the sight of me remained displeasing to him. In order the better to forget his sorrow he spent his days in hunting, and so he chanced on the event which led to all our misfortunes. For one day, as he was riding unattended in the forest, night overtook him and he knew not which way to turn. Presently in the distance he perceived a light, and advancing towards it he came upon a building which belonged to a monstrous negro; and hearing cries issuing from it, my father alighted. In the further corner of an enormous kitchen, before the fire of which an entire ox was roasting, lay a beautiful woman with hands bound, and a face betokening the deepest affliction; while at her feet a young child, between two and three years of age, stretched up its arms and wailed without ceasing.

"And as soon as the lady observed my father she cried out, imploring him to help her. And my father was filled with compassion and curiosity as to how she came to be in so sad a plight; and after he had cut her bonds she told him that she had been the wife of the chief of the Saracens, in whose service was an enormous negro of great strength in a position of trust. This, however, he had shamelessly betrayed; for having conceived a violent passion for his master's wife, he first persuaded the chief into an expedition which terminated in his death, and then returning in haste carried away by force not only the lady but her child also. But by the will of Allah her strength had sufficed to oppose the will of the negro, who every day after he had eaten and drunk, turned and addressed her saying, 'Charming Princess, why will you not accept the good things that are within your reach? Only yield to me the love that I demand and you will find in me the gentlest and most considerate of lords.' Upon that very day, however, so great had been the lady's loathing that she had been unable to refrain from crying out, 'Vile monster, every time I look at you does but increase my hatred towards you. Unchangeable as the foulness of your appearance is the disgust with which you inspire me.' At these words of violent provocation, so great had been the fury of the negro that after he had flung her into the corner in which she lay bound, he had mounted his horse, first threatening instant death to the lady and her child should she still refuse, upon his return, to comply with his demands. 'It is even now the hour of his return,' concluded the lady, 'and unless I can escape before then he will surely fulfil his threat.'

"But as she made an end of speaking a clatter of hoofs was heard in the distance; hearing which, wringing her hands, the lady started crying anew; whereupon, seeing that not a moment was to be lost, my father hurriedly mounted his horse, and spurred it towards that of the negro, who as soon as he observed my father, dashed forward brandishing his scimitar. But quicker than thought my father drew his bow and let fly an arrow with so good an aim that, pierced to the heart, the negro fell dead, after which my father re-entered the building and raised the lady from the swoon into which she had fallen.

"Thus," continued the Princess of Deryabar, "was the lady saved by my father from degradation, but though relieved of immediate danger, the wife of the Saracen chief was both solitary and friendless; for not only was she too far removed from her own land to return to it unaided, but she had small hope, should she ever arrive there, of securing for her son his rightful inheritance. This being the case, my father, moved with compassion, determined to adopt the child

[10]

as his own; and as the lady gratefully accepted his proposal, the next day as soon as it was light he returned to Deryabar bringing with him mother and son.

"Thus it came about that the son of a Saracen chief was brought up in my father's palace like a Prince of the blood royal; and so, on attaining to manhood, having both grace and good looks to recommend him, he came to forget the comparative lowliness of his origin, and aspiring to become my father's heir, had the presumption to demand my hand in marriage.

"A claim so audacious merited the severest punishment, yet my father merely remarked that he had other views concerning me, and with so lenient a rebuke would have passed the matter by. His refusal, however, excited in the proud youth the liveliest resentment; seeing that he could not obtain his ambition by fair means he immediately entered into conspiracy, and having treacherously slain my father, caused himself to be made King in his place. Fresh from this monstrous crime he renewed his suit for my hand, and was preparing to enforce it by violence, when the vizier, who alone of all my father's court had remained faithful to his memory, found means to convey me from the palace to a sailing vessel which was leaving harbour the same night.

"Here for a time I seemed to have reached safety, but when we had been only three days at sea a violent storm arose, and the ship, driving helplessly before it, struck upon a rock and went down, leaving as sole survivor the one who least wished to be spared. How I was saved I know not, nor how long I lay unfriended by the desolate shore upon which I had been cast; but scarcely had the consciousness of life returned to me when I heard a multitudinous sound of swift galloping; and presently, feeling myself lifted by men's hands, I turned and saw halting near me a troop of Arab horsemen, and at their head a youth royally arrayed and beautiful as the morning. Thus when my fortunes were at their lowest I beheld him whom Heaven had sent not only to afford me that deliverance of which I stood so much in need, but also to restore me to the rank due to my birth. For let me confess that after this young Prince had succoured me with the most tender solicitude, conducting me in all honour to his own palace and there lodging me under his mother's protection, I experienced towards him a feeling of duty and gratitude such as would have made his lightest wish my law. When, therefore, with an ardent and everincreasing devotion he desired me to become his bride, I could not, upon the completion of my recovery, refuse him the happiness he sought.

"But the festivities of our marriage were scarcely ended, when suddenly by night the city in which we dwelt was attacked by a band of travelling marauders. The attack was so unexpected and so well planned that the town was stormed and the garrison cut to pieces before any news of the event had reached the palace. Under cover of darkness we managed to escape, and fleeing to the sea shore took refuge on a small fishing boat, in which we immediately put out to sea, hoping to find in the rude winds and waves a safer shelter than our own walls had afforded us.

"For two days we drifted with wind and tide, not knowing

any better direction in which to turn; upon the third we perceived with relief a ship bearing down upon us, but as we watched its approach our satisfaction was soon changed to apprehension and dread, for we saw clearly that those on board were neither fishermen nor traders, but pirates. With rude shouts they boarded our small bark, and seizing my husband and myself, carried us captive to their own vessel. Here the one who was their leader advanced towards me and pulled aside my veil; whereupon a great clamour instantly arose among the crew, each contending for the possession of me. The dispute upon this point grew so warm that presently they fell to fighting; and a bitter and deadly conflict was maintained till at last only a single pirate was left. This one, who now regarded himself as my owner, proceeded to inform me of what was to be my fate. 'I have,' he said, 'a friend in Cairo who has promised me a rich reward if I can supply him with a slave more beautiful than any of those that his harem now contains. The distinction of earning me this reward shall be yours. But tell me,' he went on, turning towards the place where my husband stood bound, 'who is this youth that accompanies you? Is he a lover or a brother, or only a servant?' 'Sir,' said I, 'he is my husband.' 'In that case,' he replied, 'out of pity we must get rid of him, for I would not afflict him needlessly with the sight of another's happiness.' And so saying, he took my husband, all bound as he was, and threw him into the sea.

"So great was my grief at the sight of this cruel deed, that had I not been bound myself I should undoubtedly have sought the same end to my sufferings. But for the sake of future profit the pirate took the most watchful care of me, not only so long as we were on board the ship but also when, a few days later, we came to port and there joined ourselves to a large caravan which was about to start on the road to Cairo. While thus travelling in apparent safety, we were suddenly attacked by the terrible giant who lately owned this castle. After a long and dubious conflict the pirate, and all who stood by him, were slain, while I and those of the merchants who had remained timorously looking on were seized, and brought hither as prisoners destined as it seemed for a fate far more lingering and terrible. The rest of my story, brave Prince, I need not here recount, since the shaping of it was so largely in your own hands, and since to you alone is owed the happiness of its conclusion."

When the Princess of Deryabar had thus finished the tale of her wanderings, Codadad hastened to assure how deep was his sympathy in all her misfortunes. "But if you will allow yourself," he continued, "to be guided by me, your future life shall be one of safety and tranquillity. You have but to come as my bride, and the King of Harran will offer you an honourable welcome to his court; while, as regards myself, my whole life shall be devoted to securing for you that happiness which your grace and noble qualities prove that you deserve. And that you may not regard this proposal as too presumptuous, I have now to inform you, and also these Princes, concerning my birth and rank. For I, too, am a son of the King of Harran, born to him at the court of Samaria by his wife the Princess Pirouzè, whom he had sent unjustly into banishment."

THE HISTORY OF CODADAD

This declaration on the part of Codadad so accorded with the inclinations of the Princess that she at once yielded her consent, and as the castle was full of provisions suitable for the occasion, preparations were made first to solemnise the marriage, and then for all together to set forth on the return journey to Harran. As for the Princes, though they received Codadad's news with every outward protestation of joy, they were in fact more filled with apprehension and jealousy than before, for they could not but fear that his favour with the King would be greatly increased and become far more dangerous to their interests when the true facts of his birth were revealed. No sooner, therefore, had Codadad and the Princess passed to their nuptials, than his brethren entered into a conspiracy to slay him; and at the first halt upon the homeward journey, taking advantage of the lack of protection which a tent affords, they came upon their brother by night, and stabbing him in a hundred places as he lay asleep, left him for dead in the arms of his bride. They then broke up the camp and returned with all haste to the city of Harran, where, with a falsely invented tale they excused themselves to the King for their long absence.

In the meantime Codadad lay so spent by loss of blood that there remained in him no sign of life. The Princess, his wife, distraught with grief, had already given him up for dead. "O Heaven," she cried, bathing his body with her tears, "why am I thus ever condemned to bring on others disaster and death, and why for a second time have I been deprived of the one I was about to love?"

As thus she continued to cry in piteous lamentation, and to gaze on the senseless form lying before her, she thought that she perceived on the lips a faint motion of breath. At once her hope revived, and springing to her feet she ran instantly in the direction of the nearest village, hoping to find there a surgeon or one that had skill in the binding of wounds. Returning after a time with the aid that she had summoned, she found to her grief the place where Codadad had lain left vacant, nor was there any trace or indication of the fate which had overtaken him.

Overwhelmed by this final catastrophe, and believing that some wild beast must have devoured him, she suffered herself to be led away by the surgeon, who, in pity for one so greatly afflicted, placed her under the shelter of his own roof, and lavished upon her every mark of consideration and respect. So, when she had sufficiently recovered for her griefs to find utterance, he gathered from her own lips all the circumstances of her story, her name and rank, the high and valiant deeds of the Prince her husband, and the base ingratitude of his brethren. And perceiving that her grief and sufferings had so robbed her of the desire of life that without some end on which to direct her will she would presently pass into a decline, the surgeon endeavoured to arouse her to the pursuit of that just vengeance which the murder of her husband had earned. "Do not," he said, "let the death of so noble a Prince become a benefit to his enemies. Let us go together to the King of Harran, and make known to him the guilt of these wicked brethren. For surely the name of Codadad should live in story; but if you, whose honour he saved, now sink under your affliction, his name perishes with you, and you have not retrieved your debt."

These words roused the Princess from her deep despondency. Forming her resolution on the surgeon's advice, she arose instantly and prepared herself for the journey; and with such haste and diligence did she pursue her project, that within two days she and her companion arrived at the city of Harran.

Here strange news awaited them; for at all the caravanseri it was told how lately there had come to the city an exiled wife of the King, Princess Pirouzè by name, inquiring for news of her lost son; and how, as now appeared, this son had already been under a feigned designation at his father's court, and after performing many exploits and deeds of heroism had disappeared none knew whither. Forty-nine sons had the King by different wives, but all these, it was declared, he would willingly put to death so only that Codadad might be restored to him.

Now when the Princess of Deryabar heard this, she said, "I will go to the Queen Pirouzè and make known to her the fate of her son, and when we have wept together and drawn comfort from each other in our grief then we will go before the King, and demand vengeance on the murderers." But the surgeon said, "Have a care what you do; for if the Princes of Harran learn of your arrival, they will not rest till they have done to you as they did to your husband. Let us therefore proceed with secrecy, so as to ensure safety, and do you on no account let your presence here be known till the King has been thoroughly informed of the whole matter."

[17]

Then leaving the Princess in a place discreetly chosen he went forth into the streets and began to direct his steps towards the palace. Presently he was met by a lady mounted upon a mule richly caparisoned, and behind her followed a great troop of guards and attendants. As she approached, the populace ran out of their houses and stood in rows to see her go by, and when she passed all bowed down with their faces to the earth. The surgeon inquired of a beggar standing near whether this was one of the King's wives. "Yes, brother," replied the beggar, "and the best of them all; for she is the mother of Prince Codadad, whom, now that he is lost, all hold in love and reverence. And thus each day she goes to the mosque to hear the prayers which the King has ordered for her son's safe return."

Seeing his course now clear, the surgeon went and stood at the door of the mosque, waiting the Queen's departure; and when she came forth with all her attendants he plucked one of them by the sleeve and said to him, "If the Queen would have news of her son, Prince Codadad, let her send for the stranger who will be found waiting at the door of her palace." So, as soon as Pirouzè had returned to her apartments, the slave went in and gave his mistress the message. Then she sent in all haste and caused the surgeon to be brought before her. And the surgeon prostrated himself and said, "O Queen, let not the grief of the tidings which I bear be visited upon me but on them that were the cause of it!" And she answered him, "Have peace, and say on." So he told her, as has been here set forth, the full story of all the courage and prowess of Codadad, and of his generosity towards his brethren, also of his marriage to the Princess of Deryabar and of what followed after. But when he came to speak of the slaying of her son, the tender mother, as though receiving in her own body the strokes of the murderers, fell forward upon the ground, and there for a while lay motionless without sign of life. When, however, the surgeon, aided by her women, had restored her to consciousness, then Pirouzè, putting aside all personal grief, set her mind upon the accomplishment of the duty which now lay before her. "Go instantly," she said, "and tell the Princess of Deryabar that the King will shortly receive her with all the honour due to her rank. As for yourself, be assured that your services will be remembered."

Hardly had the surgeon departed, when the King himself entered, and the sight of his Queen's deep affliction at once informed him that something dreadful must have occurred. "Alas," she cried, "our son no longer exists, nor is it even possible to pay to his body those last rites which were due to his rank and virtue, for stricken by treacherous hands and left to perish unprotected he has fallen a prey to wild beasts so that not a trace of him remains." She then proceeded to inform her husband of all the horrible circumstances which the surgeon had narrated.

But before she had ended, the King became so transported with rage and grief that he could no longer delay the setting in motion of his just vengeance. Repairing in haste to the hall of audience, where courtiers and suitors stood waiting, he summoned to him his grand vizier with so much fury of countenance that all trembled for their lives. "Go instantly," he cried, "arrest all the Princes, and convey them under a strong guard to the prison assigned for murderers!" The vizier, not daring to question an order so terribly uttered, went forth and fulfilled the King's command with all speed. On his return to the palace for the presentation of his report, a further order almost equally surprising awaited him. The King described to him a certain inn lying in a poor quarter of the city. "Go thither," said he; "take with you slaves and high attendants, a white mule from the royal stables, and a guard of honour, and bring hither with all the respect due to her rank the young Princess whom you shall find there."

The vizier, with revived spirits, went forth to fulfil this second mission, so much more agreeable to him than the first; and presently there arose from the streets leading to the palace the acclamation of the populace because of the magnificence and splendour which announced the arrival of the unknown Princess. The King, as a token of respect, stood waiting at the palace gates to receive her, and taking her hand he led her to the apartments of the Queen Pirouzè. Here at the meeting of mother and wife a scene of the most tender and heart-rending affliction took place. The King himself was so moved by it that he had not the heart to refuse to them any request. So when they came and besought for the absent those funeral honours which under other circumstances would have been his due, he gave orders for a dome of marble to be erected on the plain by which the city of Harran lies surrounded. And with such speed was the work put in hand, and so large was the number of men employed upon it, that within three days the entire building was completed.

On the day following the obsequies began. All was done with the greatest solemnity and splendour. First came the King attended by his vizier and all the officers and lords of his palace; and entering the tomb, in which lay an effigy of Codadad, they seated themselves on carpets of mourning bordered with gold. Then followed the chiefs of the army mounted upon horses and bewailing the loss of him who had led them to victory; behind these came old men upon black mules, with long robes and flowing beards; and after these maidens on white horses, with heads unveiled, bearing in their hands baskets of precious stones. Now when these had approached and compassed the dome three times about, then the King rose up to speak the dismissal of the dead. Touching with his brow the tomb whereon the effigy lay, he cried in a loud voice, "O my dear son, O light of mine eyes, O joy that is lost to me for ever!" After him all the lords and the chiefs and the elders came and prostrated themselves in like manner; and when the ceremony was ended, the doors of the tomb were shut and all the people returned to the city.

Now after this there was prayer and fasting in the mosque for eight days, and on the ninth the King gave orders that the Princes were to be beheaded. But meanwhile the neighbouring powers, whose arms the King of Harran had defeated, as soon as they heard that Codadad was dead, banded themselves together in strong alliance, and with a great host began to advance upon the city. Then the King caused the execution to be postponed, and making a hasty levy of his forces went forth to meet the enemy in the open plain. And there battle was joined with such valour and determination on both sides that for a time the issue remained doubtful Nevertheless, because the men of Harran were fewer in number they began to be surrounded by their enemies. But at the very moment when all seemed lost, they saw in the distance a large body of horsemen advancing at the charge; and while both combatants were yet uncertain of their purpose, these fell furiously and without warning upon the ranks of the allies, and throwing them into sudden disorder drove them in rout from the field.

With the success of their arms thus established, the two leaders of the victorious forces advanced to meet each other in the presence of the whole army, and great was the joy and astonishment of the King when he discovered in the leader of the late-arrived troop his lost son Codadad. The Prince, for his part, was equally delighted to find in his father's welcome the recognition for which he had yearned.

When the long transport of their meeting embrace was over, the Prince, as they began to converse, perceived with surprise how much was already known to the King of past events. "What?" he inquired, "has one of my brothers awakened to his guilt, and confessed that which I had meant should ever remain a secret?" "Not so," replied the King; "From the Princess of Deryabar alone have I learned the truth. For she it was who came to demand vengeance for the crime which your brothers would still have concealed."

At this unlooked-for news of the safety of the Princess and of her arrival at his father's court, Codadad's joy was beyond words, and greatly was it increased when he heard of his mother's reinstatement in the King's favour with the honour and dignity due to her rank. He now began to perceive how events had shaped themselves in his absence, and how the King had already become informed of the bond that existed between them. As for the rest of his adventures, together with the circumstance which had led to his disappearance and supposed death, they were soon explained. For when the Princess had left Codadad in her desperate search for aid, there chanced that way a travelling pedlar; and he, finding the youth apparently deserted and dying of his wounds, took pity on him, and placing him upon his mule bore him to his own house. There with medicinal herbs and simple arts unknown in the palaces of kings he had accomplished a cure which others would have thought impossible, so that in a short time Codadad's strength was completely restored. Thereupon the Prince, impatient for reunion with those whom he loved, bestowed on the pedlar all the wealth that he possessed, and immediately set forth toward the city of Harran.

On the road news reached him of the fresh outbreak of hostilities followed by the invasion of his father's territory. Passing from village to village he roused and armed the inhabitants, and by the excellence of his example made such soldiers of them that they were able in the fortunate moment of their arrival to decide the issue of the conflict and give victory to the King's arms.

"And now, sire," said the Prince in conclusion, "I have only one request to make: since in the event all things have turned out so happily, I beg you to pardon my brothers in order that I may prove to them in the future how groundless were the resentment and jealousy that they felt toward me."

These generous sentiments drew tears from the King's eyes and removed from his mind all doubt as to the wisdom of the resolution he had been forming. Immediately before the assembled army he declared Codadad his heir, and, as an act of grace to celebrate his son's return, gave orders for the Princes to be released. He then led Codadad with all speed to the palace, where Pirouzè and her daughter-in-law were anxiously awaiting them.

In the joy of that meeting the Prince and his wife were repaid a thousandfold for all the griefs and hardships they had undergone: and their delight in each other's society remained so great that in all the world no happiness has been known to equal it. The Princes half died of shame when the means by which their pardon had been procured was revealed to them; but before long the natural insensibility of their characters reasserted itself and they recovered.

IN a town in Persia lived two brothers named Cassim and
Ali Baba, between whom their father at his death had left
what little property he possessed equally divided. Cassim,
however, having married the heiress of a rich merchant,
became soon after his marriage the owner of a fine shop,
together with several pieces of land, and was in consequence,
through no effort of his own, the most considerable merchant
in the town. Ali Baba, on the other hand, was married
to one as poor as himself, and having no other means of
gaining a livelihood, he used to go every day into the forest
to cut wood, and lading therewith the three asses which were
his sole stock-in-trade, would then hawk it about the streets
for sale.

One day while he was at work within the skirts of the
forest, Ali Baba saw advancing towards him across the open
a large company of horsemen, and fearing from their appearance that they might be robbers, he left his asses to
their own devices and sought safety for himself in the lower
branches of a large tree which grew in the close overshadow-
ing of a precipitous rock.

Almost immediately it became evident that this very rock
was the goal toward which the troop was bound, for having
arrived they alighted instantly from their horses, and took

down each man of them a sack which seemed by its weight and form to be filled with gold. There could no longer be any doubt that they were robbers. Ali Baba counted forty of them.

Just as he had done so, the one nearest to him, who seemed to be their chief, advanced toward the rock, and in a low but distinct voice uttered the two words, "Open, Sesamé!" Immediately the rock opened like a door, the captain and his men passed in, and the rock closed behind them.

For a long while Ali Baba waited, not daring to descend from his hiding-place lest they should come out and catch him in the act; but at last, when the waiting had grown almost unbearable, his patience was rewarded, the door in the rock opened, and out came the forty men, their captain leading them. When the last of them was through, "Shut, Sesamé!" said the captain, and immediately the face of the rock closed together as before. Then they all mounted their horses and rode away.

As soon as he felt sure that they were not returning, Ali Baba came down from the tree and made his way at once to that part of the rock where he had seen the captain and his men enter. And there at the word "Open, Sesamé!" a door suddenly revealed itself and opened.

Ali Baba had expected to find a dark and gloomy cavern. Great was his astonishment, therefore, when he perceived a spacious and vaulted chamber lighted from above through a fissure in the rock; and there spread out before him lay treasures in profusion, bales of merchandise, silks, carpets, brocades, and above all gold and silver lying in loose heaps or in sacks piled one upon another. He did not take long to consider what he should do. Disregarding the silver and the gold that lay loose, he brought to the mouth of the cave as many sacks of gold as he thought his three asses might carry; and having loaded them on and covered them with wood so that they might not be seen, he closed the rock by the utterance of the magic words which he had learned, and departed for the town, a well-satisfied man.

When he got home he drove his asses into a small court, and shutting the gates carefully he took off the wood that covered the bags and carried them in to his wife. She, discovering them to be full of gold, feared that her husband had stolen them, and began sorrowfully to reproach him; but Ali Baba soon put her mind at rest on that score, and having poured all the gold into a great heap upon the floor, he sat down at her side to consider how well it looked.

Soon his wife, poor, careful body, must needs begin counting it over piece by piece. Ali Baba let her go on for a while, but before long the sight set him laughing. "Wife," said he, "you will never make an end of it that way. The best thing to do is to dig a hole and bury it, then we shall be sure that it is not slipping through our fingers." "That will do well enough," said his wife, "but it would be better first to have the measure of it. So while you dig the hole I will go round to Cassim's and borrow a measure small enough to give us an exact reckoning." "Do as you will," answered her husband, "but see that you keep the thing secret."

Off went Ali Baba's wife to her brother-in-law's house. Cassim was from home, so she begged of his wife the loan of a small measure, naming for choice the smallest. This set the sister-in-law wondering. Knowing Ali Baba's poverty she was all the more curious to find out for what kind of grain so small a measure could be needed. So before bringing it she covered all the bottom with lard, and giving it to Ali Baba's wife, told her to be sure and be quick in returning it. The other, promising to restore it punctually, made haste to get home; and there finding the hole dug for its reception she started to measure the money into it. First she set the measure upon the heap, then she filled it, then she carried it to the hole; and so she continued till the last measure was counted. Then, leaving Ali Baba to finish the burying, she carried back the measure with all haste to her sister-in-law, returning thanks for the loan.

No sooner was her back turned than Cassim's wife looked at the bottom of the measure, and there to her astonishment she saw sticking to the lard a gold coin. "What?" she cried, her heart filled with envy, "is Ali Baba so rich that he needs a measure for his gold? Where, then, I would know, has the miserable wretch obtained it?"

She waited with impatience for her husband's return, and as soon as he came in she began to jeer at him. "You think yourself rich," said she, "but Ali Baba is richer. You count your gold by the piece; but Ali Baba does not count, he measures it! In comparison to Ali Baba we are but grubs and groundlings!"

Having thus riddled him to the top of her bent in order

ALI BABA AND THE FORTY THIEVES

to provoke his curiosity, she told him the story of the borrowed measure, of her own stratagem, and of its result.

Cassim, instead of being pleased at Ali Baba's sudden prosperity, grew furiously jealous; not a wink could he sleep all night for thinking of it. The next morning before sunrise he went to his brother's house. "Ali Baba," said he, "what do you mean by pretending to be poor when all the time you are scooping up gold by the quart?" "Brother," said Ali Baba, "explain your meaning." "My meaning shall be plain!" cried Cassim, displaying the telltale coin. "How many more pieces have you like this that my wife found sticking to the bottom of the measure yesterday?"

Ali Baba, perceiving that the intervention of wives had made further concealment useless, told his brother the true facts of the case, and offered him, as an inducement for keeping the secret, an equal share of the treasure.

"That is the least that I have the right to expect," answered Cassim haughtily. "It is further necessary that you should tell me exactly where the treasure lies, that I may, if need be, test the truth of your story, otherwise I shall find it my duty to denounce you to the authorities."

Ali Baba, having a clear conscience, had little fear of Cassim's threats; but out of pure good nature he gave him all the information he desired, not forgetting to instruct him in the words which would give him free passage into the cave and out again.

Cassim, who had thus secured all he had come for, lost no time in putting his project into execution. Intent on

[29]

possessing himself of all the treasures which yet remained, he set off the next morning before daybreak, taking with him ten mules laden with empty crates. Arrived before the cave he recalled the words which his brother had taught him; no sooner was "Open, Sesamé!" said than the door in the rock lay wide for him to pass through, and when he had entered it shut again.

If the simple soul of Ali Baba had found delight in the riches of the cavern, greater still was the exultation of a greedy nature like Cassim's. Intoxicated with the wealth that lay before his eyes, he had no thought but to gather together with all speed as much treasure as the ten mules could carry; and so, having exhausted himself with heavy labour and avaricious excitement, he suddenly found on returning to the door that he had forgotten the key which opened it. Up and down, and in and out through the mazes of his brain he chased the missing word. Barley, and maize, and rice, he thought of them all: but of sesamé never once, because his mind had become dark to the revealing light of heaven. And so the door stayed fast, holding him prisoner in the cave, where to his fate, undeserving of pity, we leave him.

Toward noon the robbers returned, and saw, standing about the rock, the ten mules laden with crates. At this they were greatly surprised, and began to search with suspicion amongst the surrounding crannies and undergrowth. Finding no one there, they drew their swords and advanced cautiously toward the cave, where, upon the captain's pronouncement of the magic word, the door immediately fell open. Cassim, who from within had heard the trampling of horses, had now no doubt that the robbers were arrived and that his hour was come. Resolved, however, to make one last effort at escape, he stood ready by the door; and no sooner had the opening word been uttered than he sprang forth with such violence that he threw the captain to the ground. But his attempt was vain: before he could break through he was mercilessly hacked down by the swords of the robber band.

With their fears thus verified, the robbers anxiously entered the cave to view the traces of its late visitant. There they saw piled by the door the treasure which Cassim had sought to carry away; but while restoring this to its place they failed altogether to detect the earlier loss which Ali Baba had caused them. Reckoning, however, that as one had discovered the secret of entry others also might know of it, they determined to leave an example for any who might venture thither on a similar errand; and having quartered the body of Cassim, they disposed it at the entrance in a manner most calculated to strike horror into the heart of the beholder. Then, closing the door of the cave, they rode away in the search of fresh exploits and plunder.

Meanwhile Cassim's wife had grown very uneasy at her husband's prolonged absence; and at nightfall, unable to endure further suspense, she ran to Ali Baba, and telling him of his brother's secret expedition, entreated him to go out instantly in search of him.

Ali Baba had too kind a heart to refuse or delay comfort to her affliction. Taking with him his three asses he set out immediately for the forest, and as the road was familiar to him he had soon found his way to the door of the cave. When he saw there the traces of blood he became filled with misgiving, but no sooner had he entered than his worst fears were realized. Nevertheless brotherly pity gave him courage. Gathering together the severed remains and wrapping them about with all possible decency, he laid them upon one of the asses; then bethinking him that he deserved some payment for his pains, he loaded the two remaining asses with sacks of gold, and covering them with wood as on the first occasion, made his way back to the town while it was yet early. Leaving his wife to dispose of the treasure borne by the two asses, he led the third to his sister-in-law's house, and knocking quietly so that none of the neighbours might hear, was presently admitted by Morgiana, a female slave whose intelligence and discretion had long been known to him. "Morgiana," said he, "there's trouble on the back of that ass. Can you keep a secret?" And Morgiana's nod satisfied him better than any oath. "Well," said he, "your master's body lies there waiting to be pieced, and our business now is to bury him honourably as though he had died a natural death. Go and tell your mistress that I want to speak to her."

Morgiana went in to her mistress, and returning presently bade Ali Baba enter. Then, leaving him to break to his sister-in-law the news and the sad circumstances of his brother's death, she, with her plan already formed, hastened forth and knocked at the door of the nearest apothecary. As soon as he opened to her she required of him in trembling agitation certain pillules efficacious against grave disorders, declaring in answer to his questions that her master had been taken suddenly ill. With these she returned home, and her plan of concealment having been explained and agreed upon much to the satisfaction of Ali Baba, she went forth the next morning to the same apothecary, and with tears in her eyes besought him to supply her in haste with a certain drug that is given to sick people only in the last extremity. Meanwhile the rumour of Cassim's sickness had got abroad; Ali Baba and his wife had been seen coming and going, while Morgiana by her ceaseless activity had made the two days' pretended illness seem like a fortnight; so when a sound of wailing arose within the house all the neighbours concluded without further question that Cassim had died a natural and honourable death.

But Morgiana had now a still more difficult task to perform, it being necessary for the obsequies that the body should be made in some way presentable. So at a very early hour the next morning she went to the shop of a certain merry old cobbler, Baba Mustapha by name, who lived on the other side of the town. Showing him a piece of gold she inquired whether he were ready to earn it by exercising his craft in implicit obedience to her instructions. And when Baba Mustapha sought to know the terms, "First," said she, "you must come with your eyes bandaged; secondly, you must sew what I put before you without asking question; and thirdly, when you return you must tell nobody."

Mustapha, who had a lively curiosity into other folk's affairs, boggled for a time at the bandaging, and doubted much of his ability to refrain from questioning; but having on these considerations secured the doubling of his fee, he promised secrecy readily enough, and taking his cobbler's tackle in hand submitted himself to Morgiana's guidance and set forth. This way and that she led him blindfold, till she had brought him to the house of her deceased master. Then uncovering his eyes in the presence of the dismembered corpse, she bade him get out thread and wax and join the pieces together.

Baba Mustapha plied his task according to the compact, asking no question. When he had done, Morgiana again bandaged his eyes and led him home, and giving him a third piece of gold the more to satisfy him, she bade him good-day and departed.

So in seemliness and without scandal of any kind were the obsequies of the murdered Cassim performed. And when all was ended, seeing that his widow was desolate and his house in need of a protector, Ali Baba with brotherly pity took both the one and the other into his care, marrying his sister-in-law according to Moslem rule, and removing with all his goods and newly-acquired treasure to the house which had been his brother's. And having also acquired the shop where Cassim had done business, he put into it his own son, who had already served an apprenticeship to the trade. So, with his fortune well established, let us now leave Ali Baba and return to the robbers' cave.

Thither, at the appointed time, came the forty robbers, bearing in hand fresh booty; and great was their consternation to discover that not only had the body of Cassim been removed, but a good many sacks of gold as well. It was no wonder that this should trouble them, for so long as any one could command secret access, the cave was useless as a depository for their wealth. The question was, What could they do to put an end to their present insecurity? After long debate it was agreed that one of their number should go into the town disguised as a traveller, and there, mixing with the common people, learn from their report whether there had been recently any case in their midst of sudden prosperity or sudden death. If such a thing could be discovered, then they made sure of tracking the evil to its source and imposing a remedy.

Although the penalty for failure was death, one of the robbers at once boldly offered himself for the venture, and having transformed himself by disguise and received the wise counsels and commendations of his fellows, he set out for the town.

Arriving at dawn he began to walk up and down the streets and watch the early stirring of the inhabitants. So, before long, he drew up at the door of Baba Mustapha, who, though old, was already seated at work upon his cobbler's bench. The robber accosted him. "I wonder," said he, "to see a man of your age at work so early. Does not so dull a light strain your eyes?" "Not so much as you might think," answered Baba Mustapha. "Why, it was but the other day that at this same hour I saw well enough to stitch up a dead body in a place where it was certainly no lighter." "Stitch up a dead body!" cried the robber, in pretended amazement, concealing his joy at this sudden intelligence. "Surely you mean in its winding sheet, for how else can a dead body be stitched?" "No, no," said Mustapha; "what I say I mean; but as it is a secret, I can tell you no more." The robber drew out a piece of gold. "Come," said he, "tell me nothing you do not care to; only show me the house where lay the body that you stitched." Baba Mustapha eyed the gold longingly. "Would that I could," he replied; "but, alas! I went to it blindfold." "Well," said the robber, "I have heard that a blind man remembers his road; perhaps, though seeing you might lose it, blindfold you might find it again." Tempted by the offer of a second piece of gold, Baba Mustapha was soon persuaded to make the attempt. "It was here that I started," said he, showing the spot, "and I turned as you see me now." The robber then put a bandage over his eyes, and walked beside him through the streets, partly guiding and partly being led, till of his own accord Baba Mustapha stopped. "It was here," said he. "The door by which I went in should now lie to the right." And he had in fact come exactly opposite to the house which had once been Cassim's, where Ali Baba now dwelt.

The robber, having marked the door with a piece of chalk which he had provided for the purpose, removed the bandage from Mustapha's eyes, and, leaving him to his own devices, returned with all possible speed to the cave where his comrades were awaiting him.

Soon after the robber and cobbler had parted, Morgiana happened to go out upon an errand, and as she returned she noticed the mark upon the door. "This," she thought, "is not as it should be; either some trick is intended, or there is evil brewing for my master's house." Taking a piece of chalk, she put a similar mark upon the five or six doors lying to right and left; and having done this she went home with her mind satisfied, saying nothing.

In the meantime the robbers had learned from their companion the success of his venture. Greatly elated at the thought of the vengeance so soon to be theirs, they formed a plan for entering the city in a manner that should arouse no suspicion among the inhabitants. Passing in by twos and threes, and by different routes, they came together to the market-place at an appointed time, while the captain and the robber who had acted as spy made their way alone to the street in which the marked door was to be found. Presently, just as they had expected, they perceived a door with the mark on it. "That is it!" said the robber; but as they continued walking so as to avoid suspicion, they came upon another and another, till, before they were done, they had passed six in succession. So alike were the marks that the spy, though he swore he had made but one, could not tell which it was. Seeing that the design had failed, the captain returned to the market-place, and having passed the word for his troop to go back in the same way as they had come, he himself set the example of retreat.

When they were all reassembled in the forest, the captain explained how the matter had fallen, and the spy, acquiescing in his own condemnation, kneeled down and received the stroke of the executioner.

But as it was still necessary for the safety of all that so great a trespass and theft should not pass unavenged, another

of the band, undeterred by the fate of his comrade, volun-
teered upon the same conditions to prosecute the quest
wherein the other had failed. Coming by the same means
to the house of Ali Baba, he set upon the door, at a spot
not likely to be noticed, a mark in red chalk to distinguish it
clearly from those which were already marked in white.
But even this precaution failed of its end. Morgiana, whose
eye nothing could escape, noticed the red mark at the first
time of passing, and dealt with it just as she had done with
the previous one. So when the robbers came, hoping this
time to light upon the door without fail, they found not one
but six all similarly marked with red.

When the second spy had received the due reward of his
blunder, the captain considered how by trusting to others he
had come to lose two of his bravest followers, so the third
attempt he determined to conduct in person. Having found
his way to Ali Baba's door, as the two others had done by the
aid of Baba Mustapha, he did not set any mark upon it, but
examined it so carefully that he could not in future mistake
it. He then returned to the forest and communicated to
his band the plan which he had formed. This was to go into
the town in the disguise of an oil-merchant, bearing with him
upon nineteen mules thirty-eight large leather jars, one of
which, as a sample, was to be full of oil, but all the others
empty. In these he purposed to conceal the thirty-seven
robbers to which his band was now reduced, and so to convey
his full force to the scene of action in such a manner as to
arouse no suspicion till the signal for vengeance should be
given.

Within a couple of days he had secured all the mules and jars that were requisite, and having disposed of his troop according to the pre-arranged plan, he drove his train of well-laden mules to the gates of the city, through which he passed just before sunset. Proceeding thence to Ali Baba's house, and arriving as it fell dark, he was about to knock and crave a lodging for the night, when he perceived Ali Baba at the door enjoying the fresh air after supper. Addressing him in tones of respect, "Sir," said he, "I have brought my oil a great distance to sell to-morrow in the market; and at this late hour, being a stranger, I know not where to seek for a shelter. If it is not troubling you too much, allow me to stable my beasts here for the night."

The captain's voice was now so changed from its accustomed tone of command, that Ali Baba, though he had heard it before, did not recognise it. Not only did he grant the stranger's request for bare accommodation, but as soon as the unlading and stabling of the mules had been accomplished, he invited him to stay no longer in the outer court but enter the house as his guest. The captain, whose plans this proposal somewhat disarranged, endeavoured to excuse himself from a pretended reluctance to give trouble; but since Ali Baba would take no refusal he was forced at last to yield and to submit with apparent complaisance to an entertainment which the hospitality of his host extended to a late hour.

When they were about to retire for the night, Ali Baba went into the kitchen to speak to Morgiana; and the captain of the robbers, on the pretext of going to look after his mules, slipped out into the yard where the oil jars were standing in line. Passing from jar to jar he whispered into each, "When you hear a handful of pebbles fall from the window of the chamber where I am lodged, then cut your way out of the jar and make ready, for the time will have come." He then returned to the house, where Morgiana came with a light and conducted him to his chamber.

Now Ali Baba, before going to bed, had said to Morgiana, "To-morrow at dawn I am going to the baths; let my bathing-linen be put ready, and see that the cook has some good broth prepared for me against my return." Having therefore led the guest up to his chamber, Morgiana returned to the kitchen and ordered Abdallah the cook to put on the pot for the broth. Suddenly while she was skimming it, the lamp went out, and, on searching, she found there was no more oil in the house. At so late an hour no shop would be open, yet somehow the broth had to be made, and that could not be done without a light. "As for that," said Abdallah, seeing her perplexity, "why trouble yourself? There is plenty of oil out in the yard." "Why, to be sure!" said Morgiana, and sending Abdallah to bed so that he might be up in time to wake his master on the morrow, she took the oil-can herself and went out into the court. As she approached the jar which stood nearest, she heard a voice within say, "Is it time?"

To one of Morgiana's intelligence an oil-jar that spoke was an object of even more suspicion than a chalk-mark on a door, and in an instant she apprehended what danger for her master and his family might lie concealed around her.

Understanding well enough that an oil-jar which asked a question required an answer, she replied quick as thought and without the least sign of perturbation, "Not yet, but presently." And thus she passed from jar to jar, thirty-seven in all, giving the same answer, till she came to the one which contained the oil.

The situation was now clear to her. Aware of the source from which her master had acquired his wealth, she guessed at once that, in extending shelter to the oil-merchant, Ali Baba had in fact admitted to his house the robber captain and his band. On the instant her resolution was formed. Having filled the oil-can she returned to the kitchen; there she lighted the lamp, and then, taking a large kettle, went back once more to the jar which contained the oil. Filling the kettle she carried it back to the kitchen, and putting under it a great fire of wood had soon brought it to the boil. Then taking it in hand once more, she went out into the yard and poured into each jar in turn a sufficient quantity of the boiling oil to scald its occupant to death.

She then returned to the kitchen, and having made Ali Baba's broth, put out the fire, blew out the lamp, and sat down by the window to watch.

Before long the captain of the robbers awoke from the short sleep which he had allowed himself, and finding that all was silent in the house, he rose softly and opened the window. Below stood the oil-jars; gently into their midst he threw the handful of pebbles agreed on as a signal; but from the oil-jars came no answer. He threw a second and a third time; yet though he could hear the pebbles falling among the jars, there followed only the silence of the dead. Wondering whether his band had fled leaving him in the lurch, or whether they were all asleep, he grew uneasy, and descending in haste, made his way into the court. As he approached the first jar a smell of burning and hot oil assailed his nostrils, and looking within he beheld in rigid contortion the dead body of his comrade. In every jar the same sight presented itself till he came to the one which had contained the oil. There, in what was missing, the means and manner of his companions' death were made clear to him. Aghast at the discovery and awake to the danger that now threatened him, he did not delay an instant, but forcing the garden gate, and thence climbing from wall to wall, he made his escape out of the city.

When Morgiana, who had remained all this time on the watch, was assured of his final departure, she put her master's bath-linen ready, and went to bed well satisfied with her day's work.

The next morning Ali Baba, awakened by his slave, went to the baths before daybreak. On his return he was greatly surprised to find that the merchant was gone, leaving his mules and oil-jars behind him. He inquired of Morgiana the reason. "You will find the reason," said she, "if you look into the first jar you come to." Ali Baba did so, and, seeing a man, started back with a cry. "Do not be afraid," said Morgiana, "he is dead and harmless; and so are all the others whom you will find if you look further."

As Ali Baba went from one jar to another, finding always the same sight of horror within, his knees trembled under him; and when he came at last to the one empty oil-jar, he stood for a time motionless, turning upon Morgiana eyes of wonder and inquiry. "And what," he said then, "has become of the merchant?" "To tell you that," said Morgiana, "will be to tell you the whole story; you will be better able to hear it if you have your broth first."

But the curiosity of Ali Baba was far too great: he would not be kept waiting. So without further delay she gave him the whole history, so far as she knew it, from beginning to end; and by her intelligent putting of one thing against another, she left him at last in no possible doubt as to the source and nature of the conspiracy which her quick wits had so happily defeated. "And now, dear master," she said in conclusion, "continue to be on your guard, for though all these are dead, one remains alive; and he, if I mistake not, is the captain of the band, and for that reason the more formidable, and the more likely to cherish the hope of vengeance."

When Morgiana had done speaking Ali Baba clearly perceived that he owed to her not merely the protection of his property but life itself. His heart was full of gratitude. "Do not doubt," he said, "that before I die I will reward you as you deserve; and as an immediate proof from this moment I give you your liberty."

This token of his approval filled Morgiana's heart with delight, but she had no intention of leaving so kind a master, even had she been sure that all danger was now over. The immediate question which next presented itself was how to dispose of the bodies. Luckily at the far end of the garden stood a thick grove of trees, and under these Ali Baba was able to dig a large trench without attracting the notice of his neighbours. Here the remains of the thirty-seven robbers were laid side by side, the trench was filled again, and the ground made level. As for the mules, since Ali Baba had no use for them, he sent them, one or two at a time, to the market to be sold.

Meanwhile the robber captain had fled back to the forest. Entering the cave he was overcome by its gloom and loneliness. "Alas!" he cried, "my comrades, partners in my adventures, sharers of my fortune, how shall I endure to live without you? Why did I lead you to a fate where valour was of no avail, and where death turned you into objects of ridicule? Surely had you died sword in hand my sorrow had been less bitter! And now what remains for me but to take vengeance for your death and to prove, by achieving it without aid, that I was worthy to be the captain of such a band!"

Thus resolved, at an early hour the next day, he assumed a disguise suitable to his purpose, and going to the town took lodging in a khan. Entering into conversation with his host he inquired whether anything of interest had happened recently in the town; but the other, though full of gossip, had nothing to tell him concerning the matter in which he was most interested, for Ali Baba, having to conceal from all the source of his wealth, had also to be silent as to the dangers in which it involved him.

The captain then inquired whether there was a shop for hire; and hearing of one that suited him, he came to terms with the owner, and before long had furnished it with all kinds of rich stuffs and carpets and jewelry which he brought by degrees with great secrecy from the cave.

Now this shop happened to be opposite to that which had belonged to Cassim and was now occupied by the son of Ali Baba; so before long the son and the new-comer, who had assumed the name of Cogia Houssain, became acquainted; and as the youth had good looks, kind manners, and a sociable disposition, it was not long before the acquaintance became intimate.

Cogia Houssain did all he could to seal the pretended friendship, the more so as it had not taken him long to discover how the young man and Ali Baba were related; so, plying him constantly with small presents and acts of hospitality, he forced on him the obligation of making some return.

Ali Baba's son, however, had not at his lodging sufficient accommodation for entertainment; he therefore told his father of the difficulty in which Cogia Houssain's favours had placed him, and Ali Baba with great willingness at once offered to arrange matters. "My son," said he, "to-morrow being a holiday, all shops will be closed; then do you after dinner invite Cogia Houssain to walk with you; and as you return bring him this way and beg him to come in. That will be better than a formal invitation, and Morgiana shall have a supper prepared for you."

This proposal was exactly what Ali Baba's son could have wished, so on the morrow he brought Cogia Houssain to the door as if by accident, and, stopping, invited him to enter.

Cogia Houssain, who saw his object thus suddenly attained, began by showing pretended reluctance, but Ali Baba himself coming to the door, pressed him in the most kindly manner to enter, and before long had conducted him to the table, where food stood prepared.

But there an unlooked-for difficulty arose. Wicked though he might be, the robber captain was not so impious as to eat the salt of the man he intended to kill. He therefore began with many apologies to excuse himself; and when Ali Baba sought to know the reason, "Sir," said he, "I am sure that if you knew the cause of my resolution you would approve of it. Suffice it to say that I have made it a rule to eat of no dish that has salt in it. How then can I sit down at your table if I must reject everything that is set before me?"

"If that is your scruple," said Ali Baba, "it shall soon be satisfied," and he sent orders to the kitchen that no salt was to be put into any of the dishes presently to be served to the newly arrived guest. "Thus," said he to Cogia Houssain, "I shall still have the honour, to which I have looked forward, of returning to you under my own roof the hospitality you have shown to my son."

Morgiana, who was just about to serve supper, received the order with some discontent. "Who," she said, "is this difficult person that refuses to eat salt? He must be a curiosity worth looking at." So when the saltless courses were ready to be set upon the table, she herself helped to carry in the dishes. No sooner had she set eyes on Cogia Houssain than she recognised him in spite of his disguise;

and observing his movements with great attention she saw that he had a dagger concealed beneath his robe. "Ah!" she said to herself, "here is reason enough! For who will eat salt with the man he means to murder? But he shall not murder my master if I can prevent it."

Now Morgiana knew that the most favourable opportunity for the robber captain to carry out his design would be after the courses had been withdrawn, and when Ali Baba and his son and guest were alone together over their wine, which indeed was the very project that Cogia Houssain had formed. Going forth, therefore, in haste, she dressed herself as a dancer, assuming the head-dress and mask suitable for the character. Then she fastened a silver girdle about her waist, and hung upon it a dagger of the same material. Thus equipped, she said to Abdallah the cook, "Take your tabor and let us go in and give an entertainment in honour of our master's guest."

So Abdallah took his tabor, and played Morgiana into the hall. As soon as she had entered she made a low curtsey, and stood awaiting orders. Then Ali Baba, seeing that she wished to perform in his guest's honour, said kindly, "Come in, Morgiana, and show Cogia Houssain what you can do."

Immediately Abdallah began to beat upon his tabor and sing an air for Morgiana to dance to; and she, advancing with much grace and propriety of deportment, began to move through several figures, performing them with the ease and facility which none but the most highly practised can attain to. Then, for the last figure of all, she drew out the dagger and, holding it in her hand, danced a dance which excelled all that had preceded it in the surprise and change and quickness and dexterity of its movements. Now she presented the dagger at her own breast, now at one of the onlookers; but always in the act of striking she drew back. At length, as though out of breath, she snatched his instrument from Abdallah with her left hand, and, still holding the dagger in her right, advanced the hollow of the tabor toward her master, as is the custom of dancers when claiming their fee. Ali Baba threw in a piece of gold; his son did likewise. Then advancing it in the same manner toward Cogia Houssain, who was feeling for his purse, she struck under it, and before he knew had plunged her dagger deep into his heart.

Ali Baba and his son, seeing their guest fall dead, cried out in horror at the deed. "Wretch!" exclaimed Ali Baba, "what ruin and shame hast thou brought on us?" "Nay," answered Morgiana, "it is not your ruin but your life that I have thus secured; look and convince yourself what man was this which refused to eat salt with you!" So saying, she tore off the dead robber's disguise, showing the dagger concealed below, and the face which her master now for the first time recognised.

Ali Baba's gratitude to Morgiana for thus preserving his life a second time knew no bounds. He took her in his arms and embraced her as a daughter. "Now," said he, "the time is come when I must fulfil my debt; and how better can I do it than by marrying you to my son?" This proposition, far from proving unwelcome to the young man, did but confirm an inclination already formed. A few days later the nuptials were celebrated with great joy and solemnity, and the union thus auspiciously commenced was productive of as much happiness as lies within the power of mortals to secure.

As for the robbers' cave, it remained the secret possession of Ali Baba and his posterity; and using their good fortune with equity and moderation, they rose to high office in the city and were held in great honour by all who knew them.

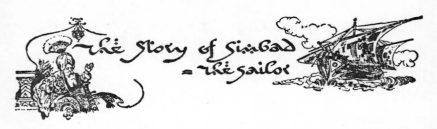

IN the time of Harun-er-Rashid there was, in Baghdad, a rich merchant named Sindbad the Sailor, the source of whose wealth was a mystery. It seemed to be inexhaustible. For long seasons he kept open house, and his entertainments were the most magnificent of all save only those of Er-Rashid himself. All that riches could buy seemed at his disposal, and he lavished the good things of this life upon his guests. Pages, slaves, and attendants there were in great number; his garden was spacious and beautiful, and his house was filled with every costly luxury.

This Sindbad the Sailor has a story to tell—the story of his life—but he never told it to any until, one day, there came to him one Sindbad the Landsman, a man of poor and humble birth. This man pleased him greatly with an apt recitation dealing with the widely different lots dispensed by God to men, and, being pleased, he was struck with the happy conceit that, now Sindbad the Sailor was at last confronted with Sindbad the Landsman, it would be no bad thing were he to narrate the story of his life so that all might know his strange adventures and conjecture no longer as to the source of his fabulous wealth.

Accordingly, Sindbad the Sailor held seven receptions on seven different days, and, although on each occasion a multitude of guests was assembled to listen, he failed not to

[50]

address his words from first to last to his simple listener, Sindbad the Landsman. Following is his narration of the strange and wonderful adventures he experienced in his seven voyages:—

THE FIRST VOYAGE OF SINDBAD THE SAILOR

My father was a merchant of high rank and rich possessions. He died when I was but a child, leaving me all his wealth. When I reached manhood's estate I used my inheritance with no thought for the morrow, living in a sumptuous manner and consorting with the richest young men of Baghdad. I continued this life for many years until, at last, when reason prevailed with me to mend my plan, I found with dismay that I had sunk to poverty. And then it was that I arose and sold what goods remained to me for three thousand pieces of silver, and girded myself, resolving to travel to other lands and rebuild my fortune by the wit of my mind and the labour of my hands.

With a part of my hoard I bought merchandise for exchange in far lands, and also such things as I should require in my travels. Thus prepared I set sail with a company of merchants in a ship bound for the city of El-Basrah. For many days and nights we sailed upon the sea, visiting islands and passing thence to other islands; and everywhere we bartered, and bought and sold. At length we came to an island unlike the others. It seemed like a garden that had floated from off the sides of Paradise and established itself in the sea. And here our ship cast anchor and we landed. Then fires were lighted, and, while some cooked, others washed in the cool stream, and yet others amused themselves admiring the beauties of the place.

When all had eaten of the food prepared, the shore became a gay scene of sport and play, in which I engaged to the full. But, suddenly, a cry from the master of the ship put an end to our gaiety. Standing at the side of the vessel he called loudly, "Hear me, and may God preserve you! Hasten back and leave everything; save yourselves from sudden death, for this that ye think is an island is not such. It is a mighty fish lying entranced in sleep on the surface of the sea since times of old, and trees have grown upon it; but your fires and your frolicking have awakened it, and lo! it moves; and, if it sink into the sea, ye will assuredly be drowned. Hasten then, and save yourselves!"

At this we all, with one accord, left everything and fled for the ship, hoping to escape with our lives. While we were making for safety the island moved with a great turmoil and sank behind us in the sea, and the waves leapt against each other above it. For a time I gave myself up as lost, for I was drawn down fathoms deep; but, by God's grace, I rose again to the surface, and to my hand was one of the large wooden bowls which some of the passengers had taken on shore for the purpose of washing. This I seized, and established myself in it, and thus combated the leaping waves, steadying myself with my hands and feet. In vain I called on the master of the ship. He heard me not. He had spread his sails and pursued his way, thinking that none beside those who had been taken up were left alive.

Astride my wooden bowl I gazed longingly at the ship until it was out of sight. Then I prepared for death as the night was closing around me. Perchance I swooned, for I remembered naught else until I found myself stranded upon a mountainous island. There were trees overhanging, and I grasped a drooping bough and drew myself up from the fretting wave. My limbs were benumbed, and, on looking at my legs, I saw the marks made by the nibbling teeth of fish, and marvelled at my salvation from death.

Staggering forward, I flung myself high on the beach like one dead, and so I remained until the dawn of the next day, when the sun, rising upon me, woke me to a sense of such a condition as I had never known before. Long—long it was before I could rise to a sitting posture, and longer still before I could crawl on my hands and knees to a space of grass that was shielded from the sun. Thence, in time, I staggered till I came to a brook, of which I drank; and strength returned to me. I found luscious fruits and ate of them, and drank again of the clear waters of the brook. And so I continued many days roaming the island and wondering at its beauties until I was strong again as before.

And it chanced, as I took my way to and fro in the island, revelling in the sight of things that God had set there, that on a day when the sea was sounding loudly on the shore I beheld something in the distance which excited my curiosity. It seemed like a wild animal of gigantic size, and, as I approached, I feared it was some fabulous beast of the sea.

But, as I drew still nearer, I was overcome with amazement to see a beautiful mare standing high, with mane and tail floating on the breeze. She was tethered to a stake on the shore, and, at sight of me, she screamed loudly and stamped her fore-feet on the sand; but, ere I turned to flee, I beheld a man come forth from a cave near by, and he ran after me, calling on me to give an account of myself and my presence in that place. Thereupon I laid my story before him, sparing no detail, even to the wooden bowl by means of which and the grace of God I had come thither.

Gladness seized him at my recital, and he took my hand. Saying, "Come with me!" he led me into his cave and set food before me. I ate until I was satisfied; and, being at my ease, I repeated my story more minutely, and he wondered thereat. Then I said, "Thou hast the truth of my adventures upon the sea; now I pray thee, O my master, tell me who *thou* art, that thou dwellest hidden in a cave while thy mare is tethered on the shore." He was in no way displeased at my curiosity, but answered me in plain words. "I am one of the grooms of the King El-Mihraj," he said, "and the others are scattered about the island. For, look you, friend, it is the time of the new moon, when the sea-horse cometh up out of the sea; and it is our plan to bring our best mares hither and tether them by the shore so that they may lure the sea-horses into our hands."

While I was wondering at the manner of this cunning device a magnificent sea-horse rose from the waves, shaking the foam from its crest and neighing loudly. As it approached, my companion drew me into the cave and placed himself at the opening with a long coil of thick cord in his hand. Presently by means of this he leashed the sea-horse with great dexterity, and fettered him, and subdued him. Then, with the mare and the sea-horse, he led me to his companions, who, when they had heard my story, were all of one mind that I should accompany them to the city of the King. So they mounted me on one of the mares and I rode with them to the King's palace.

As soon as we had arrived at the palace gates they went in to the King and informed him of my strange adventures; whereupon he sent for me, and they led me before him. He greeted me very courteously and bade me tell him my story, which, when he had heard it, filled him with amazement, so that he cried, "By Allah! my son, of a truth thou art favoured by fate; for how else could'st thou escape so great a peril? Praise God for thy deliverance!" And he made much of me and caused me to be treated with honour; and he appointed me master of the harbour and comptroller of the shipping.

My condition then was no longer that of a wayfarer. I rose day by day to a higher and a higher place in the King's favour, and he took me into his council in all affairs of State. For a long time I served him well, and he ceased not to recompense me with a liberal hand. Yet my thoughts turned ever to Baghdad, the Abode of Peace; but when I inquired of merchants and travellers and masters of ships in which direction it lay, and how one might come at it, they one and all shook their heads at the name of a strange city of which they had never heard. At last, weary of the wonders of that island and the sea around it—wonders the which, if I had time to tell you, would cause you the greatest amazement,—wearied, too, with my arduous duties, but most of all with my prolonged absence from my own land, I stood one day on the seashore when a great ship drew near and a number of merchants landed from it.

The sailors brought forth their merchandise, and, when I had made an account of it, I inquired of the master of the ship if that were the whole of his cargo. "All, O my master," he replied; "all save some bales whose owner was drowned on our voyage hither; but even these, being in my charge, I desire to sell on behalf of his family in Baghdad." "Sayest thou so?" I cried. "Tell me, I pray thee, the name of the owner of these goods." And he replied, "His name was Sindbad the Sailor, and he was drowned on our way hither."

When I heard this I regarded him more closely and recognised him. Then I cried out, "O my master, I am he; and they are my goods that are in thy hold." But he neither recognised me nor believed my words; whereupon I narrated to him the history of my supposed death; but he shook his head and called upon Allah to witness that there was neither faith nor conscience in any. "Look you!" he said. "Thou heardst me say the owner was dead, and therefore thou desirest the goods for thyself free of price. I tell thee we saw him sink into the sea with many others." "O my master," I answered, "hear me and then judge of my veracity." With this I narrated to him many trivial things which happened before we reached the great-fish island, and which could never be known to me had I not been on the ship. And then it was that he and many of the merchants regarded me with fixed looks and recognised me. "By Allah!" said they one and all, "we truly believed thee drowned, but here we find thee alive." And they pressed upon me and congratulated me, and the master of the ship gave me my goods, at sight of which I was overjoyed; and they all rejoiced with me.

Mindful of the King I served, I at once opened my bales, and, selecting the most costly articles, went in to him and laid them at his feet, telling him how I had regained the goods of which they were a part. And the King wondered greatly at my good fortune and graciously accepted my gifts. He also showed me great favour and honour in that he bestowed upon me gifts in return for mine.

Then, having sold my remaining goods at a profit, I bought largely of the merchandise of the city, and when the ship was about to sail, I approached the King and thanked him for his great kindness to me, and humbly begged his leave to depart to my own city and family. So he gave me his blessing and a great wealth of merchandise and rare commodities, and bade me farewell. And soon thereafter, having stowed all my goods in the hold of the ship, I set sail with the others for Baghdad.

Our voyage was fortunate, and, with the aid of favourable winds, we reached the city of El-Basrah in safety. Thence I repaired to Baghdad, and my family and my friends gave me a joyous welcome. And when I had sold my merchandise I set up a large establishment, sparing no cost. And I bought land and houses, and gathered round me wealthy companions, in whose society I soon forgot the dangers and terrors I had suffered in other lands.   Such is the story of my first voyage; and, to-morrow, by God's grace, I will narrate to you the strange adventures of my second voyage.

THE SECOND VOYAGE OF SINDBAD THE SAILOR

As I related yesterday, I was living here in Baghdad in the midst of every delight, surrounded by companions after my own heart.   But a time came when the wandering spirit seized me again and I longed for the sight, even for the perils, of other and unknown lands.   This, and the fact that I had decreased my substance by large expenditure, led me to adventure a second journey, at once to relieve the monotony of life and to replenish my exhausted store.

The step was quickly taken.   Having collected suitable merchandise I repaired to the river, and, without a word to any one, embarked on a new ship finely rigged and manned by a large crew.   Together with a goodly part of merchants I sailed away, and we passed over the deep from island to island and from sea to sea, with fair winds filling the sails. And at every place at which we cast anchor we bought and sold and bartered.   So we continued until we came to an uninhabited island of great beauty.   The trees hung with ripe fruits; birds of bright plumage flew hither and thither over the shining foliage, and their songs were heard in the topmost branches; rare flowers laid their scent upon the breeze, and pure clear streams coursed everywhere. When we landed, we fell to extolling these master touches of the Creator's hand, for, indeed, the place was, as it were, born of fragrant musk—so fresh and beautiful and full of all delights not made by man. Selecting a rare spot on the bank of a stream, I sat apart, meditating upon the wonderful works of the Omnipotent One. There the soft zephyrs singing in the trees, and the stream murmuring at my feet, lulled me to slumber; and, when I awoke later, I looked forth upon the sea and lo, the ship was far out on the wall of the ocean sloping to the sky. They had forgotten me and I was left alone upon the island.

Despair fell upon me as I gazed around and realised that I was desolate. And I said within myself, "What if I escaped from dangers in the past when all seemed lost—it still remains that here at least there is no escape." Then I blamed myself for leaving my comfortable life in Baghdad to undertake this voyage; for here there was neither strong food nor strong drink; nor rich apparel, nor gold, nor goods. As I pondered to the point of madness on these things a restless spirit came upon me, and I ran to and fro in the island, retracing my steps and crossing them; but I found naught to lessen my despair.

At last I climbed to the top of a high tree, and, looking forth in every direction, saw only sky and sea and trees and watercourses. As I gazed, however, my eye reverted again and again to an object in a distant part of the island. It was round and white, and of enormous size. This aroused my curiosity, and I resolved to find out what it was. Having marked its position I descended from the tree and made my way towards it. When I reached it I found to my astonishment that it was a gigantic dome, white and shining. My first thought was to walk round it to ascertain if there were some door or opening, but none could I find in its whole circumference, which was about fifty paces.

While I was meditating on some means to gain an entrance to this strange structure, behold, the sky darkened; and on looking towards the sinking sun, I saw it was hidden by a great black cloud,—an unwonted thing, as it was the summer season. While I continued to gaze the object drew rapidly nearer, and now I could discern in it the shape of a monstrous bird approaching swiftly through the air; and this it was that blotted out the sun.

Marvelling greatly I recalled a story told by travellers about certain islands where was found a bird of immense size called the rukh, which fed its young on elephants. It was then I knew that the great white dome I had discovered was one of this bird's eggs,—at which, not the least of the Creator's works, I wondered greatly. Then, while I so wondered, the giant bird alighted over the egg, and, crouching down, spread its wings and brooded over it, and composed itself to sleep.

Here, thought I, was a chance of escaping from the island. Unfolding my turban I twisted it into a rope, and bound one end of it tightly about my waist; then I approached the great bird cautiously, and fastened the other end securely to one of its feet; for thus, when it flew away, it might perchance bear me through the air to some inhabited region. The whole night long I lay awake thinking of my pro-jected flight, but it was not until morning that the bird awoke, and, with a loud cry, rose from the egg, bearing me aloft. Higher and higher it soared, until I thought it must reach the stars; then, gradually, in vast circles, it descended, and finally came to earth on a high table-land. In great fear lest the bird should discover my presence I made haste to loose the turban from its foot, and, having done so, I crept away, trembling in every limb. Then, as I watched the bird from a distance, I observed it pick something from the ground and soar away with it clutched in its talons; and I looked again and saw that it was an enormous serpent twist-ing and writhing in the grasp of the bird as it flew swiftly towards the sea. And at this strange thing I wondered greatly as I folded my turban.

But what desert place had I come to by this daring mis-adventure? On the one side of the table-land was a deep valley, and, on the other, a steep mountain which no foot of man could climb. Had I only remained in the island I should at least have had fruit to eat and water to drink, but here was nothing but desolation, from which I had no hope of escape. There was no course but to descend into the valley; and this I did, little caring whither I went.

Now, I had not walked therein but a few furlongs when I observed that the ground I trod was strewn with diamonds of large size, but—and this gave me cause for wild alarm—coiled here and there amongst the stones were gigantic serpents such as the one I had seen the bird bear away in

[61]

its talons. As soon as I was aware of these sleeping serpents, which were of the same hue as the ground whereon
they lay, I stept warily lest I should waken them and be
devoured.

In this way I was proceeding down the valley, my flesh
quaking and my knees a-tremble, when suddenly the flayed
carcase of a slaughtered beast fell with a great noise before
me. This aroused great wonder in my mind and also called
to my recollection a story I had heard in my youth from a
merchant traveller who had visited lands whence none else
had ever come to deny the truth of it—a story confirmed by
others who claimed a reputation for wide knowledge, and
feared to lose it. It was this—that in a far land, where
diamonds are as thickly strewn as the venomous serpents
and other deadly perils which render it difficult to come at
them, the daring merchants who seek these precious stones
employ a cunning stratagem. They take a beast and
slaughter it on the heights above the valley, and, having
skinned it and lacerated the flesh, they throw it down. And,
when it reaches the bottom of the valley whereon the diamonds lie, the stones adhere to the moist flesh. From the
depths of the sky descends the watching vulture of the giant
kind, and this bird, seizing the carcase in its talons, soars with
it to the mountain tops; whereupon the merchants spring
out and frighten the bird away with loud cries, and then take
the stones adhering to the meat and bear them to their own
country. I had my whole life long regarded this story with
a half-shut eye, but now, beholding the slaughtered beast before me, and guessing full well the meaning of its presence

there, I said within myself, "By Allah! no marvel is past belief, for here is the verification." I surveyed that carcase and, having measured in a glance the distance to the mountains whence it had descended, I gazed into the blue sky in whose depths lurked the watching vulture. A plan of escape then came to me and I hastened to put it into operation. First I gathered as many diamonds as I could well dispose within my garments. Then, unfolding my turban, I approached the slaughtered beast, and, lying on my back, drew it over me and bound myself firmly to it.

I had not lain long in that position, with the heavy weight of the beast upon me, when a monstrous vulture came out of the sky, and, seizing upon the carcase with a loud scream, gripped it in its powerful talons and rose up and away with it and me. And it rose higher and higher, with a mighty flapping of its wings, until at last it alighted on a broad ledge near the summit of the mountain—a place which, judging by the bleached bones lying on every hand, was the favourite feeding-place of these birds. This was clearly known to the merchant who had cast the carcase down, for, no sooner had the vulture deposited his burden and started to tear at the flesh, then he sprang out with loud cries and scared it away.

Half smothered by the weight of the slaughtered beast I lost no time in freeing myself, and soon I struggled to my feet and stood there with my clothes stained and polluted with its blood. When the merchant saw me his fear was great; but his disappointment was even greater when, his fear mastered by the lust of gain, he turned the carcase over and found no diamonds sticking to the flesh. Pitying him in his sad case—for he was smiting hand on hand and calling out against fate—I advanced and said, "Curse not fate, nor fear me, for I am of thy kind, and I bear with me an abundance of these stones the loss of which thou lamentest; and they are of the largest that a man can carry upborne by a vulture's wings. Of these will I give unto thee; therefore forget thy fear and bury thy disappointment."

On hearing this the merchant thanked me and prayed fervently for me and my family; and he ceased not to pray for the prolongation of my life until I had bestowed upon him the largest diamonds I could find within my garments. While he was thanking me for this there came his companions, each of whom had cast down a carcase; and, when they had heard the story of my escape, they congratulated me and bade me come with them, for they said, "By Allah! thou art greatly favoured by fate, since none but thee hath been in that valley and escaped to tell the tale."

After my perilous adventures, and my despairing sojourn in the valley of serpents, I was filled with the utmost joy at finding my fellow mortals around me; and, seeing this, they made me welcome among them, and I partook of their food and wine. We passed the night in a safe place, and, when morning came, we set forth over the mountain ranges overlooking the valley of the serpents and at length descended to a stretch of sea. This we crossed by means of the boats which they had moored by the shore, and came thus to a low-lying island where grew camphor trees in abundance, each of which might shield a hundred men from the sun. Here, too, upon the plains roamed the wild rhinoceros, of which wonderful tales are told by people who return from unknown lands. This beast impales an elephant upon its horn with ease, and wanders thus, with little hindrance to its pasturing, until the fat of the elephant, melting in the heat of the sun, and flowing down into its eyes, renders it blind; whereupon it seeks the seashore and lies down until such time as the rukh may find it and carry both it and the elephant away as a morsel for its young. But I speak of what I know, and, as I saw naught of this kind, I can but say that I know not.

I continued with my companions for some space, journeying from island to island and exchanging the diamonds we had acquired for rich merchandise. And, in passing through many countries unheard of in this city, I separated from them and went my way, coming at length to El-Basrah with a princely cargo of goods. Thence I journeyed to Baghdad, the Abode of Peace, and rejoined my family. Wealth I had in abundance, and I resorted to my former life of luxury, bestowing gifts and alms, wearing rich apparel, and eating and drinking with my companions. This is the story of my second voyage; and by the grace of God (whose name be exalted!) I will narrate, to-morrow, the still more remarkable adventures that befell me on my third voyage.

THE THIRD VOYAGE OF SINDBAD THE SAILOR

HAVING rested for a space in Baghdad, where I lived surrounded by every happiness and delight, I began again to experience that restless desire for travel and commerce which had drawn me forth on my former voyages. When the desire grew so great that I could no longer withstand it, I set out with a large stock of merchandise and arrived at the city of El-Basrah, where I took ship, together with a goodly company of merchants, and others of high standing and repute.

For many days we sailed outwards, buying and selling among the islands; until, one day, while we were in the midst of the ocean, a storm descended upon us and blew the ship out of its course. The wind continued from one quarter with great violence, and for a day and night we were hurled before it. When morning came it abated, and the master of the ship looked forth on every hand to ascertain where we were. Suddenly he uttered a loud cry and plucked his beard. "God preserve us!" he said. "The gale hath driven us to an evil fate. See! yonder is the Mountain of Apes! None hath ever come near it and escaped."

We looked and beheld a high mountain on an island, and, while we were gazing at it, and wondering where lay the danger at so great a distance, behold, the sea around us was swarming with apes which had swum out from the island. They were hideous black beasts, not of large size, but of malignant aspect; and so great was their number that we were powerless to stand against them. They climbed up the sides of the ship and seized upon the ropes, which they severed with their sharp teeth so that the sails were powerless and the vessel drifted with tide and wind to the shore. There we were seized by the apes and set on the land, after which they returned to the ship and bent fresh ropes and set the sails and departed over the sea we knew not whither. But we ceased to wonder at the manner of their going, for we were in a desolate plight, since all sailors feared the Mountain of Apes and no ship would ever approach the island to rescue us.

In our wanderings through the island, eating of its fruits and drinking of its streams, we came at length to an open space in which stood a house of gigantic size. The walls and the folding doors of ebony were very lofty, and, when we walked into an immense apartment—for the doors were open—we found everything within it of a corresponding size. The cooking utensils were large enough to cook an ox whole, and, on the couch at the upper end, a hundred men might sit with comfort. But no occupant could we find, so we seated ourselves and rested for a while, and then we slept.

It was about sunset when we were awakened suddenly by a loud noise and a trembling of the earth; and lo, we beheld coming from the further end of the apartment a gigantic being in the shape of a man. His skin was black, and his eyes blazed like fire; two gleaming tusks protruded from his great mouth, his enormous ears drooped to his shoulders, and his nails were like the sharp claws of a beast of prey. We were stricken with great fear at the approach of this frightful being, so that we could neither move nor cry out while he advanced to the couch and disposed his huge limbs thereon. Then, on turning his head, he caught sight of us and arose and came towards us. As I was nearest to his hand he seized me, and, taking me from the ground, turned me over and over in his palm, feeling my limbs to see if they were fat. But, by the grace of God (whose name be exalted!) I was lean and wasted with fatigue and affliction; so he set me down and seized another, whom he turned over and felt in the same manner. He, too, was lean, and he let him go; but he took one after another until he came to the master of ship—a big man and fat. With him he was satisfied. Then, seeing what he was about to do, we hid our eyes, and did not look again until the ogre, having cooked and eaten our master, threw his bones upon a heap of others on one side of the apartment. Afterwards he arose and laid himself down upon the couch and slept, and his snoring was like the roll of thunder.

We crept forth from that house in terror, feeling that it were happier to be killed by apes or drowned in the sea than to be roasted on live coals—a terrible death for a man! We then considered means of hiding, or escaping from the place. But there was no place to hide, and the ship, our only way of escape, was gone. While we were lamenting, a spell seemed to be cast over us, so that our very excess of fear drew us back to the ogre's house, wherein we sat as before, and slept.

Again we were awakened by the thunder of the ogre's approach, and again he came and selected one of our number. When, having eaten, he slept upon the couch, we conversed together, thinking to find some way of escape. One said, "By Allah! by Allah! let us kill him!" and he proposed a plan. "Listen, O my brothers!" I said on hearing this;

"if we seek to kill him let us first prepare some rafts on which to escape, for we may fail of our purpose; and on these rafts we can at worst be drowned, which is better than being roasted." They answered me, "Thou art right!" So we set to work and gathered stout pieces of wood and carried them to the seashore, where we constructed rafts and stowed food upon them in readiness for a hasty departure. Then we returned to the giant's house to carry out our plan.

The sound of his snoring told us he still slept, so we took two sharp-pointed iron spits and heated the points red-hot in the fire. Then we approached him cautiously, and, at a given signal, thrust the red-hot points one into each of his eyes, and bore upon the spits with our combined weight. He arose with a mighty roar, and we fled right and left; for, his sight being destroyed, we feared his blind rage. He searched for us, but, not finding us, he groped for the door, and went forth uttering loud cries which shook the earth.

In great haste, and lashed by mortal fear, we gained the seashore and launched the rafts; but, scarcely had we gained the water, when we saw the ogre approaching, led by a female more gigantic and more hideous than himself. We swam out, pushing the rafts before us; but they hurled great rocks after us, and many of our number were killed. Three alone, including myself, escaped, and, after much stress and peril, reached another island.

We had gained at length what seemed to us a place of safety, high and dry above the wave and far from the ogre's domain; and there, when night came on, we slept, but only to awaken to fresh terrors. Lo! in the act of coiling round us was a serpent of enormous size, its folds contracting and its head raised to strike.   At sight of this, another and myself were more nimble than our companion, for we sprang clear of the serpent's embrace while he was seized in the huge jaws and slowly swallowed with a horrible crackling of bones.   And we mourned our companion and went thenceforth in fear for ourselves.   Dreading to sleep again on the ground we climbed a high tree, and, binding ourselves each in a safe position with our turbans, we slept fitfully. But alas! God hath given to all serpents the wisdom of the Evil One.   That night the serpent mounted the tree, and, seizing my companion, proceeded to swallow him, while I looked on in helpless fear.   Then, in descending the tree, it coiled its vast bulk round the trunk, and I heard my companion's bones crack within its paunch.

When morning had come I descended from the tree feeling that my safest course was to drown myself in the waves, for where else could I hide that the serpent could not find me?   But life is sweet, and I pondered long upon a cunning plan to protect myself.   Then, repairing to the seashore, I selected some pieces of wood from the raft, and took them to a dry place.   Towards evening, when I had eaten of the fruits of the island and drunk of its streams, I bound a long piece of wood crosswise upon the soles of my feet and another crosswise upon my head; I secured a wide flat piece to my right side, another to my left side, and another to the front of my body; and there, having thrust my arms under the side pieces, I lay encased.   And, as the evening wore on, the serpent saw me, and drew near; but it could not swallow me because of the pieces of wood. All through the night it tried to come at me, attempting in all ways to effect its purpose; but in every way it failed, while I lay like a dead man, gazing in speechless horror at the terrible creature. And it ceased not in its efforts to engulf me till morning broke, when it went its way consumed with rage and vexation. Then I freed myself from the pieces of wood and arose, trembling in every limb, but thanking God for my deliverance; for, look you, I was sorely tried by what I had endured from that serpent.

Not many hours later I had the good fortune to espy a ship far out upon the sea, and, as it was making as if to pass a headland of the island somewhat closely, I ran with all speed and established myself on the furthest point. There I waved my unfolded turban to attract the notice of those on the vessel. At last they saw me, and came and took me on board. They listened to my story with great astonishment, and congratulated me on my escape. Then they gave me clean raiment, and set food and drink before me, so that I was revived and comforted. And, as we proceeded on our way, I was emboldened to look back on all I had suffered as nothing more than a terrible dream.

In the course of our journey we came to an island where the sandal wood grows, and here I landed with the other merchants. But they had goods to sell, while I, alas! had none. Then, strange to relate, the same kind Providence that had befriended me on my first voyage was at my service once more, and in the same guise. The master of the ship, seeing me without merchandise, came to me, and, taking compassion upon my poor condition, told me of some goods in the hold which belonged to a man whom they had lost during the voyage. He offered me these goods to sell upon the island, so that, when an account had been rendered to the owner's family in Baghdad, there would be a recompense for my trouble and service. I thanked him gladly for this, and he ordered the goods to be brought up and landed on the island. And lo! when I saw the bales, I knew them, and showed how they were marked with the name of Sindbad the Sailor. Then, seeing that they were perplexed, I shouted in my excitement, "Do you not hear me? *I* am Sindbad the Sailor, and these are my goods!"

While some believed and others doubted I related by story from the time I had awakened upon the island to find myself alone; and, when I mentioned the valley of diamonds, a merchant came forward and confirmed my words, for it was he whose slaughtered beast had helped me to safety. "Hear me, ye doubters!" he said. "When I related this very thing to you, you believed me not; but see—this is the man I spoke of, and now you have it independently from his own mouth. Learn from this, O my brothers, never while living, doubt a true tale because it is marvellous." Then the master asked me what was the distinguishing mark of my goods, and I replied that it was such and such a mark, and I also called to his mind some conversation between him and me before the ship left El-Basrah. He was then convinced that I was Sindbad the Sailor, and he congratulated me and embraced me, saying that my story was extraordinary.

SINDBAD THE SAILOR

The remainder of this, my third voyage, was occupied in buying and selling among the islands on the way to El-Basrah, whence, in good time, laden with wealth and rich merchandise, I proceeded to Baghdad to dwell in peace again, surrounded by my family and friends. Here, for a season, charmed with every delight, I forgot the perils and horrors I had endured. But the longing for travel and adventure found me out again, impelling me to undertake a fourth voyage; and the events of this—more marvellous than those of the preceding voyages, O Sindbad the Landsman—I will narrate to you to-morrow.

THE FOURTH VOYAGE OF SINDBAD THE SAILOR

LED by the desire to associate with other races, and to buy and sell for gain,—for the soul is prone to evil,—I departed from Baghdad with many precious bales, and set sail from El-Basrah in a large ship on which a company of other merchants embarked in like fashion.

For many days we had a pleasant journey among the islands, and all went well with us until, on reaching the wider sea beyond, a mighty wind came up against us. The sea rose in great waves as the tempest increased, and we were in dire peril. More and more violent grew the gale, lashing the sea into fury. The sails were rent, the masts were blown away, we sprang a leak, and slowly the vessel began to sink. We gave ourselves up for lost, and, indeed, when the waves passed over us and we sank, many perished. But, in the seething turmoil, it was my good fortune to be cast against a broad plank, which I seized and held. Others were struggling for life near by, and I was able to draw some of them to me. Sore buffeted as we were by wind and wave we mounted that plank and sat astride of it. Thus, through a whole day and night, we drifted before the gale, now descending into despairing hollows of the sea, and now flung up on the mountain tops of billows. At dawn on the following day the sea cast us like dead men upon an island, where, for many hours, we lay exhausted. Albeit, strength began to return to us again, and we arose feebly, and staggered forth into the island. Fruit and herbs there were in abundance, and clear fresh water; so we ate and drank and were revived.

That night we slept upon the shore, and in the morning we arose strengthened and invigorated. When we had broken our fast we set ourselves to explore the island, and had not gone far in this before we came to a great building. As we stood at the door of this, wondering who dwelt within, a party of naked men came out, and without a word, seized us and led us into a spacious apartment, where we found ourselves standing before their King. He commanded us to be seated, and they brought us food of a strange kind, such as we had never seen. My companions ate largely of this, but my stomach revolted at it, and I ate but little—a thing which preserved me from a terrible fate. For, as my companions ate, they became mad with a ravenous hunger, and ate more and more. Presently they were given cocoanut oil to drink, and, when they had swallowed it, their eyes rolled in their heads, and they continued to eat in a frenzy horrible to behold.

I was consumed with fear at these things and said within myself, "This is a tribe of the Magi and their King is a ghoul!" As I observed them attentively I remembered a story of these people: how they seize on travellers and set this loathsome food before them to eat, and give them the oil to drink, so that they swell out and eat more and more until they are fattened to an enormous degree and their minds are rendered like those of idiots; whereupon, in due time, they kill and roast them and serve them up as food to their King. And all these things I saw in the days that my companions were fattening, for there were others who had been seized before us, and each day one of these was killed and roasted and set before the King.

While I was wasting away with fear and hunger—and it was on this account that they forgot me and left me to die in my own way—my companions had come to be like dull, heavy, stupid beasts of the field, so that they were placed in the care of a beastherd, who led them forth every day to the pasturage. As for myself, as soon as I observed that I was a failure in that I would not fatten, and that none took heed of me nor marked my coming or going, I arose in the night and crept away among the trees surrounding the King's dwelling. Then, when morning came, I went forth with a heart of fear, knowing not what fresh terror I should encounter. In my wanderings back and forth I came about midday to a stretch of green pasture, where I beheld with sorrow my late companions grazing on all fours, and fatten-

ing like beasts for the slaughter, while the beastherd sat
upon a rock and piped on an oaken reed. I breathed a silent farewell to them as to those I should never see again,
and turned sadly away.

My heart was cold within me, and my steps were falter-
ing as I wandered on, pausing here and there to gather edible
herbs and roots, which, for want of something better, served
to sustain life in my body. Journeying in this way I came
at length to a grove of pepper trees, and there were men at
work in it, gathering the berries. Their aspect seemed to
me to be peaceable, so I exposed myself, and they approached
me and pressed upon me, asking my name and whence I
had come, for my aspect excited their curiosity. Then I
unfolded to them the tale of the adventures, the perils, and
the horrors that had befallen me; and, when I had related
the sad case of my companions, they wondered greatly at
my escape. While they resumed their work, they made
me welcome amongst them, and set nutritious food before
me, the like of which I had not tasted for many days. I
regaled myself on their bounty and rested and was content.

When they had finished their work at the setting of the
sun they took me with them to the seashore, and I accompanied them in their vessel to an island not far distant,
where they brought me to their King. And, there, before
them and his Court, at his command I narrated my adventures since leaving Baghdad, at which his interest was
kindled, and he bade me sit with him and eat. And I did so
gladly, for my body was thin and meagre, and my vigour
was sorely wanting. After that, having shown my gratitude

to the King and offered praise to God for His saving grace,
I rose, and, with the King's permission, went forth into
his city. It was a well-conditioned, flourishing place,
thronged with buyers and sellers; and there was an abundance of food and rich merchandise.

As day followed day and time drew on I had cause to
rejoice at my arrival in that city, for I found favour with the
King, and he magnified me over his people and his great
men. Observing the ways of the people, I saw that the
horses that they rode were without saddles; whereupon I
went in to the King and spoke to him on the matter, describ-
ing a saddle and the ease and comfort of it. At this the
King desired me to make him one, and placed at my disposal
his cleverest carpenter with many tools and instruments.
And I sat with the carpenter and instructed him how to
proceed, so that the saddle, covered with polished leather
and stuffed with teased wool, was soon complete. I attached
stirrup-straps and girths, and showed the blacksmith how
to fashion the stirrups. Then, with the aid of costly fringes
and trappings, the work was complete. Full of satisfaction
I sent for one of the King's finest horses, saddled and bridled
him, and led him before His Majesty. He was greatly
pleased at the sight of what I had done, and, when he had
mounted the horse and sat in the saddle, he was overjoyed
at the ease and pleasure of it, and bestowed upon me a large
reward.

When the King's chief officials and the grandees of his
Court saw the saddle which I had made, they each and all
desired me to make others like it. Then, with the carpenter

and the blacksmith, I employed many days in the construction of numerous saddles, and for these I received much gold, and rose to an assured position in the land.

The high rank and honour which the King had bestowed upon me had but half expressed his heart towards me. I was yet to learn that he had a further favour in store. One day, while I was sitting at his right hand discussing affairs of state, he said to me, "O my son, seeing thou hast now become as one of us and we cannot part with thee, I desire that thou give ear to a matter which I have planned and which will bind thee more closely to us." And I answered him, "For thy great kindness to me, O King, I am now and henceforth thy faithful servant. What dost thou desire me to do?" And he looked at me intently and said, "I would marry thee to a woman of high rank among us—one possessed of great beauty and wealth—so that thou mayest continue to dwell with us in pleasure and comfort and with a good heart. Thus shalt thou advantage greatly and receive every good thing at my hands; wherefore, refuse me not, nor oppose my wish."

I remained silent, for I was overwhelmed by his proposal and the stress of bashfulness it brought to my face. Seeing this, he rallied me and said, "Art thou dumb? Is not thy heart with us?" Then of a sudden I replied, "O King! Thy words took away my breath. As thou commandest, so I obey."

Pleased at my compliance the King immediately ordered his officials to bring the lady and the witnesses, and forthwith I was married to her with the King's blessing and the acclamation of all his Court. She was of surpassing loveliness, and she brought me a dowry of abundant wealth and possessions. And to this the King added a magnificent house with servants and slaves, and assigned me a handsome salary. And I lived in ease and comfort, our days being full of delights. Gone was all thought of the perils and hardships I had endured, and gone was the fear of adversities in store. But there is no strength nor power but in God, and He orders the fate of men as He will. On an evil day a great fear suddenly came to me by reason of a thing which I will make known to you.

A companion of mine suffered a bereavement in that his wife died; whereupon I went to him, and mourned with him, saying, "Take heart, O brother; God will fill her place to thee with one far better." But he continued to weep, saying, "Alas! How can I marry another when this very day I depart this life?" "Nay," said I, "that is not within reason, for thou art in good health and not like to die." He then raised his head and dried his tears, and said to me very slowly, "Hear me, O my brother! Knowest thou not that, to-day, they will bury my wife, and that they will bury me also in the same tomb with her? For such is our custom. When husband or wife is buried the other must be buried also, so that neither may continue to enjoy life alone."

"By Allah!" said I, smiting palm on palm, "this custom is wholly vile, and it toucheth me closely." Then, as we continued to discuss this matter, there came others who condoled with my companion, grieving not only for the loss of his wife, but also that they should never see him more. And, later in the day, came yet others bearing a bier; and on this they laid the woman and carried her forth prepared for burial with all her jewels and raiment and wealth. And the husband went with them.

Through sympathy with my companion, and to bid him a last farewell, I followed this funeral procession till it halted in a distant spot on the seashore. There a great stone was lifted and a vault exposed. Into this they threw the body of the woman, and then, by means of a stout cord, they lowered the husband gently till he rested by her side. A pitcher of water and seven cakes were then let down to him, and, when he had freed himself from the cord, they drew it up and closed the sepulchre and went their ways.

"By Allah!" said I within myself as I smote myself on my breast, "this manner of death is the worst of all!" And on my return I went in to the King with grief and fear gnawing at my heart. "O King!" I said, "Tell me why is this: that ye bury the living with the dead?" Said he, "O my son, it is the custom of our country and has descended to us from our ancestors: husband and wife are one, in death as in life." And I answered him with a question that concerned me nearly. "O my lord," I said, "and the stranger that sojourneth with thee: if his wife die, do ye treat him in like manner?" "Yea," he replied, "in like manner, even as thou hast seen." Then I departed from him in grief and mourning lest I should perchance be bereft of my wife. In vain did I say to myself, "Be comforted! Maybe thou wilt die before her—none knoweth." In vain did I give myself up to my manifold occupations. The fear was not to be dispelled.

And, within a short time, what I had feared came to pass. My wife was stricken with fever, and, when I had reason to hope she would recover, she suddenly relapsed and died. My grief at this was overwhelming, but, as if to add to it, there came many to condole with me on her death and to mingle their tears with mine for that I should soon be departing this life. The King himself came and commiserated with me on my most unhappy fate. And he said, "There is no strength nor power in any but God. Farewell, O my son!"

And they prepared my wife for burial, arraying her in her richest garments and her finest jewels. But, when they carried her to the burial place and cast her down into the pit, and all my companions pressed upon me to bid me farewell, my gorge rose and I cried out upon them that their custom was vile. Loudly I spoke my bitter mind on the abominable nature of this thing; they would not listen, but took me by force and lowered me into the pit, together with the seven cakes and the pitcher of water. And when I had reached the floor of a vast cavern they called down to me: "Untie the ropes that we may draw them up!" I answered, "Draw me up with them!" "Nay, nay"; they replied, "we do but follow our custom." "To the ravens with you and your custom!" I retorted, for I had no stomach for this proceeding. Then, as I steadily refused to loose the ropes, they at last threw them down upon me, and, having closed the mouth of the pit, went their way.

Now was I in worse plight than I had ever been. On that cavern floor there were the bodies and bleached bones of those that had died a natural death cheek by jowl with those who had perished in the fulfilment of this abominable custom. And I said to myself, "Better to remain single and live, than to marry and be buried alive."

Nevertheless, knowing not night from day, I kept myself from death by eating sparingly of the cakes and drinking some of the water, for I was in no mood to die in so vile a manner after having come through great perils by mountain and sea. At length, when I had eaten all the cakes and drunk all the water, and hunger and thirst began to cry out within me, I arose and wandered to and fro in the cavern, stumbling and falling over dead bodies and biting the dust of bones that had crumbled long since. By dint of much groping in the dark I at length found the wall of the cavern, and, selecting therein a cavity free from bones and corpses, I stretched myself and slept.

I was awakened later as if by hunger and thirst knocking at the door; and, while I sat in gloom thinking of the plenty in Baghdad—fool that I was to leave it!—I heard a sudden noise. Looking forth from my cavity, I saw that the stone had been removed from the opening of the cavern and a dead body was being lowered. It was the body of a man, and after him was let down the living body of his wife. She was weeping and wailing for him and for herself. Then the mouth of the cavern was closed again and all was dark and silent save for the wailing of the woman echoing through the cavern. "Alas!" she cried, "that I should die this lingering death! Had I the means to end my life, then would I do it. Would that there were one here to slay me!"

When I heard this I remembered that I had never been able to resist the pleadings of a woman. So I arose, and, taking a stout leg-bone in my hand, I slew her according to her desire. And I took her seven cakes and the pitcher of water, which she would no longer need, and, retiring to my cavity, I ate and drank. This thing occurred many times during my sojourn in that cavern, for a number of married men and women chanced to die. And, though they did not always cry out for me to slay them, I knew their prayer beforehand and answered it speedily. Thus the cakes and the water bequeathed to me stayed my spirit and I continued to live.

Time passed slowly, but yet it passed. I had no other means of measuring it except to call an hour a day and a day a year. And I was weary to death of it all when an unwonted thing occurred. I was awakened suddenly from sleep by a noise at the far end of the cavern. Then I heard footsteps as of some beast. I arose, and, arming myself with a stout bone, advanced upon the intruder; but it heard me and fled from me, and I could not come at it. Yet, as I followed its footsteps, I saw its form darken a pin-spot of daylight at the end of a crevice of the cavern. This gave me a glimmer of hope, for, where that beast had passed, I myself might pass, and so gain the outer air. Over jagged points of rock I clambered towards that opening, now losing sight of it, and now gaining view of it again, until at last I reached it and found that it was indeed a communication with the outer country. With some difficulty I forced my way through it and climbed down by a perilous pathway to the seashore.

I had escaped from the sepulchre of the living and the dead, and I praised God for the sight of the sky and the sea; but, when I had looked into my position and found behind me an impassable precipice, before me the wide stretching sea, and above me the dome of heaven, I sat down on the shore with my head on my knees and said within myself, "There is no way out! I cannot scale the sheer cliff, neither can I tread the fishes' pathways in the sea, nor walk in the tracks made by birds in the air. There is no way out!"

Day followed day, and I strove to stay my hunger with what shell-fish I could find; but the supply was meagre, and again and again I was forced to return to the cavern to receive reward of cakes and water in return for merciful death dealt by my hand. Far be it from me to rob the dead, and none can say I did so. It was in the spirit of a last gift generously bestowed by those about to die that chains of pure gold were hung about my neck and rich jewels thrust upon me. These keepsakes of many I retained, assured that later I should carry them with me to a nameless grave in a desolate spot.

But God, in His infinite mercy, willed it otherwise, for one day, sitting sadly on the shore as was my wont, I espied a vessel on the sea. Hope surged high within my breast and I arose and stripped myself of a white garment and mounted it on a staff and ran wildly to and fro, waving it above me. And, when my signal was observed, the vessel stayed its course and sent a boat ashore.

"Who art thou, and what doest thou here?" cried one from the boat as it ran upon the beach. "Know ye not that this is a desolate coast, and none has ever been seen upon it?" And I greeted them with joy, and answered them, telling my strange experience in a few words. Then, their wonder strong within them, they took me across to the ship and led me before the master, who marvelled greatly at finding a man where none had ever seen a human being before. He asked me many questions, and when I answered him, giving him the whole history of my adventures as heretofore set down, he was a man bewildered. Raising his eyes to heaven he said, "By Allah! thy case is extraordinary!" And all around wondered that a man could experience such things and live.

In return for his kindness in rescuing me from my terrible plight, I tendered him some of the rarest jewels I had brought with me from the cavern. But he refused me courteously, saying, "Nay, O my brother; if we find one in like case with thee, we succour him and give him to eat and drink; and, if he be naked, we clothe him. Then, at the first city we reach, we set him on land with some valuable token of our goodwill; for so it is with us of the sea that we are not unmindful of the sufferings of others." And, when I heard this, I prayed for him and his family, that he and they might live long in health and prosperity.

Our journey from that place, where I had suffered so

much, took us from island unto island towards the city of El-Basrah. As we proceeded, the places where we cast anchor grew more and more familiar to me, and, as of old, I bought and sold as merchants do. At length we arrived at the city of El-Basrah, whence, having transacted business there for some days, bartering and selling the jewels I had acquired, I journeyed to Baghdad. There, in the bosom of my family, and surrounded by my companions, I returned to my former habit of life. These, then, were the experiences of my fourth voyage; and, O my brother, Sindbad the Landsman! if thou wilt honour me by thy presence tomorrow, I will relate to thee still stranger things that befell me in my fifth voyage.

THE FIFTH VOYAGE OF SINDBAD THE SAILOR

LOOKING back from the position of safety and comfort to which I had returned I came in time to make light of the perils I had encountered and the sufferings I had endured. The advantages that had come to me through these perils and sufferings now stood in the foreground of my thoughts, and I said within myself, "It is the life for a man; for how otherwise can he come at the meaning of the great book of the world than by treading its pages?" And, moreover, I had conceived the wish to become the owner of a ship, for thus the gain accruing from a voyage to other lands would be so much greater.

Having considered the matter deeply, I arose from my

life of luxury and ease and departed with many bales of merchandise for the city of El-Basrah. There in the river I found at length a splendid vessel, which I purchased. I found a master and a crew, over whom I set my own trusty servants; and, having secured a goodly company of merchants as passengers, I embarked their bales and mine, and we set sail. We worked our way outwards, calling at island after island, and doing the usual business that merchants find in those places, until one day we came to a large uninhabited island.

Here, while I was engaged in matters concerning the vessel, the merchants landed and, as I afterwards learned, they found there the great egg of a rukh, such as I had met with on a former voyage. Mistaking it for a deserted structure, and, failing to find an entrance, they had amused themselves by casting stones at it, so that it broke; whereupon a young rukh came forth from the shell. And they set upon this monstrous chicken in its helpless condition, and slew it, and brought great slabs of its flesh back to the ship.

When I heard what they had done I was sore afraid and reproached them for their rash action. "For, look you," I said, "there is not a doubt the mother rukh will seek to revenge the loss of her young, and, seeing our ship, will attribute the deed to us, and attack us and destroy us." But they neither heeded my warning nor repented them of their rash action.

The vengeance of the rukh was sudden and dire. Scarce had I spoken when the sun was obscured from our sight, and, looking up, we beheld the gigantic bird descending upon the island. When it saw that its egg had been broken and its young one destroyed it flew above us, looking down at the ship and shrieking in a voice that filled the sky. On this it was joined by its mate, and the two circled round us, their hoarse cries of rage falling like thunder on the sea. In great fear I bade the master and the sailors hoist the sails and seek safety in flight.

Then, as soon as we began to draw off from the island, the rukhs left us and flew inland, so that we thought we had made good our escape. But soon they reappeared and came after us, each bearing in its talons a huge mass of rock. One of them flew above us and dropped the rock, so that we saw death descending upon us. But the great mass missed the ship by a narrow space, and, falling close astern, raised such a commotion of waves that the ship was flung up on a mountain of water and then hurled down against the bottom of the sea before little by little she came to rest on the level tide. Then the other rukh dropped the rock from its talons, and fate ordained that it struck the ship astern with a mighty crash. Amid cries of fear and despair we sank into the sea, and all seemed lost.

How I survived the shock and turmoil of that sudden shipwreck I cannot describe clearly, for I was like one stunned or wrenched from his mind apart. How I sought to save myself is gone from me by reason of the extreme peril. I can imagine only that I touched some wreckage and clung to it, for, when my mind returned to me, I found myself on the shore of an island sitting upon a plank, which, it seemed had borne me hither. That I had fought against wind and wave I knew, for I was well nigh exhausted. I could do nothing more than drag myself painfully to a sheltered spot, where I rested and slept.

When I arose later in the day, I was refreshed; and, having found both fruit and water, I ate and drank and my strength returned to me. I went forth upon the island, and to and fro in it, but I found no other's footprint on the shore, nor any sign of human habitation from coast to coast. But that there *was* a dweller there I was soon to learn, and to my cost.

It was on the following day towards evening, when I was walking among the trees, that I came upon an old man sitting on the bank of a stream. He was a comely old man, with flowing silver locks and an ample white beard. He was clothed from the waist downward, with the leaves of trees threaded together. As I regarded him for some moments I felt that his whole aspect betokened a disposition of simplicity and mild benevolence. Advancing upon the bank I spoke to him, but he shook his head sadly and sighed; and I saw that his speech was gone. Then he made signs with his hands as if to say, "Mount me upon thy neck and carry me across the stream."

I felt kindly disposed towards this mild and gentle old man, and wished to do him a service; so I mounted him upon my neck and took him across the stream. "Now," I said, "Thou canst dismount when it pleaseth thee!" But, instead of dismounting, he wound his legs still more closely round my neck, and pressed his feet into my chest, so that I cried out with pain and rage and attempted to throw him from my shoulders. But my frantic efforts were in vain; he stuck like a leech, and I could not dislodge him. Indeed he clung so tight that he nearly throttled me, and I fell to the ground exhausted. Then he belaboured me sorely with his feet until I arose with him again, and, in this way, he compelled me to obey him. When he would go in among the trees he made a sign with his hand, and, if I obeyed not with alacrity, he beat me with his feet unmercifully. By reason of his behaviour I was at last compelled to cancel my first opinion of him and, though he cleaved to me night and day, we were by no means friends. I was his captive and he ceased not to remind me of it. If I dallied by the way, or stumbled, his hard feet would rain blows upon me; and, at night, when he slept with his legs wound tightly round my neck, he would often dream that I had disobeyed him and would beat me violently with his feet and hands.

For many many days I was ridden hither and thither at the will of this obstinate old fellow, who, though he could not torment me with speech, was truculent enough in his manner. And I reproached myself for having desired to do him a service, saying constantly in my mind, "By Allah! never again while living will I do a service to any!"

At length one day the old man guided and belaboured me into a space on the island where pumpkins grew in abundance. While he was eating some of these I took others that were ripe, and, having cleaned out the seeds and coarse matter through a small aperture, filled them with the juice of grapes; then I filled up the apertures and laid the pumpkins in the sun. Thus in a few days I procured pure wine, and, every day thereafter, while the old man on my neck ate of the pumpkins, I drank of the wine until I became intoxicated, and laughed and sang and danced about with him among the trees. And when, with fist and heel, he desired to know the cause of this, I showed him the wine that I had made. Seeing that its effect upon me was so agreeable he sought to achieve the same happy result by drinking largely of it himself, so that he grew hilarious and broke a pumpkin over my head, rocking and rolling in his seat with laughter. Then, as he continued to drink, he gradually lost control of his limbs and lolled from side to side; whereupon I grasped his feet and unwound them from my neck and threw him on the ground. And so at last, to rid the earth of such a monster, I slew him, and left him there for the vultures.

After this, happiness returned to me and I went about the island like one relieved of a heavy burden, as indeed I had been. And day by day I sat by the sea watching for a vessel. But I lived upon the island many days before at last I saw a ship approach and cast anchor off the shore. When the passengers had landed I ran towards them and welcomed them, answering their many questions respecting my condition. They listened to my story with great amazement. Then some one said, "This old man of whom thou speakest is surely he whom they call the Old Man of the Sea. He hath ridden many to death, and none hath escaped but thee. Therefore, praise God for thy deliverance."

They took me to the ship and set food before me, and, after I had eaten, they brought me some clean clothes and I clad myself decently. As the ship set sail for El-Basrah my thoughts went before it to Baghdad, The Abode of Peace; but I was destined to mischance, for a strange thing befell me. We had journeyed but a few days when we came to an island whereon was a city with lofty spires and splendid houses. This was the City of Apes, of which I had heard that at night-time the people, fearing the apes, put out in boats upon the sea, so to sleep in safety.

I landed on this island with some companions, and, in our going about the city, I missed them. While I was searching everywhere they must have returned to the ship, thinking I had preceded them, for, when I reached the shore later, the vessel had gone. I reproached myself for this mishap, for I had already suffered once at the hands of the apes. So I sat on the seashore bemoaning my fate.

While I was doing this, one of the people of the city came to me and inquired as to my trouble, and I told him. "Then come with us in our boat," he said, "for the night is falling, and if thou remain in the city the apes will devour thee." So I went with them, and we pushed off together with a multitude of other boats until we rested about a mile from the shore; and there we remained and slept till the morning, when every one returned to the city and went about his occupation. And in like manner as the inhabitants sleep upon the sea by night, and dwell in the city by day, so the apes infest the city by night and sleep in the forests by day. Woe betide any remaining in that city after the sun goes down, for he will of a certainty be torn limb from limb and devoured.

I earned my bread in that island in a strange manner,

and was able to set by a small store of gold. It was in this way. I observed many of the people gathering pebbles on the shore and placing them in bags, and, when they had collected a sufficient quantity, they went forth into a valley filled with lofty trees. Here slept the apes among the branches, for the trees were so high that none but an ape could climb them. It was the way of the people then to pelt the apes with the pebbles, whereupon they awoke screaming and chattering, and plucked the fruit from the trees, and hurled it down at their tormentors. And I saw that the fruit was the cocoanut. When a sufficient number of these nuts had been secured the people gathered them up and returned to the city, where they sold them. Very soon, I, too, was gathering pebbles and pelting the apes in the trees, and in this way I amassed a great store of cocoanuts. These I sold, and bought merchandise and traded and prospered in the city.

In this way I continued for a long time, until at last I took to buying cocoanuts from the people and storing them against the arrival of a ship, when I hoped to sell them in bulk. At length a large vessel anchored off the island, and I bargained with the merchants thereon. They agreed with me upon a good price for my store. With the money thus obtained I bought more of the merchandise of the place, and embarked it on the ship; then, bidding farewell to my companions in the city, I took my departure.

The ship was bound for El-Basrah, but on the voyage we lingered to visit many islands that I had not seen before. Upon one we found an abundance of cinnamon and pepper, and here I noted a peculiar thing. On every bunch of pepper was a large leaf that hung down when the sun shone, but, when it rained, this leaf twisted and erected itself above the tendrils to shield them. And this is truth.

So we sailed onwards, past the islands of the aloes-wood, where the people are depraved and know not the call to prayer, until we came at length to the Island of Pearls. Here I gave some cocoanuts to the divers, saying, "Dive for me for luck!" And they dived in the sea and returned to the surface with pearls of great size, which they gave to me, assuring me that my fortune was of the best. So that when we reached El-Basrah I was rich with pearls and merchandise, some of which I sold there, and some here in Baghdad.

Once more in the lap of luxury, and reposing in the bosom of my family, I returned to my former life of revelry and ease, and soon forgot the hardships I had endured. And this is the whole story of my fifth voyage. Return tomorrow, O Sindbad the Landsman, and thou shalt hear from me the adventures of my sixth voyage, for they are even yet more wonderful.

THE SIXTH VOYAGE OF SINDBAD THE SAILOR

ON a day when I was living happily in Baghdad, having forgotten the perils and dangers of my former voyages, I was sitting at ease in my garden when a party of merchants came to me, and their tales of travel aroused within my bosom a great longing to engage again in the hazardous delights of those things. I pondered long upon the matter, and, though I had said within myself, "never will I set forth again," I found that my mind was made up in spite of me. Therefore I set about collecting merchandise, and, having packed a goodly number of bales, I departed for El-Basrah, where I took ship with a company of merchants and others of high repute.

The outward voyage was pleasant and fortunate, and we did as others do, buying and selling and amusing ourselves in different cities. But there came a day of disaster, when the master of the ship suddenly discovered that we had wandered from our course, and had lost our reckoning. He plucked his beard and smote his breast, and cried out in despair that we had sailed into an unknown sea, where dire perils awaited us. And so it proved, for not long afterwards, while we were sailing in a calm sea, a sudden wind burst upon us and, before the sails could be loosed, the rudder was broken and the ship drifted and was driven at last upon the sides of a high mountain rising up to heaven. She was dashed to pieces by the violence of the waves, and, from that terrible wreck, few survived. There were some others besides myself who clung to the sides of the mountain, and, by tooth and nail, climbed to a place of safety.

Little by little, when the tide receded, we made our way down among the crags until we came to a strip of seashore, and from this point we could see that the island was of large size, its interior being sheltered from storms by the front of the mountain. But what took our wonder was this: on the seashore was amassed the wealth of a thousand wrecks.

Scattered here, there, and everywhere, in foam and high dry, were flotsam and jetsam of richest merchandise, much of it spoiled by the sea, but much more cast high up and still of great value. All along the shore were planks and fragments of many vessels that had been wrecked on this inhospitable coast. And this was not all, for, when we proceeded through the island, we found a spring of pure ambergris overflowing into the sea; and by this the whales are attracted, but when they have swallowed it and dived to the depths of the sea it turns in their stomachs and they eject it, so that it rises to the surface in solid lumps such as are found by sailors. But the ambergris that is cast about the opening of the spring melts in the heat of the sun, and its perfume is blown about the island, wafted sweet upon the breeze like fragrant musk.

When we had explored the island and wondered at the many strange things it contained, we searched among the wreckage on the shore and found some few barrels of preserved meats, and on these we stayed our hunger. With the provisions on the shore and the fruit we secured on the island we were in no danger of starvation, but a kind of fever seized upon our company and one after another sickened and died. This was a time of stress and despair. Day after day the living buried the dead until there was only one left, and that one was I. And I wept and waited, and, as if death would not come uninvited, I arose and dug myself a grave in readiness, for there was none left to bury me when I died. It was on the seashore that I made my grave, so that, when I should come to lie in it in my last moments, the wind should blow the sand upon me and bury me. And in this state of mind I blamed myself for setting out on this voyage in disregard of the lessons learned from former perils.

But God in His mercy led my footsteps forth and I roamed in the island, restless for the end. In my wanderings I came to a river gushing forth out of the side of a mountain, and, after flowing for a space between banks of verdure in a valley, entering again another mountain. Having followed it to this point, I sat down upon a bank against the mountain wall and pondered. And I said within myself, "This river flowing through caverns within the mountain must have an opening somewhere, perchance in a fertile country where people dwell." For a long time I turned the chances of this within my mind, and at last decided to build a raft and commit myself upon it to the current; for at most it were better to die that way than in my present desolation.

By means of rope and wreckage from the seashore my raft was soon constructed, and in its construction I omitted not to measure it according to the width of the river. Then, full of a wild hope that I might at length reach an inhabited region, I stowed upon it rich goods from the shore, ambergris from the spring, and the rarest jewels I could find in the beds of the watercourses. As I set myself upon the raft and launched it, I said, "If I perish, I perish; but if I come to the haunts of men, I come to them rich in precious things."

No sooner had I entered into the aperture of the mountain than I was suddenly encased in darkness, and, having no choice which way I went, flung myself flat on the raft lest my head should be shattered against the roof of the tunnel. Like this I floated on, sometimes feeling there was a wide space around me, and sometimes clinging to the raft lest some narrowing of the passage should sweep me to destruction. And all this time my terror was so acute that at last I swooned and lay face downward on the raft, the plaything of fate and the sport of the rushing current.

When I awoke I found myself in the open air. The sun was shining above and the birds were singing in the trees around me. I was still lying on the raft, which was tied to a stake on the shore of a beautiful lake. As soon as I had raised myself and looked about me a number of dark-skinned people gathered round and questioned me in an unknown tongue; but I shook my head, understanding nothing of what they said. At last one advanced from among them, and, addressing me in Arabic, said, "Peace be with thee, brother!" Then I seized him joyfully by the hand and greeted him, but I was weary and hungry and could give no account of myself because of my utter exhaustion. Seeing my state he called for food and wine, and they hastened to set them before me. When I had eaten and drunk and my strength had returned to me I told what I had come through, and the one who had addressed me in Arabic interpreted it to the others. They were filled with wonder at my story, and insisted that I should accompany them to their King and acquaint him with the history of my strange adventure.

So they took me, with the raft and all the riches I had laid upon it, and led me before their King; and, from his state and magnificence, I knew that I beheld the King of

Sarandib, whose name and power and learning are known through all the earth. He saluted me in the custom of my own people, addressing me in Arabic which fell easily from his tongue. This set me at my ease and I told him my story, to which he listened with great attention. When I had finished, he raised his hand and said, "By Allah! thou hast endured much, and thy case is extraordinary. Thou art greatly favoured by fate: wherefore I join my happiness with thine at thy deliverance and safety."

I was greatly moved at his words, and, begging his acceptance of a gift at my hands, I took the rarest jewels from the raft, together with a quantity of ambergris and aloeswood, and laid them at his feet. He graciously accepted my present and immediately established me in a position of honour, bidding me dwell with him in his palace. I accepted his hospitality and remained in his land in great happiness and honour, associating with the grandees and the people of rank. And I said to myself, "I care not if the rest of my days are passed in this kingdom of splendour and magnificence."

It was indeed a land of wealth and abundance. And there the day is equally divided with the night the whole year round; and, when the sun rises, light bursts suddenly upon the earth, and, when it sets, the darkness descends like a curtain that is loosed. There is a lofty mountain whose glittering streams contain the richest jewels, with rare minerals; and everywhere, on hill and valley, are wafted the fragrant odours of spices. The delights of this realm held me enthralled for a long time, so that I forgot my own country, wherein is the Abode of Peace.

But, on a day when I ascended the high mountain and looked far out across the sea, I seemed to hear the voice of my own land calling to me. Then, with that far call still in my ears, I went in to the King and asked him to let me go. At first he demurred, and tried to induce me to remain with him and his people; but, when I pressed for his permission, he relented and gave me a large sum of money for my journey, and also many gifts.

When I was about to depart the King called me to him and handed me a letter written on fine parchment. This he asked me to give into the hands of the Khalifeh, Harun Er-Rashid. The substance of the letter was this:—"The King of Sarandib sends greeting. Peace be on thee, O Brother, from the King of Sarandib, who commands a thousand elephants, and in whose palace are ten thousand jewels. By the bearer of this we send thee a gift, for we have a deep affection for thee. The gift is all too trifling, but we beseech thee to accept it graciously and reply to us. Peace be upon thee!" The present with which I was entrusted was a goblet of ruby, the inside of which was set with sparkling diamonds and priceless pearls—truly a kingly gift.

Having bade farewell to the King and such of his people that I had associated with I embarked in a large ship which was bound for El-Basrah. In good time we reached that port and I journeyed up the river to Baghdad.

My first thought was to deliver the letter and the gift into the hands of the Khalifeh. So I lost no time in approaching him and fulfilling my pledge to the King of Sarandib. He was greatly pleased with the letter, and, when he saw the sparkling goblet of ruby and precious stones, he was filled with delight.

"O Sindbad," he said, "this King must be exceedingly wealthy and powerful; what sayest thou?" And I told him of the wonder and magnificence of the land of Sarandib: how the King's seat of state is in a splendid throne placed upon a gigantic elephant with his courtiers and officials standing about him on a highly decorated platform; how there are around His Majesty a thousand other elephants on which sit the princes of the land; and, surrounding all, on every hand, ten thousand horsemen clad in silk and gold; and how a crier goes before the King exalting him to heaven, and another behind him proclaiming "Great is he, but he will die! Again, again and again I say it: he will die!"

And as I continued to tell of these things the Khalifeh marvelled greatly at the wisdon and power of this King. "Report hath spoken truly," he said. "As thou hast witnessed to me, O Sindbad, the tales of his might and dominion have exaggerated nothing."

He then thanked me for my faithful service and bestowed rich gifts upon me, and bade me seek my own house in peace and content. There in the bosom of my family, I lived at ease, having put behind me the perils of travel and set fixedly before me the determination never to seek them again. Yet O Sindbad the Landsman my determination was over-ruled by the direct command of the Khalifeh; and, if thou wilt honour me by thou presence again to-morrow, I will re-late to thee the events of my seventh and last voyage.

THE SEVENTH VOYAGE OF SINDBAD
THE SAILOR

IN adhering to my vow never again to fare forth from my
native land in search of strange wonders at the risk of
deadly peril, I was contented and happy in my state.
While I was sitting one day thinking on this and saying
within myself, "I am here in the Abode of Peace, and Allah
be praised! I shall never quit it for the haunts of trouble";
lo! there came a messenger summoning me to the Khalifeh.
I arose and followed him, and presently I was before His
Majesty, saluting him and kissing the ground. "Welcome,
O Sindbad!" he said. "Know that I have a matter of
importance for thee to execute." "Sire," I answered, "I am
thy slave."

Then the Khalifeh unfolded to me his wish: which was
that I should go to the King of Sarandib bearing a letter and
a gift. "By Allah!" I cried when I heard this. "O my
lord, be not displeased, but have I not already taken a vow
that I will not go forth again upon the sea lest I suffer worse
things than have already befallen me? The bare mention
of a voyage causes my knees to shake." And I repeated to
him the terrible sufferings and perils I had encountered in
my travels; whereupon the Khalifeh raised his hands and
said no man had endured worse things. "Nevertheless," he
added, smiling upon me, "thou wilt go forth once more, for
my sake, and thou wilt bear my letter and gift to the King
of Sarandib."

[102]

SINDBAD THE SAILOR

It was not for me to disobey the command of the Prince of the Faithful, and I bowed my head in submission. I took from his hands the account of the items composing the gift, together with a letter and a sum of money for my expenses; and, bidding him farewell, went forth, saying to myself that fate was against me.

The Khalifeh's gift to the King of Sarandib was one of great magnificence. First there was a splendid white horse, the equal of which was not to be found in the length and breadth of Arabia. Its saddle and trappings were adorned with gold and set with brilliant jewels. Then, in addition to this, there were a priceless robe, fit for the king of all the earth; a great quantity of rich stuffs from Egypt and Greece, and a wonderful crystal goblet of such a kind that a man's whole lifetime would be required to make it. And the Khalifeh's letter ran as follows:—"Peace be on thee from the King of Er-Rashid, highest in any land but thine—under God (whose name be exalted!) We rejoiced greatly at thy letter, and we have sent thee some royal trifles, thy gracious acceptance of which will give us joy and happiness. Peace be with thee!"

With all these things I embarked upon a large vessel and set sail from El-Basrah with a company of merchants. We journeyed for long days and nights until at length we came to the island of Sarandib. There I went in to the King in his palace, and he gave me a joyous welcome.

"By Allah!" he said, "we have often thought of thee, O Sindbad; and now we rejoice to see thy face again." Then he bade me sit beside him, and asked with courtesy the reason

[103]

of my visit. I informed him and told him of the Khalifeh's gift handing him the letter. When he had read it he was overjoyed, and when at length he saw the gift and the richness of it, he marvelled greatly and conferred upon me all the honours befitting the ambassador of the Prince of the Faithful.

After some days of pleasure and happiness in his land, I made known to him my desire to depart speedily to my own country, but it was with difficulty that I obtained his permission. At last he allowed me to go, bearing friendly messages to the Khalifeh; and I set sail for my own land, glad that I was now free to return to the life to which I had vowed myself.

But, O Sindbad the Landsman! the chances of long voyages upon the sea are such as thou know'st not of. We had not been many days on our course when, as we were passing near an island, a fleet of boats put off from the shore and surrounded us. They were manned by a host of men clad in suits of mail. They looked more like demons than men and were armed with swords and daggers. They drew in on us and attacked us, slaying those who offered resistance, and taking the rest prisoners. They towed the ship to the island and took all the merchandise in the hold. Then they led us away to be sold as slaves.

It fell to my lot that I was purchased by a rich man of gentle mien. He took me to his house, gave me food and drink, clothed me well and treated me in a friendly fashion. Somewhat comforted I rested, giving my hands to light tasks about his house. After some days he called me to him and said, "Art thou skilled in any art or trade?" I answered him that I was a merchant, and was skilled only in the art of buying and selling. "Canst thou not use the bow?" he asked. Now, I was skilled in archery, and I offered to give him proof in the matter. He then placed a bow and arrow in my hands and I pierced a mark at fifty paces. "It is well," he said; "thou art skilled."

The next day he sat me behind him on an elephant, and, at nightfall, we journeyed to a place where there were some high trees. One of these he bade me climb and sit there with arrow on bowstring till the elephants came at dawn, when I was to shoot; and, if I was so fortunate as to kill one, I was to run to him in all haste and inform him of it. He then went away on his elephant, leaving me in the tree, full of terror.

When at last the sun rose, a great number of elephants came straying about among the trees, and when one came beneath mine I sent my arrows at him. Late in the morning a well-aimed shaft pierced the brain of a monstrous beast, and, with loud roarings, he fell and died. At evening time, when the other elephants had retired from the spot, I descended from the tree and ran with all haste to my master, who rejoiced at my news and sent his slaves to bring the beast in.

Day after day I continued at this sport, each day securing at least one elephant. But a day came when trouble gathered round that tree in which I sat. It appeared in the form of countless elephants of large size and ferocious aspect. One who seemed to be king among them led the others to my tree. After he had thundered round it many times until the whole world trembled, he made a dash at it, and winding his trunk round it, tore it up by the roots and threw it down. When, half stunned, I found my way out from among the broken branches, the great elephant came upon me bellowing loudly, and, seizing me with his trunk, bore me aloft. In this manner he led the whole herd of elephants in a wild stampede that made the earth shake; and they ceased not in their career until they came to a valley in which were a great number of elephant's bones and teeth and tusks. On a heap of these the king-elephant set me down very gently; and, after that, he and the others turned and walked away, leaving me there.

I looked about in the valley and saw a wealth of gleaming white tusks on every hand, and I said within myself, "The elephants liked not the death of one of their number every day, and they have done this to show how I may come by an abundance of tusks without further slaughter."

Then I found my way back over a great distance to the abode of my master. He welcomed me as one returned from the dead, for, when he had found the tree torn up by the roots, he had concluded that the elephants had made an end of me. I told him what had befallen me and described the position of the valley where the tusks lay. When he heard this he was greatly excited and lost no time in mounting me behind him on an elephant and setting forth to find the spot where so much wealth was stored. We reached the valley without mishap and I showed my master the ivory, at sight of which his joy knew no bounds. We then laded the el-

ephant with as much as he could carry and returned with it to
the house.

This adventure of mine placed me in a most favourable
light in my master's eyes; and, because I had been the means
of revealing to him a source of enormous wealth, he set me
free and gave me permission to return to my own country.
He was even better than his word, for, not many days
later, he set me on board a vessel bound for El-Basrah and
presented me with a large sum of money for my passage and
expenses, together with many bales of merchandise. And
my return journey was very fortunate. The traffic I did
at the different cities on the way brought me great profit,
and I bought many rare things suitable for gifts.

On my arrival at Baghdad I went in to the Khalifeh and
told him all that had befallen me; and he was so astonished
thereat, and so delighted at my return, that he commanded
his scribes to write my story in letters of gold. And he said
to me, "O Sindbad, my son; thou hast done well, and now
thou shalt have the wish of thine heart and keep thy vow;
for, unless thou so desirest, thou shalt go forth no more upon
the sea."

.   .   .   .

This, O Sindbad the Landsman, is the end of the story
of my voyages; and now, as I have conceived an affection
for thee, thou shalt dwell with me and be my boon companion; and we shall pass our lives together in a state of
the utmost joy and happiness, strengthened by God (whose
name be exalted!) the Great! the Omnipotent Creator of sea
and land!

ONCE upon a time, in a far city of Cathay, there dwelt a poor tailor who had an only son named Aladdin. This boy was a born ne'er-do-well, and persistently resisted all his father's efforts to teach him a trade by means of which he would be able in future to earn a livelihood. Aladdin would sooner play at knuckle-bones in the gutter with others as careless as himself than he would set his mind to honest business; and, as to obeying his parents in the smallest matter, it was not in his nature. Such was this boy Aladdin, and yet—so remarkable is the favour of fate—he was strangely predestined for great things.

Stricken with grief because of the waywardness and idle conduct of his son the father fell ill and died, and the mother found great difficulty in supporting herself, to say nothing of the worthless Aladdin as well. While she wore the flesh off her bones in the endeavour to obtain a meagre subsistence Aladdin would amuse himself with his fellow urchins of the street, only returning home to his meals. In this way he continued until he was fourteen years of age, when his extraordinary destiny took him by the hand, and led him, step by step, through adventures so wonderful that words can scarce describe them.

One day he was playing in the gutter with his ragged companions, as was his wont, when a Moorish Dervish came by, and, catching sight of Aladdin's face, suddenly stopped and approached him. This Dervish was a sorcerer who had discovered many hidden secrets by his black art; in fact, he was on the track of one now; and, by the look on his face as he scrutinised Aladdin's features, it seemed that the boy was closely connected with his quest.

The Dervish beckoned to one of the urchins and asked him who Aladdin was, who his father was, and indeed all about him. Having thus learned the whole history of the boy and his family the Dervish gave his informer some coins and sent him away to spend them. Then he approached Aladdin and said to him, "Boy, I seem to recognise in thee a family likeness. Art thou not the tailor's son?" Aladdin answered him that he was, and added that his father was dead.

On hearing this the Dervish cried out with grief and embraced Aladdin, weeping bitterly. The boy was surprised at this and inquired the cause of such sorrow. "Alas!" replied the Dervish with tears running down his cheeks, "my fate is an unhappy one. Boy, I have come from a distant country to find my brother, to look upon his face again, and to cheer and comfort him; and now thou tellest me he is dead." He took Aladdin's face in his hands and gazed searchingly upon it as he continued: "Boy, I recognise my brother's features in thine; and, now that he is dead, I will find comfort in thee."

Aladdin looked up at him in wonder, for he had never been told that he had an uncle; indeed, he was inclined to doubt the truth of the matter; but, when the Dervish took ten pieces of gold from his purse and placed them in his hand, all doubt was out of the question, and he rejoiced at having found so rich an uncle. The Dervish then asked him concerning his mother and begged him to show him the way to her house. And, when Aladdin had showed him, he gave the boy more gold and said, "Give this to thy mother with my blessing, and say that her brother-in-law, who has been absent forty years, has returned and will visit her to-morrow to weep with her over the place where his brother is buried." With this he departed, and Aladdin ran to his mother to tell her the news.

On the morrow the Dervish sought Aladdin in the street where he had seen him the day before, and found him there among his disreputable friends. Taking him aside he kissed him and embraced him; then, placing ten gold pieces in his hand, he said, "Hasten now to thy mother and give her these gold pieces, and say that her brother-in-law would come to sup at her house this night."

So Aladdin left him and ran home to his mother with the gold pieces and the message. Then the widow busied herself and prepared for the coming of this new-found relative. She bought rich food, and borrowed from the neighbours such dishes, utensils, and napery as she required. When the supper was ready, and the widow was about to send Aladdin to hasten the guest, the Dervish entered, followed by a slave bearing fruit and wine, which he set down, and then went his way. The Dervish, weeping bitterly, saluted the widow and immediately fell to asking questions about the departed.

ALADDIN AND THE WONDERFUL LAMP

Then, when he was comforted and they all sat at supper together, the Dervish turned to Aladdin and asked him if he knew any art or trade. At this Aladdin hung his head, and, as he was too ashamed to answer, his mother dried her tears and answered for him. "Alack!" she said, "he is nothing but an idler. He spends his time as thou didst find him, playing with ragamuffins in the street, and is never at home except at meal times. And I—I am an old woman and ugly through toil and hardship, and grief at his behaviour. O my brother-in-law! It is he who should provide for me, not I for him."

"I am grieved to hear this of thee," said the Dervish, turning to Aladdin; "for thou art no longer a child. Wouldst thou like to be a merchant?" he asked. "If so I will give thee a shop with all kinds of merchandise, and thou shalt buy and sell and get gain, and rise to a position of importance."

At this Aladdin clapped his hands with glee, and his mother was rejoiced. And she chid her boy for his own good, and counselled him straitly to obey his uncle in all things. The Dervish also gave Aladdin much sound advice on the conduct of trade, so that the boy's head was bursting with buying and selling, and he could not sleep that night for dreams of rich stuffs, and bales of merchandise. At last, when the Dervish arose and took his departure, promising to return for Aladdin on the morrow and take him to buy his merchant's dress, the wizard felt that he had proved himself undoubtedly the best of brothers-in-law, and the best of uncles.

True to his word the Dervish came on the morrow, and Aladdin, holding him affectionately by the hand, went with him forth to the market. There they entered a shop full of the finest materials, and the Dervish asked to be shown some dresses such as a wealthy merchant might wear. The owner of the shop laid a great variety before him, and the Dervish said, "Now, my son, choose what dress you like." This delicate favour of choice pleased Aladdin greatly, for it seemed that he had now at last reached the age of discretion. He picked out one that he liked, and the Dervish paid the price without any attempt at bargaining. Then they went together to the Hammam, and, when they had bathed and rested, Aladdin clothed himself in his new dress and came forth in great delight, kissing his uncle's hand and thanking him again and again.

After they had rested the Dervish suggested a walk, and he led Aladdin through garden after garden until they came to the confines of the city, beyond which stood a high hill. "Shall we return, O my uncle?" said Aladdin, who was in no mood for climbing the hill. "There are no more gardens outside the city." "Nay," replied the Dervish, "on the hillside is the loveliest garden of all. Bear up, my son, and be a man; we shall soon be there." And, as they went, he beguiled the boy with anecdotes, so that Aladdin forgot both the length of the way and his weariness.

At last they came to a place on the hillside where the Dervish paused and looked about him, saying to himself, "This is the spot I have journeyed so far to find." But to Aladdin he said, "Rest here awhile, O my son, and, when thou art refreshed, gather some wood and we will make a fire; then, if thou wish to see a most wonderful thing, I will show thee that which will take thy breath away."

At this Aladdin's curiosity was excited, and with no thought of resting, he began at once to gather wood. When he had collected a sufficient quantity the Dervish lighted the fire, and, taking from his wallet a little box, drew some fine powder from it and scattered it over the fire, uttering an incantation. Immediately, amid rumblings of thunder, the earth reeled and opened. At this Aladdin fled in terror, but the Dervish, powerless to effect his purpose without the boy's aid, flew after him in a rage, and smote him over the head, so that he fell to the ground stunned.

When, presently, he regained his senses, he sat up and cried out, "What have I done, O my uncle, that thou shouldst strike me?" "Nay, my son," replied the Dervish, "I intended not to hurt thee. Come, now, be a man, and obey my wishes if thou wouldst see the wonderful things that I will show thee." With such words as these he banished Aladdin's fears and smoothed him over. Then he directed him to the opening in the earth, where there was revealed a slab of marble with a brass ring let into it. The Dervish stooped and began to draw figures upon the ground, saying as he did so, "Obey me, Aladdin, in all that I say, for so thou shalt become richer than all the kings of the earth. Know, O my son, that beyond that slab of stone lies vast treasure which none but thee can acquire and live. Therefore, advance, my son, and take the brass ring in thy hand, and lift the slab from its place; for it is predestined that thou art the only one on this earth that hath the power to do this thing." And Aladdin, stirred to great wonder by the words of the Dervish, would have done his bidding with alacrity, but, on looking at the marble slab, he saw that it was far too heavy for him.

"Never can I raise that alone, O my uncle," he said. "Wilt thou not help me?" "Nay," answered the Dervish, "it will yield to no hand but thine. Grasp the ring and repeat the names of as many of thine ancestors as thou canst remember, beginning with thy father and mother; for thine ancestors are my ancestors, O my son! By this the stone will come away quite easily in thy hand as if it were a feather. Am I not thine uncle, and have I not said it? And did I not cleave the hillside with my incantations? Wherefore, pluck up courage, and forget not that all the riches beyond that stone are for thee."

Thus encouraged Aladdin advanced to the stone, repeating the names of all the ancestors he could remember; and, taking hold of the ring, lifted the heavy slab from its place with perfect ease, and threw it aside. Then within the aperture lay revealed a stairway of twelve steps leading into a passage.

While Aladdin was gazing at this wonder the Dervish took a ring from his finger and placed it upon the middle finger of the boy's right hand, saying impressively as he did so, "Listen to me, O my son! fear nothing in what I am about to bid thee do, for this ring will be thy protection in all dangers and against all evils. If thou shouldst find thyself in evil case thou hast only to——, but of that I will tell thee presently. What is more important now is this. In order to come at the treasure, O my son, steady thyself and listen attentively, and see to it that thou fail not a word of these my instructions. Go down the steps and traverse the passage to the end, where thou wilt find a chamber divided into four parts, each containing four vessels of gold. Touch not these on thy life, for if so much as the fringe of thy robe cometh in contact with any of them, thou wilt immediately be turned into stone. Linger not to gaze upon them, but pass right through to the end, where thou wilt find a door. Open this, repeating again the names of thine ancestors, when lo, thou wilt behold a beautiful garden before thee. Take the pathway that is ready for thy feet and proceed forty-nine cubits until thou comest to an alcove, where is set a stairway of forty-nine steps. Look not to ascend that stairway: it is not for thee nor me; but direct thine attention to a lamp hanging above the alcove. Take it from its fastening, and pour out the oil therein; then put it in thy breast securely, and retrace thy steps to me. Is it clear to thee, my son?"

"O my uncle, it is quite clear," replied Aladdin, and he repeated the instructions he had received. "Pull thy wits together then, my son," said the Dervish, well pleased; "and descend, for verily thou art a man of mettle, and not a child. Yea, thou, and thou only, art the rightful owner of all this great treasure. Come now!"

Filled with courage from the wizard's words, and enticed by the dazzle of untold riches, Aladdin descended the twelve steps and passed through the fourfold chamber with the utmost care lest he should touch any of the golden jars therein with so much as the fringe of his garment. When he came to the door at the far end he paused to repeat the names of his ancestors, and opened it; then, lo, before him lay a beautiful garden where the trees were laden with many coloured fruit, while sweet-voiced birds sang in the branches. He took the pathway that lay before his feet, and, as he followed it, he looked up and noticed that the trees bore, not fruit as he had supposed, but sparkling jewels, flashing with many colours.

But Aladdin, though dazzled by the glitter, thought these sparkling things were but coloured glass; and it was for such that he plucked them with boyish delight until his pockets were full. "These are lovely things to play with," he said, and proceeded to fill his girdle also.

As he made his way along the garden path, plucking the bright jewels as he went, he caught sight of the alcove at the far end, and, remembering his uncle's instructions, hastened towards it. There was the stairway of forty-nine steps, and there, hanging from a crystal beam, was the Lamp. He paused, looking up at it. How should he reach it?" His uncle had said that the stairway was neither for Aladdin nor for himself, and yet he saw at a glance that the only way of reaching the Lamp was by mounting seven steps of the stair-way. He hesitated, then, concluding that the Lamp was the whole object of his quest, and that he must reach it at all costs, he ventured. With some misgivings he mounted the seven steps and, reaching out, took the Lamp from its fastening and descended with it. Then, emptying out the oil, he placed it securely in his bosom, saying, "Now, as my uncle said to me, with this Lamp in my bosom all is mine!"

As Aladdin was returning along the pathway among the trees, laden with the precious jewels, fear assailed him lest his uncle would be angry at his delay, for it was borne in upon him that no great delight can come to a mortal without his having to suffer for it. Whereupon he hastened his footsteps, and, passing through the fourfold chamber without touching the golden jars—for the fear of that was still upon him—he arrived quickly at the foot of the stairway of twelve steps. Heavily weighted at he was with the jewels and the Lamp he proceeded to mount the stairs at a run. But the jewels grew heavier, and the Lamp weighed upon his bosom, so that he was exhausted by the time he was half-way up. Kneeling on the seventh step he looked up and saw the Dervish urging him on with the greatest impatience.

"Bear with me, O my uncle," he said. "I am heavily weighted and am out of breath. I will soon come to thee." Then he climbed three steps and one step more, and sank exhausted before the last, which was far higher than the others. The jewels and the Lamp oppressed him with heaviness and he could not mount that last step. "O my uncle, give me thy hand and help me up," he cried. But the wizard dare not touch him, for so the spell of fate was worded and he must abide by it. "Nay," he called down, "thou art man enough! It is the Lamp that hampers thee. Reach up and place it on the ledge here; then thou canst mount easily thyself."

The Dervish held out his hand expectantly for the Lamp and his eyes glittered. Aladdin saw the evil light in them, and, having some mother wit, replied, "O my uncle, the Lamp is no weight at all; it is simply that I am exhausted and this step is too high for me. Give me thy hand and help me up." "Give me the Lamp!" cried the Dervish, holding his hand out for it, and beginning to rage. "Place it on the ledge before thee, and then I will help thee up." "Nay," returned Aladdin, growing obstinate, "if thou wilt not give me thy hand I will not give thee the Lamp, for it is in my thoughts that thou wantest the Lamp more than thou wantest me."

This enraged the Dervish to a point beyond control, and he said within himself, "If I get not the Lamp then may it perish with him!" And, taking a box from his wallet, he threw some powder on the embers of the fire, muttering curses and incantations as he did so. Immediately a flame shot up, and its many tongues went hither and thither, licking the air. The earth shuddered and groaned with a hollow thunder; then the marble slab closed of itself over the aperture, the hillside rushed together above it, and all was as before, save that Aladdin was sealed within that cavern without hope of escape.

Long and loud did Aladdin call to his supposed uncle to save him from a living death; but there was no answer to his cries, and, at last, when he was almost exhausted, he took counsel of himself and plainly saw the truth of the matter. The Dervish was no uncle of his, but a cunning wizard who had made a cat's-paw of him to secure treasure which, by the laws of magic and destiny, he was powerless to come at in any other way. The whole thing, from the very beginning, was a trick; and he saw it clearly now that it was too late. The way out was sealed, and the darkness pressed heavily upon him. Frantic with the desire to escape from this dungeon he thought of the garden and the stairway in the alcove; but, when he had groped his way to the end of the passage, he found the door closed, and all his efforts failed to open it. The names of his ancestors were of no avail against the magic of the Dervish. At this he wept loudly, and continued to weep throughout the night, until his rage and despair were spent. At last he sank down exhausted on the lowest step of the stairway by which he had first descended, and, feeling himself utterly abandoned by man, he raised his hands to God, praying for deliverance from his calamity.

Now, while he was holding his hands in supplication, he felt the ring upon his middle finger—the ring which the Dervish had placed there saying, "In whatever difficulty thou mayst find thyself this ring will be thy protection; thou hast only to——, but of that I will tell thee later." The Dervish had perhaps given him the ring to gain his confidence, and had purposely omitted to reveal its secret. But now, in answer to Aladdin's prayer, the power of the ring was revealed as if by the merest chance; for, when he felt the ring, he looked at it; and, seeing a light from the jewel therein, he breathed upon it and rubbed it with his palm to increase its lustre. No sooner had he done this when, lo, the

Slave of the Ring appeared, and gathered shape before before, first in a luminous haze, and then, gradually, in clearer and clearer contour.

"Ask what thou wilt, and it shall be done," said the apparition; "for know that I am the Slave of the Ring and the slave of him on whose finger my master placed the ring."

Aladdin, seeing before him an Efrite after the order of those invoked by the Lord Suleiman, was terrified, and his tongue clave to the roof of his mouth, so that he could not speak. But the Efrite reassured him with kindly speech. "Thou hast only to ask," he said, "and thy wish will be fulfilled; for, since my master's ring is on thy hand, I am thy servant."

At this Aladdin took heart, and, having considered his wish, resolved to put the matter to the test. "O Slave of the Ring!" he said, "my wish is that thou take me from this dungeon and place me in the light of day where the sun shines and the breezes blow—if indeed it *is* day, for here have I been for many, many hours."

Scarcely had he spoken the words when there was a clap of thunder. The cavern opened, and, by some mysterious power, he was conveyed through the opening. Then, when he sat up and looked around him, he was in the light of day upon the hillside, and everything was as it had been when he and the Dervish had first reached the spot.

Aladdin marvelled greatly at this, and said within himself, "I wonder if it was all a dream!" But, when he looked at the ring upon his finger and felt the Lamp and the jewel-fruit he had gathered from the trees in the garden, he knew it was not a dream. Besides, there was the spot where the fire had been; and it was now but a heap of grey ashes on the ground. Turning himself about, he saw the path by which they had ascended, and the gardens stretching below. Nothing had changed. The side of the hill which the Dervish by his magic had opened for his entrance, and the Slave of the Ring had now closed up behind him, was as it had been when he first saw it.

Seeing that he was safe and sound in the outer world, Aladdin fell on his knees and gave thanks to the most High for his deliverance from a terrible death. Then straightway he arose and took the path that led down the hillside and through the gardens of the city in the direction of his home. At length, with wearied body, but elated mind, he reached the doorway of his dwelling, and, entering, found his mother weeping.

"Where hast thou been, my son?" she cried. "All night long I lay awake, anxious for thee; and now it is again near nightfall, and thou comest like one about to die. Where hast thou been, and where is thine uncle?"

But Aladdin could not answer her. What with utter weariness, and the joy of gaining his home once more, he fell in a swoon at her feet. Quickly she dashed water on his face and restored him. Then, when she had made him eat, she inquired gently what had befallen him.

"O my mother," said Aladdin, "how much thou art to blame! Thou gavest me over to a devil of a sorcerer who tried, by his evil arts, to compass my ruin." And thus, having vented his anger at the false conduct of the Dervish, he proceeded to tell his mother, first about the Lamp and the jewel-fruit, then about all that had happened on the hillside, from the opening of the earth by a magic spell, to the closing of it again, and his subsequent escape through the Slave of the Ring.

Then Aladdin took the Lamp and the precious stones from his bosom, and placed them before his mother, albeit neither knew why the Lamp had been so coveted by the Dervish, or that the stones were more valuable than any possessed by kings.

Now, neither Aladdin nor his mother had rested for two days and two nights, so that, exhausted at length with weeping and with heaping maledictions on the Dervish, they slept; and, when they awoke, it was about noon of the following day. Aladdin's first words on pulling his wits together were to the effect that he was hungry. "Nay, O my son," replied his mother, "there is nothing to eat in the house, for thou didst eat yesterday all that there was. But stay, I have some spinning that is ready for the market. I will take and sell it and buy some food."

She was busying herself about this when Aladdin suddenly called out to her, "Mother! bring me the Lamp, and I will take and sell that; it will fetch more than the spinning." Now, although Aladdin and his mother knew that the Dervish had greatly coveted the Lamp, they both imagined that he had some strange reason of his own for this; and, as the Lamp was an article that would command a ready sale, the mother quickly agreed to Aladdin's proposal and brought the Lamp to him in answer to his call. On regarding it closely, however, she observed that it was very dirty. Well knowing that it would fetch a better price if it were clean and bright, she set to work to polish it with some fine sand; when lo, as soon as she started to rub the Lamp, the air before her danced and quivered and a chill gasp of wind smote her in the face. Then, looking up, she saw, towering above her, a being monstrous and terrible, with a fierce face in which gleamed fiery eyes beneath frowning brows. She gazed at this apparition in fear and astonishment, for she knew it was surely a powerful Efrite such as were under the power of the Lord Suleiman. Then the being spoke: "Thou hast invoked me; what is thy wish?" But she only gazed at him, dumb with terror. Again the awful being spoke: "Thou hast summoned me, for I am the Slave of the Lamp which is in thy hand. What is thy desire?" At this the poor woman could no longer endure her fear, and, with a cry, she fell in a swoon.

Aladdin had heard the Efrite's words and had hastened to his mother's side. He had already seen the power of the Slave of the Ring, and he guessed that now the Slave of the Lamp had appeared, and was ready to do the bidding of the one who held the Lamp. So he quickly took it from his mother's hand, and, standing before the Efrite, plucked up courage and said, "I desire food, O Slave of the Lamp! the finest food that ever was set before a king."

No sooner had he spoken than the Efrite vanished, but only to reappear immediately, bearing a rich tray of solid silver, on which were twelve golden dishes with fruits and meats of various kinds. There were also flagons of wine and silver goblets. As Aladdin stared in amazement at this magnificent repast the Efrite set the tray down before him and vanished in a flash. Then Aladdin turned to his mother and dashed cold water on her face, and held perfumes to her nostrils until she regained consciousness and sat up. And when she beheld the sumptuous repast set out upon the golden dishes she was greatly astonished, and imagined that the Sultan had sent it from his palace. But Aladdin, who was very hungry, fell to eating heartily; and, while persuading his mother to eat, he would tell her nothing.

It was not until they had satisfied their hunger, and placed the remainder aside for the morrow, that Aladdin informed her what had happened. Then she questioned him, saying, "O my son, was not this the same Efrite that appeared to thee when thou wast in the cavern?" "Nay," he answered. "That was the Slave of the Ring; this was the Slave of the Lamp." "At all events," said she, "it was a terrible monster that nearly caused my death through fear. Promise me, O my son, that thou wilt have naught further to do with the Ring and the Lamp. Cast them from thee, for the Holy Prophet hath told us to have no traffic with devils."

"Nay, nay, O my mother," protested Aladdin; "it were wiser to keep them, for did not the Slave of the Ring deliver me from death? and has not the Slave of the Lamp brought us delicious food when we were hungry?" "That may be so," replied his mother, "but hear my words, my son; no good thing can come of these dealings with accursed spirits, and it were better for thee to have died in the cavern than to invoke their aid." And thus she pleaded with him to cast away the Ring and the Lamp, for she was sore afraid of the power of the Evil One. But Aladdin would not undertake to do this, although, in respect for her wishes, he agreed to conceal the objects so that she might never need to look upon them. He also agreed to invoke neither of the Efrites again, unless it were a case of dire necessity. And with this his mother had to rest content.

Mother and son continued to live on the food that remained, until, in a few days, it was all gone. Then Aladdin took up one of the dishes from the tray, and, not knowing that it was of pure gold, went out to sell it and buy food with the proceeds. In the market he came to the shop of a merchant—a man of exceeding vile methods of buying and selling; and he showed the dish to him. This man, as soon as he saw the dish, knew it for pure gold and glanced sharply at Aladdin to find whether he knew its value. Then, preferring that others might call him a rogue rather than that the event might prove him a fool in his own eyes, he took a single gold piece from his pocket and handed it to Aladdin.

As for Aladdin, he hastened home and gave the gold piece to his mother, begging her to buy food with it. She did so, and they ate, and were comforted. And so, from day to day, they lived on the proceeds of one dish after another, which the unregenerate merchant bought at cheaper and cheaper prices, saying always that the metal was inferior, and that the demand for such goods was not what it used to be. And, when at last the dishes were all sold, Aladdin, who, in deference to his mother's wishes, had concealed the Lamp

[125]

and the Ring against a necessitous occasion, brought forth
the former and rubbed it, for so, he concluded, was the Slave
invoked. His conclusion was right, for no sooner had he
rubbed the Lamp than the Efrite suddenly appeared before
him, immense and of terrible aspect.

"What is thy wish, O my master?" said the Efrite; "for
I am the Slave of the Lamp and of him who holds it." "My
wish," answered Aladdin, "is that you bring me another tray
of food similar to the one you brought before." Immediately the Efrite vanished, and, in a moment, appeared again,
bearing a tray of food exactly similar to the one he had
brought before. He set this down before Aladdin and then
disappeared.

And they ate and drank and were merry, the food lasting
them some days. Then, when the food was all gone,
Aladdin proceeded to dispose of the dishes as before. Taking one of them he went forth to find the merchant, but it
chanced that on his way he passed the shop of a fair-dealing
man who had no vile methods of buying and selling, but was
just, and feared God. When this man saw Aladdin passing
he called to him, and told him that he had frequently seen
him selling things to the wicked merchant, and warned him
about it.

Then Aladdin showed him the dish of gold and he took
it, and weighed it on the scales. "My son," he said, "here
is the price if thou wouldst sell."

He counted out seventy gold pieces and handed them to
Aladdin, who took them and thanked the merchant heartily
for his honest exposure of the merchant's wickedness. And

thereafter he brought the remaining dishes, and at last the tray, to that merchant, and received from him their full value; so that Aladdin and his mother were placed above want and in a comfortable position for people of their station in life.

During this time Aladdin had changed his ways greatly. He no longer consorted with the ragamuffins of the street, but selected for his friends men of standing and integrity. Often he would watch the jewellers at their work, and the goods they handled; and, through knowledge thus acquired, he began to suspect that the jewel-fruit he had gathered in the garden of the cavern was not glass, as he had imagined, but real gems. By this and that, and by comparing and asking questions, he came at length to the certainty that he actually possessed the richest jewels in all the earth. The smallest among them was bigger and more sparkling by far than the largest and finest he could see in any jeweller's shop.

One day he was in the jewellers' market, taking note of things, when a herald came by, crying to all people: "Take heed! By command of the Sultan, King of the Age and Lord of the Earth, let all doors be closed, and let none come forth from shop or dwelling on pain of instant death, for the Sultan's daughter, Bedr-el-Budur cometh to the bath! Take heed!"

Now, on hearing this, a great longing arose in Aladdin's breast too look upon the face of Bedr-el-Budur, the sultan's daughter. "All people extol her loveliness," he said to himself; "and I—even if I die for it—I will look upon her face;

for something—I know not what—impels me to gaze on Bedr-el-Budur the beautiful."

Hastening to the Hammam he secreted himself behind the door so that, unobserved himself, he might see her when she came in. And presently the Sultan's daughter arrived; and, as she entered, she lifted the veil from her face, so that Aladdin saw her features clearly.

What a wondrous beauty was there! The witchery of her eyes! The ivory of her skin! The jet of her glossy tresses! These, and the swaying of her graceful body as she walked, caused Aladdin's heart to turn to water and then to spring wildly into flame.

Like one walking in a dream Aladdin went home and sat him down in dejection of spirit. For a long time he answered not his mother's questions as to what ailed him, but continued like one who had beheld a vision so lovely that it had deprived him of his senses. At last, however, he looked up, and said, "O my mother, know that until to-day I had believed that all women were of thy fashion of face, but now 1 find they are not; for to-day I saw the Sultan's daughter, and she is more beautiful than all others on earth." And Aladdin told her how he had hidden behind the door of the Hammam, so that, when Bedr-el-Budur had entered and lifted her veil, he had seen her clearly; and how, on that, a great love had leapt up in his heart and filled him to the exclusion of all else. "And there is no rest for me," he concluded, "until I win the Lady Bedr-el-Budur, and make her my wife."

At these daring words Aladdin's mother regarded him

sharply with fear on her face. "Art thou mad, my son?" she cried. "Nay, O my mother," he answered, "I am not mad. But, as I risked my life to see her, so will I risk it again to win her; for, without her, life is of no account to me. I will go to the Sultan and ask him to give me the lovely Bedr-el-Budur for my lawful wife."

Seeing his determination his mother was sore afraid, and knew not what to do. For a long time she reasoned with him anxiously, pointing out what a scandal it would be for the son of a poor tailor to aspire to the Sultan's daughter.

These arguments, and more, his mother put before him; but Aladdin shook his head at all of them, and remained firm in his determination. "And further, O my mother," he said, "I wish now that thou go thyself to the Sultan and put my request to him, for am I not thy child? And is it not thy duty to perform this office for me?"

"O my son," she cried in despair, "wilt thou bring me into thy madness? I, a poor woman of humble birth, to go in to the Sultan and demand the princess for my son! Besides, O my son, How shall I even gain access to the Sultan's presence for this purpose without bearing a rich gift to offer him?"

"Mother," answered Aladdin, "thy words have served me well, for they have called to my recollection a thing which, through excess of love for the Lady Bedr-el-Budur, I had forgotten. Thou sayest that thou canst not approach the Sultan without a rich gift. Then, O my mother, if I place in thy hands an offering richer than any King in the world can make to any other, wilt thou carry out my desire?"

Thinking his words were wild as the wind, and that he could produce no such offering, his mother agreed; but, remembering the Slave of the Lamp, and what had already been done in that way, she stipulated with Aladdin that she would carry out his wish only on condition that it required no further invoking of the Efrite. Aladdin assured her on this, and asked her to fetch him a china bowl. Wondering greatly she arose, and brought the bowl to him. Then Aladdin emptied into it all the sparkling jewels which he carried within his garments, and, when they were heaped together in the bowl they shone with a dazzling splendour. But, since he realized that it was not impossible that the project might fail, and that he might have to seek too the Slave of the Lamp for advice and help in difficulty, he spoke to his mother on the matter. "O my mother," he said, "it was the condition of thy promise that I should not invoke the Slave of the Lamp in the furtherance of this my desire; yet it must be understood between us that if thou make a blunder—which thou needst not do—then, to extricate us from a dire calamity, I am free to rub the Lamp and see what its Slave can do for our salvation."

His mother assented to this, for she knew, if she failed with the Sultan, all was lost; and, in such case, even the aid of a demon would be acceptable.

When morning dawned Aladdin's mother arose and prepared herself for the visit to the palace, and, wrapping the bowl of jewels in a cloth, went forth early. When the audience was full the Sultan came in and seated himself on the royal divan. All bowed down before him, and then stood waiting with folded arms for his permission to be seated. And, when he gave permission, all sat down in their due order of precedence. Then he listened to their petitions in the same order, and gave his decisions, until the hour grew late, and the audience was declared closed. The Sultan arose and went into the palace, and the princes, with the nobles and the people, went their ways. Among them went Aladdin's mother, thinking to herself that this would be a matter of many days. And every day thereafter she stood in the audience with the bowl of jewels under her arm and heard the petitions, but dared not for very timidity address the Sultan. And in this way she continued for a whole month, while Aladdin was nursing his impatient soul and waiting on the issue.

Now the Sultan, being observant, had noticed the woman present herself constantly at the levee. So he commanded the Vizier to see to it that, should the woman present herself again, she be instantly brought before him.

And it came according to the Sultan's command to the Grand Vizier; for one day the Sultan saw her waiting in the audience chamber and ordered the Vizier to bring her forward that he might consider her affair.

Now, at last, she was face to face with the Sultan, making obeisance to him and kissing the ground at his feet. "I have seen thee here, O woman, for many days," said the Sultan; "and thou hast not approached me. If thou hast a wish that I can grant, lay it before me." At this she kissed the ground again, and prayed fervently for the prolongation of his life. Then she said, "O King of all Ages, I have a request; but, peace be on thee, it is a strange one! Wherefore I claim thy clemency before I state it."

These words whetted the Sultan's curiosity, and, as he was a man of great gentleness, he spoke her softly in reply, and not only assured her of his clemency but ordered all others present to withdraw, saving only the Grand Vizier, so that he might hear her petition in secret.

"Now, woman," said the Sultan, turning to her, "make thy petition, and the peace and protection of God be on thee." "Thy forgiveness, also, O King," she said. "God forgive thee if there is aught to forgive," he replied. And at this Aladdin's mother unfolded the tale of her son's exceeding love for Bedr-el-Budur, the Sultan's daughter: how life had become intolerable to him because of this, and how his only thought was to win the Lady Bedr-el-Budur for his wife, or die—either of grief, or by the Sultan's anger. Wherefore, his life being in the balance in any case, she had come as a last resort to beg the Sultan to bestow his daughter on her son. And she concluded by beseeching the Sultan not to punish either her or her son for this unparalleled hardihood.

The Sultan looked at the Grand Vizier, whose face was of stone—for the Lady Bedr-el-Budur had already been promised to his son. "What sayest thou?" said the Sultan, regarding him with merriment in his eyes. But the Grand Vizier only cast a contemptuous look at Aladdin's mother, and answered him: "O King of the Age! Thou knowest how to deal with this petition." At this the Sultan laughed outright, and, turning a kindly face to the humble suppliant, observed her minutely. "What is that bundle thou hast under thine arm?" he said at last, remembering that she had brought it with her on every occasion.

Aladdin's mother, greatly relieved to see the Sultan laughing, unfolded the wrappings of the bowl and handed it to him. As soon as he took it in his hand, and saw the size and splendid sparkle of the jewels, the Sultan laughed no longer, but gazed at them, speechless with wonder and admiration. Then, at length, he handed the bowl to the Grand Vizier, saying, "Upon my oath, this is a marvellous thing! Tell me, O Vizier, have I in my treasury a single jewel that will compare with even the smallest of these?"

The Grand Vizier also was taken aback by their dazzling loveliness and beauty. He would have lied, saying they were glass or crystal, but the stones themselves flashed back the purposed lie in his teeth. All he could reply was, "Never O my lord the King, have I beheld the like of these; nor is there one in thy treasury that could equal the beauty of the smallest of them." And, saying this, the Vizier turned very pale, for neither he nor his son could approach the Sultan with such a gift. And it was as he had feared, and as Aladdin had prophesied: the Sultan required to know nothing further than what was before him in the bowl.

"O Vizier," said the Sultan. "What sayest thou? The man who sends me this kingly gift is worthy of my daughter. I, the Sultan, King of the Age, having power over all men, do withdraw my former promise to thee to bestow her on thy son. Bedr-el-Budur, the one beautiful jewel in the treasury of my heart, is my gift in return to the man who has sent me these priceless jewels."

The Grand Vizier bit his lips and pondered awhile. Then he spoke. "Peace be on thee, O King of all the Earth. But is not thy promise worth most of all? Thou didst pledge me thy daughter for my son, and with that pledge I went, thinking that the whole earth and all therein were not its value. Wherefore, O King, I pray that thou wilt allow this matter time. If thou wilt pledge this foster-mother of a prince that thou wilt comply with her request in three months' time, then it seems to me that, by so doing, thou wilt cement the good feeling and loosen the griefs of all parties concerned. And in the meantime—yea, I have good reason for saying it—there will come before thee, O King of the Age, a gift compared to which this thou hast seen is but dross."

The Sultan weighed the Grand Vizier's words in his mind, and accordingly, he said to the woman, "Tell thy son that he hath my royal assent, and that I will give him my daughter in marriage; but, as every woman knows, these things cannot be hastened, for there are garments and necessaries to be prepared; wherefore thy son (on whom be peace) must abide in patience, for, let us say, three months. At the end of that time he may approach me for the fulfilment of my promise."

Satisfied with this, Aladdin's mother thanked and blessed the Sultan, and, buoyed up with a burden of delight, almost flew back to her house. There Aladdin was awaiting for her, and, when he saw her hastening, and noticed that she had returned without the bowl of jewels, his heart rose high to meet her.

Then she related to him the details of the interview, laying stress upon the fact that, although the Sultan had been moved at the sight of the jewels to make immediate arrangements for the marriage, a private word from the Grand Vizier had led him to delay the ceremony for three months. "Take heed, my son!" she concluded. "The Grand Vizier hath a motive for this counsel of delay. He is thine enemy. I saw it in his face. Beware of him!"

Aladdin was greatly relieved by her news. He felt like one jerked out of the grave; and, where the Sultan was favourable to his suit, he was in no mood to fear a Grand Vizier. "Nay, nay," he said, "the jewels have the eye of the Sultan more than the Grand Vizier hath his ear. Fear nothing, O my mother! The Sultan's word is good, and I rest content to wait; though I know not how such a long time as three months can be got into the calendar."

Two of these long, weary months went by, and Aladdin nursed his soul in patience. Then a thing happened which gave him seriously to think. On a day in the first week of the third month his mother went forth into the market place about sunset to buy oil, and she saw that all the shops were closed, and the people were adorning their windows with bright garlands as if for some festivity. She wondered greatly at this, thinking the Sultan had either changed his birthday or that another child had been born to him. Yet she had gleaned nothing of any great event from the gossip of her neighbours. Having, after much difficulty, found an oil shop open, she bought her oil, and questioned the man. "Uncle," she said; "what is abroad in the city that the people close their shops and place candles and garlands in their windows?" "Thou art evidently a stranger," replied the man. "Nay, I am of this city," said she. "Then must thou cleanse thine ears," he retorted. "Hast thou not heard that the Grand Vizier's son is to take to himself this evening the beautiful Bedr-el-Budur? Surely, woman, thou hast been sleeping all day on thine ears, for the news went abroad early this morning. The Vizier's son is at the Hammam, and these soldiers and officials you see in the streets are waiting to escort him to the palace. And, look you, you are fortunate to get oil to-day, for all those who purvey oil to the Grand Vizier and his household have closed their shops as a mark of respect."

Aladdin's mother went home in a state of great consternation. Though her feet hastened, her heart lagged behind her, for she knew not how to tell her son the terrible news. She was afraid that after his joy at the Sultan's promise, and his patient waiting, this blow would send him from his mind. Then she contrived it in her thoughts that it was best to provoke her son's anger against the Sultan, rather than his grief at the loss of Bedr-el-Budur. Accordingly, as soon as she entered the house and found him sitting thinking, as was his wont of late, she said, "O my son, there is no faith nor trust but in God. Said I not to thee that the Grand Vizier was thine enemy? Out on him and the Sultan, for their word is but hot wind, and there is no faith in the promise of a King." "I see by thy face and by thy speech," said Aladdin, "that thou hast some bad news. What is it, O my mother?"

Then his mother told how that the Sultan had violated his covenant, and how the marriage of the Lady Bedr-el-Budur to the Grand Vizier's son was to take place that very evening. For this she heaped abuse upon the Grand Vizier, saying that it was only the worst of men that could so lead the Sultan to break his promise. When she had told all, and Aladdin understood how the matter lay, he arose, more in anger than in grief, and cried out against the Grand Vizier and cursed all the parties concerned in the affair. But presently he remembered that, when all seemed lost, he still had the Lamp, and that was something in time of trouble and difficulty.

With this he arose and retired to his own chamber, where he brought out the Lamp. Then, having considered well the manner of his wish, he rubbed it. Immediately the Efrite stepped out of the unseen and stood before him, saying, "Thou hast invoked me: what is thy desire? I am the Slave of the Lamp in thy hand, and am here to do thy bidding." And Aladdin answered: "Know, O Slave of the Lamp, that the Sultan promised me his daughter for my wife, but he has broken his word, and this night she is to be united with the Grand Vizier's son; wherefore I wish that, as soon as the pair retire, thou take them up, with the couch whereon they lie, and bring them hither to me." "I hear and obey," said the Slave of the Lamp, and immediately vanished.

Aladdin waited expectantly for some time, for he guessed that the moment would not be long delayed when the wedded pair would retire from the ceremonies. And his guess was right, for when he had waited a little longer, suddenly a cold blast of air swept through the chamber; the wall opened and there appeared the Efrite bearing in his arms the wedded pair upon the nuptial couch. They had been transported in the twinkling of an eye, and, when the Efrite had set the couch down at Aladdin's feet, they were both stupefied with astonishment at this proceeding.

"Take that scurvy thief," said Aladdin to the Efrite, pointing to the Vizier's son, "and bind him and lodge him in the wood-closet for the night." And the Efrite did so. He took up the Vizier's son in one hand, and, reaching with the other for cords, drew them from the invisible and bound the miscreant securely. Then he placed him in the wood-closet and blew an icy blast upon him to comfort him. Returning to Aladdin he said, "It is done, O Master of the Lamp! Is there aught else thou dost desire?" "Naught but this," replied Aladdin. "In the morning, when the Sultan is proceeding towards their chamber to wish them long life and happiness, convey them back thither in a state of sleep so that the Sultan's knock at their door may wake them." "I will obey," said the Efrite, and, in a moment, the air closed over him and he was gone.

And Aladdin smiled to himself to think that this thing had been done. Then he turned to the Lady Bedr-el-Budur, who was sitting weeping on the couch. "O lovely one," said he, "weep not; for I would not hurt one hair of thy head,

nor sully thine honour in any way. Know that I love thee
too much to harm thee; but, since thy father the Sultan
promised me thee, and has violated his word, I am determined
that none other shall call thee his. Rest in peace, lovely
lady; for neither am I thy husband nor the thief of thy
husband's honour. Wherefore, weep not, but rest in peace."

So saying he took a sword that hung on the wall of his
chamber, and, having placed it by her side in token of secu-
rity, he stretched himself upon the couch so that they lay with
the sword between them. Thus they passed the night. The
Sultan's daughter wept the long night through, and Aladdin
could not close his eyes for thinking of his unfortunate rival's
condition in the wood-closet. Towards morning Bedr-el-
Budur, utterly exhausted with weeping, fell asleep; and,
as Aladdin gazed upon her, he saw that indeed her loveliness
was rare; and, the more he gazed, the more he thought of
the unhappy fate of the Vizier's son. Never was a man so
badly treated as to be bound fast on his wedding night and
laid in a wood-closet in deadly fear of the dreadful apparition
that had placed him there.

In the morning, while Bedr-el-Budur still slept, the Slave
of the Lamp appeared according to Aladdin's command.
"O my master," he said, "the Sultan hath left his couch and
is about to knock at the door of the bridal chamber. I am
here to perform thy bidding on the instant." "So be it,"
answered Aladdin. "Convey them together on the couch
back to their place." And scarcely had he spoken when the
Efrite vanished and reappeared with the Vizier's son, whom
he quickly unbound and laid upon the couch beside the sleep-

ing Bedr-el Budur. Then, lifting the couch with the two upon it, he vanished, and Aladdin knew that, before the Sultan had knocked at the door of the bridal chamber, everything would be as it had been. Everything? No, not everything; for the Lady-el-Budur must awake as from a terrible nightmare; and, as for the Vizier's son, would he sing a song to the Sultan about spending the night in the wood-closet? Aladdin pondered over this and decided that nothing less than a repetition of the affair would wring the truth from either of them.

At this moment the Sultan knocked at the door of the bridal chamber in the palace, and the Vizier's son, still cold from the wood-closet, arose and opened to him, The Sultan advanced to the couch, and kissed his daughter, and asked her if she was happy and content. By way of answer she glared at him in sullen silence, for she had not forgotten in dreams or in waking, what had happened to her. The Sultan, not understanding what had befallen, and feeling annoyed, turned and left the chamber to lay the matter before the Queen, to whose ear their daughter's tongue might the more easily be loosed. So he came to the Queen and told her how Bedr-el-Budur had received him, concluding his recital with the remark, "Thus it is; there is trouble behind the door of that bridal chamber."

But the Queen smiled at his serious fears and answered him: "O my lord the King, thou knowest little of the heart of a woman. When it is happiest, a trifle makes it sad; and, when it would send tears of laughter and joy to the eyes, it sometimes turns perverse against itself for very gladness, and sends tears of pain instead. Wherefore, be not angry with her, but let me go and see her. She will surely confide in me."

So saying, she arose and robed herself, and went to the bridal chamber. At first sight of her daughter's dejected attitude and pained expression she imagined that some lovers' quarrel over a mere trifle had occurred; but when she kissed her, wishing her good morning, and Bedr-el-Budur answered no word to her salutation, she began to think that some grave trouble rested on her daughter's mind. And it was not until she had coaxed her, and used every argument known to a mother, that she received an answer to her questions. "Be not angry with me, O my mother," said Bedr-el-Budur at last, raising her sad beautiful eyes, "but know that a terrible thing has happened—a thing which I hardly dare tell thee lest thou think I have lost my reason. Scarcely had we retired, O my mother, when there suddenly appeared a huge black shape—terrible, horrific in aspect; and this—I know not what nor who—lifted the couch whereon we lay and conveyed us in a flash to some dark and vile abode of the common people." And then to her mother's astonished ears she unfolded the tale of all that had happened during the night till, suddenly, in the morning, she awoke to find the monstrous shape replacing them in the bridal chamber at the moment her father the Sultan had knocked at the door. "And that, O my mother," she concluded, "is why I could not answer my father, for I was so bewildered and stricken with unhappiness that I thought I was mad; though, now I have thought about the affair from beginning to end, I know that I have my wits like any other."

"Truly, O my daughter," said the Queen with great concern, "if thou wert to tell this story to thy father he would say thou wert mad. Wherefore, I counsel thee, child, tell it to him not; neither to him nor to any other one." "Nay, O my mother," answered Bedr-el-Budur, "dost thou doubt me? I have told thee the plain truth, and, if thou doubt it, ask my husband if my tale be true or not." But the Queen replied, "Sweep these fancies from thy mind, O my daughter; and arise and robe thyself to attend the rejoicings which this day have been prepared in the city in thine honour. For the whole people is in glad array, and the drums will beat and music will delight the ears of all; and the musicians will sing thy praises and all will wish thee long life and happiness."

Leaving Bedr-el-Budur, then, with her tire-women, the Queen sought the Sultan, and begged him not to be angry with their daughter, for she had been distressed with unhappy dreams. Then she sent for the Vizier's son to come to her secretly, and, when he stood before her, she related to him what Bedr-el-Budur had told her, and asked him if it were true or if he knew aught of it. "Nay," he answered, for he had thought the matter over and feared that the truth might rob him of his bride; besides, his acquaintance with the wood-closet seemed to him discreditable, and he felt little inclined to boast of it. "Nay, O my lady the Queen," said he; "I know naught of these things beyond what thou hast told me."

ALADDIN AND THE WONDERFUL LAMP

From this there was no doubt left in the Queen's mind that her daughter had suffered from a nightmare so vivid that she had been unable easily to cast it from her. Nevertheless, she felt assured that, as the day wore on, with its gaieties and rejoicings, Bedr-el-Budur would be enabled to rid herself of these troublous imaginings of the night, and resume her former self.

At eventime, when the wild rejoicing of the city had fatigued itself against the replenishment by wine, Aladdin retired to his chamber and rubbed the Lamp. Immediately the Slave appeared and desired to know his wish. "O Slave of the Lamp," said Aladdin, "do as thou didst last night. See to it that thou convey the bridal pair hither again as man and maid at the eleventh hour of their innocence." The Slave of the Lamp vanished in a moment, and Aladdin sat for a long time; yet he was content, for he knew that the wily Efrite was but waiting his opportunity. At length the monster reappeared before him, bearing in his arms the bridal couch with the pair upon it, weeping and wringing their hands in excess of grief and terror. And, at Aladdin's word the Slave took the Vizier's son as before and put him to bed in the wood-closet, where he remained, bound fast in an icy chill. And when it was morning, and the Sultan was about to knock at the door of the bridal chamber in the palace, the Slave of the Lamp appeared and conveyed the bride and bridegroom swiftly back to their place.

The Sultan had come to wish his daughter good morning, and to see also if she would behave towards him as on the former occasion.

Then Bedr-el-Budur wept and supplicated him, and told him what had befallen on the second night as on the first.

The Sultan repaired immediately to the Grand Vizier and told him all; and asked him whether he had received the same version of this matter from his son. But the Grand Vizier shook his head in the manner of one who might be lying and might not. "Then," said the Sultan, "go at once and question him, for it may be that my daughter hath seen visions and dreamed dreams; albeit, I am unable to disbelieve the truth of her story."

So the Grand Vizier went and inquired of his son, and presently returned to the Sultan in great perplexity of face, for his son, whatever he had admitted before, had now confessed to everything, even to the wood-closet. And, moreover, he had begged and implored his father to obtain his release from this most unhappy marriage, since it was better to be without a bride and sleep in peace than to have one and perish with cold in a wood-closet. Thus it was with the Vizier's son.

"O King of the Age," said the Grand Vizier, who could not see his way to conceal the truth, "my son telleth the same tale as thy daughter, the Lady Bedr-el-Budur. Wherefore I beseech thee that thou set a guard this night, so that——" "Nay," broke in the Sultan angrily; "it is an unhappy marriage and bodes no good. Thou didst persuade me that my promise to that woman in respect for her son was not binding, but these unhappy events and ill-omened affairs make me think thou wast mistaken. Abide not another night, for worse may happen. Go forth, O Vizier, and proclaim the marriage annulled. Bid the people cease to rejoice, and command all to go their own ways and comport themselves as if the marriage had not been."

At this the Grand Vizier bowed his head and went forth exceeding wroth, and proclaimed the annulment of the marriage to all the people.

Whether the Sultan had swiftly forgotten, or tardily remembered, his pledge, Aladdin troubled not to inquire. He waited patiently until the three months had expired, and then sent his mother to demand of the Sultan the the fulfilment of his promise.

The Sultan, who had not now the bowl of jewels before him to blind his vision, regarded her intently, and saw that she was of humble state. "What is thy thought on this, O Vizier?" he said. "My word is my word, and I regret that thou shouldst have explained it away; yet it seems to me that this woman is not of the kind that could mother-in-law my daughter. Hast thou a plan which is not a trick? If thou hast, whisper it in mine ear."

The Grand Vizier was pleased to hear the Sultan appealing to his ready wit in this way. "O King of the Age," he said, "thy pledge holds good, as ever it did; yea, as good as marriage vows. But verily, if this common woman's son desireth thy daughter for his wife, there should be a settlement befitting such a suit. Wherefore ask of him forty bowls of gold filled with jewels of the same blood and tincture as the woman brought at first, with forty female slaves to carry them, and a fitting retinue of forty. This thing, which is a Sultan's right to ask, it seemeth to me he cannot contrive to execute, and thus thou shalt be free of him."

"By Allah!" said the Sultan, "thou art of ready wit, O Vizier! Truly a marriage settlement is needed." Then, turning to Aladdin's mother, he said: "O woman! know that when one asketh the daughter of the Sultan one must have standing, for so it is in royal circles; and, to prove that standing, the suitor must show that he is able to provide for the Sultan's daughter and keep her in that state to which she has been accustomed. Wherefore he must bring to me forty bowls filled with jewels such as thou didst bring, with forty beautiful female slaves to carry them and forty black slaves as a retinue. Coming like this, thy son may claim my daughter, for the Sultan's word is the Sultan's word."

A sad woman then was Aladdin's mother. She returned to her son sick at heart. "O my son," she exclaimed, weeping, "said I not to thee that the Grand Vizier was thine enemy? The Sultan remembered his pledge, but the Vizier —may his bones rot!—spake in his ear, and the outcome is this: forty golden bowls of jewels, forty female slaves to carry them, and forty slaves as an escort. With this dowry, O my son, thou mayest approach the Sultan and claim his daughter as thy bride."

Loudly Aladdin laughed to scorn. And when his mother had brought him food, and he had eaten, he arose and went into his chamber. There he brought out the Lamp, and, sitting down, he rubbed it. Immediately the Slave appeared.

ALADDIN AND THE WONDERFUL LAMP

In less than an hour he returned and led before Aladdin forty beautiful maidens, each carrying a golden bowl of jewels on her head, and each accompanied by a magnificent black slave. And when Aladdin's mother saw this array she knew that it was done by the Lamp, and she blessed it for her son's sake. Then said Aladdin, "O my mother, behold, the dowry is ready according to the Sultan's requirement. It is for thee to take it to him, to show him what is in my power, and also that no time hath been lost in complying with his request."

Then the maids, with the golden bowls of precious stones, arrayed themselves in the street outside the house, and by each maid stood a slave. Thus, led by Aladdin's mother, they proceeded to the Sultan's palace; and the people crowded in the streets to see this unwonted sight, for the maids were richly dressed, and all, with the sun shining on their raiment and flashing in the jewels they bore, made a magnificent spectacle. Never had the people seen such jewels, never such beauteous damsels, never such magnificent slaves.

Thus, in due course, came Aladdin's mother before the Sultan, leading the cortège into the Audience Hall. The maidens took the bowls of jewels from their heads and set them on the ground. Then they made obeisance, they and the slaves prostrating themselves before the Sultan; and, having done this, they all rose and stood before him in humble reverence. And, when the Sultan's gaze at last left the beauteous damsels and fell upon the bowls of jewels at their feet, he was beside himself with wonder and admiration.

When he found words, he commanded that the whole cortège should present itself, with the jewels, to the Lady Bedr-el-Budur in her palace. Then he added to Aladdin's mother: "Tell thy son he need fear not but that I shall keep my promise; but bid him come hither to me with all haste, so that I may look upon his face and accept him as my son-in-law; for the marriage shall be this very night."

The Grand Vizier turned white with rage—whiter than his false heart had ever been, even when a boy. After a dagger-thrust of glances between them, Aladdin's mother made obeisance to the Sultan and thanked him. Then, with contempt for the Grand Vizier written plainly on her face, she withdrew, and returned home, walking on the air.

Now Aladdin, when he saw his mother returning swift-footed and on wings of joy, knew that good tidings came with her. But, before he could speak, his mother burst in upon him and embraced him, crying, "O my son! thy heart's wish is fulfilled. This very night thou art to wed the Sultan's daughter, and so it is proclaimed before all the world." Then did Aladdin rejoice that his expectations were fulfilled, and was continuing to rejoice when his mother addressed him suddenly. "Nay," she said, "I have not told thee all. The Sultan bids thee go to him immediately, for he desires to see his son-in-law. But how shalt thou approach the Sultan in thy merchant's garments? However, I have done all I can for thee, and it is now thine own affair."

So saying, she withdrew to rest a little, and Aladdin,

ALADDIN AND THE WONDERFUL LAMP

having blessed her, retired to his chamber and brought forth the Lamp. With a set purpose in his mind, he rubbed it, and at once the Slave appeared. "Thou knowest me: what is thy desire?" "I wish," answered Aladdin, "that thou take me to a bath which hath no equal in all the kingdoms, and provide me there with a change of raiment of resplendent glory, richer than any the Sultan has ever worn."

No sooner had he spoken than the Efrite bore him away in his arms, and deposited him in a bath the like of which no King could compass nor any man describe. Then he sought the jewelled hall and found there, in place of his merchant's garb, a set of robes that exceeded all imagination. At the door of the bath, he was met by the Efrite in waiting, who took up and bore him in a flash to his home.

"Hast thou still some further need?" asked the Slave of the Lamp, about to vanish. "Yea," replied Aladdin. "Bring me here a Chief of Memluks with forty-eight in his train—twenty-four to precede me and twenty-four to follow after; and see that they have splendid horses and equipments, so that not even the greatest in the world can say, 'This is inferior to mine.' For myself I want a stallion such as cannot be equalled among the Arabs, and his housings must be for value such as one could purchase only in dreams. And to each Memluk give a thousand gold pieces, and to the Chief Memluk ten thousand; for we go to the Sultan's palace and would scatter largesse on the way. Wait! Also twelve maidens of unequalled grace and loveliness in person to attire and accompany my mother to the

Sultan's presence. And look you! whatever of grace and beauty is lacking in my person supply it to me on my natural plan of being. See to it, O Slave of the Lamp!"

"It is already done," said the Slave of the Lamp; and, vanishing on the instant, he reappeared at once at the doorway of the house, leading a noble white stallion gorgeously equipped, while behind came the twelve damsels and forty-nine Memluks on magnificent chargers.

Now, when the Sultan had received word that Aladdin was coming, he informed his nobles and grandees of the meaning of this thing; so that, when Aladdin arrived, there was a vast concourse of people, and all the stateliest of the land were there awaiting his entry. As the sun rises in glory upon a waiting world, so came Aladdin to the palace. At the door of the Hall of Audience he dismounted, while hands held his stirrup that had never performed such an office before.

The Sultan was seated on his throne, and, immediately he saw Aladdin, he arose and descended and took him to his breast, forbidding all ceremony on so great an occasion. Then he led him up affectionately, and placed him on his right hand. In all this Aladdin forgot not the respect due to kings. Forbidden to be too humble, he was not too lofty in his bearing. He spoke:

"O my lord the Sultan! King of the Earth and Heaven's Dispenser of all Good! Truly thou hast treated me graciously in bestowing upon me thy daughter the Lady Bedr-el-Budur. Hear me yet further, for I have a request to make. Grant me a site whereon to build a palace, unworthy as it may prove, for the comfort and happiness of thy daughter, the Lady Bedr-el-Budur?"

Then the Sultan conversed with Aladdin and was greatly charmed with his courtliness and eloquence. Anon he ordered the musicians to play, and together they listened to the music in the utmost content. Finally he arose, and, taking Aladdin by the hand, led him forth into the palace banqueting-hall, where a splendid supper was awaiting them, with the lords of the land standing ready in their proper order of degree. Yet above them all sat Aladdin, for he was at the Sultan's right hand. And, while they ate, the music played and a merry wit prevailed; and the Sultan drew nearer to Aladdin in their talk, and saw, from his grace, his manner of speech, and his complaisance, that indeed he must have been brought up and nurtured among kings. Then, while they conversed, the Sultan's heart went out with joy and satisfaction to Aladdin, and the whole assemblage saw that it was not as it had been with the Vizier's son.

The Grand Vizier himself would have retired early had it not been that his presence was required for the marriage ceremony. As soon as the banquet was over and the tables cleared away, the Sultan commanded the Vizier to summon the Kadis and the witnesses, and thus the contract between Aladdin and the Lady Bedr-el-Budur was duly executed. Then, without a warning word, Aladdin arose to depart. "Wherefore, O my son?" said the Sultan. "Thy wedding is duly contracted and the festivities are about to begin.'

"Yea, O my lord the King," replied Aladdin; "and none rejoiceth at that more than I; but, if it please thee, it is my thought to build a palace for the Lady Bedr-el-Budur; and if my love and longing for her be anything, thou mayest rest assured that it will be completed so quickly as to amaze thee." At this the Grand Vizier tugged the Sultan's sleeves, but received no attention. "It is well," said the Sultan to Aladdin; "choose what site seemeth best to thee and follow thine own heart in the matter. See! this open space by my palace! What thinkest thou, my son?" "O King," replied Aladdin, "I cannot thank thee enough, for it is the summit of my felicity to be near thee."

Then Aladdin left the palace in the same royal manner as he had approached it, with his Memluks preceding and following; and again the people praised and blessed him as he passed. When he reached his house he left all other affairs in the hands of his chief Memluk with certain instructions, and went into his chamber. There he took the Lamp and rubbed it. The Slave appeared on the instant and desired to know his pleasure. "O Slave," answered Aladdin, "I have a great task for thee. I desire thee to build for me in all haste a palace on the open space near the Sultan's Serai—a palace of magnificent design and construction, and filled with rare and costly things. And let it be incomplete in one small respect, so that, when the Sultan offers to complete it to match the whole, all the wealth and artifice at his command will not suffice for the task." "O my master," replied the Efrite, "it shall be done with all speed. I will return when the work is finished." With this he vanished.

It was an hour before dawn when the Slave of the Lamp

returned to Aladdin, and, awakening him from sleep, stood before him. "O Master of the Lamp," he said, "the palace is built as thou didst command." "It is well, O Slave of the Lamp," answered Aladdin; "and I would inspect thy work." No sooner had he spoken than he found himself being borne swiftly through the air in the arms of the Efrite, who set him down almost immediately within the palace.

Most excellently had the Slave done his work. Porphyry, jasper, alabaster, and other rare stones had been used in the construction of the building. The floors were of mosaics the which to match would cost much wealth and time in the fashioning, while the walls and ceilings, the doors and the smallest pieces of detail were all such that even the imagination of them could come only to one dissatisfied with the palaces of kings. When Aladdin had wondered at all this, the Slave led him into the Treasury, and showed him countless bars of gold and silver gems of dazzling brilliance. Thence to the banqueting-hall, where the tables were in a manner to take one's breath away; for every dish and every flagon was of gold or silver, and all the goblets were crusted with jewels. But, when the Slave led him farther and showed him a pavilion with twenty-four niches thickly set with diamonds and emeralds and rubies, he fairly lost his wits. And the Slave took him to one niche and showed him how his command had been carried out in that this was the one small part of the palace that was left incomplete in order to tempt and tax the Sultan to finish it.

When Aladdin had viewed the whole palace, and seen

the numerous slaves and beautiful maidens therein, he asked yet one thing more of the Efrite. "O Slave of the Lamp," he said, "the work is wonderful, yet it still lacketh an approach from the Sultan's palace. I desire, therefore, a rich carpet laid upon the intervening space, so that the Lady Bedr-el-Budur may come and go upon a splendid pathway of brocade worked with gold and inwrought with precious stones." "I hear and obey," said the Slave, and vanished. Presently he returned and led Aladdin to the steps of the palace. "O my lord," he said, "what thou didst command is done." And he pointed to a magnificent carpet extending from palace to palace. The gold and the precious stones in the brocade gleamed and sparkled in the stars' last rays before the rise of dawn. When Aladdin had gazed upon it and wondered at it, the Efrite carried him in the twinkling of an eye back to his own home.

Shortly afterwards, when the dawn had arisen, the Sultan opened his eyes, and, looking forth from his window, beheld a magnificent structure where the day before had been an open space. Doubting the evidence of his senses, he turned himself about and rubbed his eyes and looked again. There, undoubtedly, was a palace more splendid and glorious than any he had ever seen; and there, leading to it, was a carpet the like of which he had never trod. The news of it spread through the palace like wildfire. The Grand Vizier came rushing to the Sultan, and, finding him at the window, had no need to tell him the cause of his excitement. "What sayest thou, O Vizier?" said the Sultan. "Yonder stands a palace surpassing all others. Truly Aladdin is worthy of my daughter, since at his bidding such a royal edifice arises in a single night."

Then the Vizier's envy found vent. "O King," he said, "thinkest thou that such a thing as this could be done save by the vilest of sorcery? Riches and jewels and costly attire are in the hands of mortals, but this—this is impossible!" "Impossible?" said the Sultan. "Behold!"—and he pointed towards the palace—"there it stands in the light of day, and thou sayest it is impossible. Verily, O Vizier, it seems thy wits are turned with envy at the wealth of Aladdin. Prate not to me of sorcery. There are few things beyond the power of a man in whose treasury are such jewels as those sent me by Aladdin." At this the Grand Vizier was silent; indeed, his excess of envy well-nigh choked him, for he saw that the Sultan loved Aladdin greatly.

Now when Aladdin awoke in the morning and knew that he must set forth for the palace where the nobles and grandees were already assembling for the wedding celebration, he took the Lamp and rubbed it. The Slave appeared on the instant and desired to know his wish. "O Slave of the Lamp," said Aladdin, "this is my wedding day and I go to the Sultan's palace. Wherefore I shall need ten thousand gold pieces."

When all was ready Aladdin mounted his steed and rode through the city while the Memluks before and behind distributed largesse all the way. And the people were loud in their praises of his dignity and grace, and loved him greatly for his generosity. Anon the palace was reached, and there the high officials, who were looking for Aladdin and his train, hastened to inform the Sultan of his approach. On this the Sultan arose, and going out to the gates of the palace to meet him, embraced and kissed him.

Anon the Sultan commanded the wedding banquet to be served. And, when it was all ready, Aladdin sat on the right hand of the Sultan; and they, with all the nobles and foremost in the land, ate and drank. On every hand were honour and good will for Aladdin.

When the banquet was over Aladdin repaired with his Memluks to his palace to make ready for the reception of his bride, Bedr-el-Budur. And, as he went, all the people thronged him, shouting, "God give thee happiness! God bless thy days!" And he scattered gold amongst them.

Bedr-el Budur, watching him from a window in her father's palace, felt her heart turn over and over in her bosom, and then, saying within herself, "He is my husband and none other," she renounced herself to the exquisite joy of sudden love.

At eventime the Sultan commanded an escort to conduct the Lady Bedr-el-Budur to her husband's abode. On this the captains of guards, the officers of state and nobles, well equipped, were mounted in readiness and waiting at the door of Bedr-el-Budur's apartments. Presently, preceded by female slaves and eunuchs bearing lighted tapers set in jewelled candlesticks, came forth a vision of loveliness. Bedr-el-Budur, aflame with love for Aladdin, appeared on the threshold like a pure white bird about to fly into space. All too slow was the procession that escorted her to Aladdin's palace. The stately pomp and splendour accorded not with the beating of her heart. She saw not Aladdin's mother nor the beauteous damsels, nor the mounted guards, nor the emirs, nor the nobles—her only thought was Aladdin, for her heart was consumed with love.

Thus from the Seraglio to Aladdin's palace, where Bedr-el-Budur, as one floating in a dream, was taken to her apartments and arrayed for presentation to the Court assembled. And of all that Court and multitude of people the only one who had no voice was Aladdin, for, when he looked upon his bride in her surpassing loveliness, he was reft of speech or thought, and stood silent before a joy too great for tongue to tell.

At last, when the presentation was over, Aladdin sought the bridal chamber where he found his mother with Bedr-el Budur. And there, in the apartment all sparkling with gold and precious stones, his mother unveiled her and Aladdin gazed into her eyes and took no thought for the lustre of jewels. And while his mother went into raptures over the splendour of the palace, Aladdin and Bedr-el-Budur exchanged one look of love—a thing which none could purchase with all the treasures of the earth. And so it was with Aladdin and his bride.

Great was the Sultan's wonder and admiration when he saw the architecture and masonry of the structure, for, even without, it was all of the rarest and most costly stone inwrought with gold and silver and fashioned with consummate skill; but when he entered and viewed the entrance hall his breath was snatched away from him, for he had never seen anything so magnificent in his life. At length, finding speech, he turned to the Grand Vizier and said, "Verily, this is the greatest wonder of all. Hast thou ever, from first to last, beheld a palace like this?" "O King of the Age," replied the Vizier gravely, "there hath never been the like of this among the sons of men. It would take ten thousand workmen ten thousand days to construct it; wherefore, as I told thy Felicity, its completion in a single night is the work of sorcery." At this the Sultan was not pleased. "Verily, O Vizier," he replied, "thou has an envious heart, and thou speakest foolishly with thy mouth."

At this moment Aladdin approached the Sultan to conduct him through the rooms of the palace. And as they went from one to another, the Sultan was simply astounded at the wealth of metal and precious stones on every hand, and at the workmanship thereof. As for the Vizier, he had said all he had to say, and followed sullenly, nursing an evil heart. At length they came to the kiosk, which was a crowning work of jewel-clusters so rich and splendid that the Treasuries of the earth must have been emptied to fill them. The Sultan nearly went from his wits in the effort to calculate the fabulous wealth of this apartment alone. For relief he turned this way and that, gazing upon the niches, which were the most precious and wonderful of all. And in this way he came at length to the niche that had been left incomplete. This gave him speech. "Alas!" he said, relieved to find a flaw, "this niche, at least is imperfect." Then, turning to Aladdin, he inquired the reason of it. "Yea, O my lord," answered Aladdin, "woe unto it; it is indeed unfinished, for the workmen clamoured to be allowed to prepare themselves for the wedding festivities and I had not the heart to say to them nay. So they left it as thou seest it." Then, while Aladdin stood by observing intently the effect of his words, the Sultan stroked his beard in contemplation. "O my son," he said presently, "the thought has come to me to complete it myself." "On the head and eye, O King!" cried Aladdin. "And may thy life be prolonged! If thou wilt honour me thus it will be a fitting perpetuation of thy memory in the palace of thy daughter." At this the Sultan, vastly pleased, summoned his jewellers and artificers, and, empowering them to draw on the Royal Treasury for all they might require, he commanded them to complete the niche.

Scarcely had the Sultan finished his directions in this matter when Bedr-el-Budur came to greet him. And his heart leapt with joy at her radiant face when he looked upon her. Then, when she had confided to him how happy she was, Aladdin led them into the banqueting-hall, where all was ready.

When the Sultan's soul was well-nigh weary with excess of enjoyment he rose, and, bethinking himself of the unfinished niche, repaired to the kiosk to see how his workmen had progressed with their task. And when he came to them and inspected their work he saw that they had completed only a small portion and that neither the execution nor the material, which was already exhausted, could compare with that of the other niches. Seeing this he bethought him of his reserve Treasure and the jewels Aladdin had given him. Wherefore he commanded the workmen to draw upon these and continue their work. This they did, and, in due course, the Sultan returned to find that the work was still incomplete. Determined to carry out his design at whatever cost the Sultan commanded his officials to seize all the jewels they could lay their hands on in the kingdom. Even this was done, and lo, still the niche was unfinished.

It was not until late on a day thereafter that Aladdin found the jewellers and goldsmiths adding to the work the last stones at their command. "Hast thou jewels enough?" he asked of the chief artificer. "Nay, O my master," he replied sadly. "We have used all the jewels in the Treasuries; yea, even in all the kingdom, and yet the work is only half finished."

"Take it all away!" said Aladdin. "Restore the jewels to their rightful owners." So they undid their work and returned the jewels to the Treasuries and to the people from whom they had been taken. And they went in to the Sultan and told him. Unable to learn from them the exact reason for this, the Sultan immediately called for his attendants and his horses and repaired to Aladdin's palace.

Meanwhile, Aladdin himself, as soon as the workmen had left, retired to a private chamber; and, taking out the Lamp, rubbed it. "Ask what thou wilt," said the Slave, appearing on the instant. "I desire thee to complete the niche which was left incomplete," answered Aladdin. "I hear and obey," said the Slave, and vanished. In a very short space of time he returned, saying, "O my master, the work is complete." Then Aladdin arose and went to the kiosk, and found that the Slave had spoken truly; the niche was finished. As he was examining it, a Memluk came to him and informed him that the Sultan was at the gates. At this Aladdin hastened to meet him. "O my son," cried the Sultan as Aladdin greeted him, "why didst thou not let my jewellers complete the niche in the kiosk? Wilt thou not have the palace whole?" And Aladdin answered him, "O my lord, I left it unfinished in order to raise a doubt in thy mind and then dispel it; for, if thy Felicity doubted my ability to finish it, a glance at the kiosk as it now stands will make the matter plain." And he led the Sultan to the kiosk and showed him the completed niche.

The Sultan's astonishment was now greater than ever, that Aladdin had accomplished in so short a space that which he himself could command neither workmen nor jewels sufficient to accomplish in many months. It filled him with wonder. He embraced Aladdin and kissed him, saying there was none like him in all the world. Then, when he had rested awhile with his daughter Bedr-el-Budur, who was full of joy and happiness, the Sultan returned to his own palace.

As the days passed by Aladdin's fame went forth through all the land.

Now it chanced that the Sultan's enemies from distant parts invaded his territory and rode down against him. The Sultan assembled his armies for war and gave the chief command to Aladdin, whose skill and prowess had found great favour in his eyes. And Bedr-el-Budur wept when

Aladdin went forth to the wars, but great was her delight when he returned victorious, having routed the enemy in a great battle with terrible slaughter.

Now the fame of Aladdin penetrated even to distant parts, so that his name was heard even in the land of the Moors, where the accursed Dervish dwelt. This sorcerer had not yet made an end of lamenting the loss of the Lamp just as it seemed about to pass into his hands. And, while he lamented, he cursed Aladdin in his bitter rage, saying within himself, " 'Tis well that ill-omened miscreant is dead and buried, for, if I have not the Lamp, it is at least safe, and one day I may come by it." But when he heard the name "Aladdin," and the fame attached to it, he muttered to himself, "Can this be he? And hath he risen to a high position through the Lamp and the Slave of the Lamp?" Then he rose and drew a table of magic signs in the sand in order to find if the Aladdin of Destiny were indeed alive upon the earth. And the figures gave him what he feared. Aladdin was alive and the Lamp was not in the cavern where by his magic he had first discovered it. At this a great fear struck him to the heart, and he wondered that he had lived to experience it, for he knew that at any moment Aladdin, by means of the Slave of the Lamp, might slay him for revenge. Wondering that this had not occurred to Aladdin's mind he hastened to draw another table; by which he saw that Aladdin had acquired great possessions and had married the Sultan's daughter. At this his rage mastered his fear, and he cursed Aladdin with fury and envy. But, though his magic was great, it could not cope with that which

ALADDIN AND THE WONDERFUL LAMP

slumbered in the Lamp, and his curses missed their mark, only to abide the time when they might circle back upon him. Meanwhile, in great haste, he arose and journeyed to the far land of Cathay, fearing every moment that Aladdin would bethink him of revenge by means of the Slave of the Lamp. Yet he arrived safely at the City of the Sultan and rested at an inn where he heard naught but praises of Aladdin's generosity, his bravery in battle, his beautiful bride Bedr-el-Budur and his magnificent palace.

Taking his instruments of divination, he soon learned that the Lamp was not on Aladdin's person, but in the palace. At this he was overjoyed, for he had a plan to get possession of it. Then he went out into the market and bought a great number of new lamps, which he put in a basket and took back to the inn. When evening was drawing nigh, he took the basket and went forth in the city—for such was his plan—crying, "New lamps for old! Who will exchange old lamps for new?" And the people hearing this, laughed among themselves, saying he was mad; and none brought an old lamp to him in exchange for a new one, for they all thought there was nothing to be gained out of a madman. But when the Dervish reached Aladdin's palace he began to cry more lustily, "New lamps for old! Who will exchange old lamps for new?" And he took no heed of the boys who mocked him and the people who thronged him.

Now Fate so willed it that, as he came by, Bedr-el-Budur was sitting at a window of the kiosk; and, when she heard the tumult and saw the pedlar about whom it turned, she

bade her maid go and see what was the matter. The girl
went, and soon returned, saying, "O my lady, it is a poor
pedlar who is asking old lamps for new ones; and the people
are mocking him, for without a doubt he is mad." "It seems
proof enough," answered Lady Bedr-el-Budur, laughing.
"'Old wine for new' I could understand, but 'old lamps
for new' is strange. Hast thou not an old lamp so that
we might test him and see whether his cry be true or false?"

Now the damsel had seen an old lamp in Aladdin's apartment, and hastened to acquaint her mistress with this. "Go
and bring it! said the Lady Bedr-el-Budur, who had no
knowledge whatever of the Lamp and its wonderful virtues.
So the maid went and brought the Lamp, little knowing
what woe she was working Aladdin. Then the Lady Bedr-
el-Budur called one of the Memluks and handed him the
Lamp, bidding him go down to the pedlar and exchange it
for a new one. Presently he returned, bearing a new lamp,
and, when the Princess took it and saw that it was a far better
one than the old one, she laughed and said, "Verily this man
is mad! A strange trade, and one that can bring him small
profit. But his cry is true, therefore take him this gold to
cover his losses." And she gave the Memluk ten gold pieces,
and bade him hasten. But the Memluk returned anon with
the ten pieces, saying that the pedlar had disappeared, having left all his new lamps with the people. The Lady Bedr-
el-Budur wondered at this, but knew not, nor guessed the
terrible consequences of her act.

As for the Dervish, as soon as he had got the Lamp, he
recognised it. Placing it in his bosom, he left all else and

ran, which to the people was only a further proof of his madness. On and on he ran, through the city and its outskirts, until he came to the desert, where at last he was alone. Then, and not till then, he took the Lamp from his bosom and rubbed it. In a flash appeared the Slave of the Lamp. "What is thy wish? I am the Slave of the Lamp which is in thy hands." And the Dervish replied, "I desire thee to take the palace of Aladdin, with all it contains, and convey it to the land of the Moors in Africa, and set it down upon the open space within the gardens of my dwelling in that land. Take me also with it. I have spoken." "O my master," said the Slave, "in the twinkling of an eye it is done. If thou carest to close thine eyes for one moment, when thou openest them thou wilt find thyself within the palace, in thy garden in the land of the Moors." And ere the Dervish could say, "I have closed my eye and opened it again," he found that it was even so, as the Slave had said. The palace and all in it were in his own garden, in his own country, with the sun of Africa shining in upon him.

Now the Lady Bedr-el-Budur was within the palace, but Aladdin was not. He had not yet returned from the chase. This thing had taken place after nightfall, so that as yet none had perceived it. But at the hour of the rising of the full moon, the Sultan looked forth from a window to admire Aladdin's palace in its silver light; what was his surprise to find that there was no palace there! All was bare and open space just as it had been before this wonderful palace was built. "By Allah!" he cried in distress and alarm. "Can it be that the Vizier was right, and that this splendid thing was but a fabric of sorcery, built in a single night and dissolved in a moment like a dream on waking? And my daughter, where is she? Oh woe! oh woe!" And the Sultan wrung his hands in grief. Then presently he summoned the Grand Vizier, and bade him look forth at the palace of Aladdin. And when the Vizier looked forth and saw no splendid edifice giving back the rays of the moon, but all as bare as it had been before, he turned to the Sultan, his face pale and twitching with excitement. "O King of the Age," he said, "doth thy Felicity now believe that the palace and all Aladdin's wealth were the work of sorcery?" And the Sultan did not reply, but beat his breast and plucked his beard; for, apart from sorcery, it was enough for him to know that Aladdin's palace was gone and his daughter with it. "Where is Aladdin?" he demanded at last in wrath. "At the chase," replied the Vizier. "Then I command thee to have him brought before me at once, and pinioned and shackled."

A glad man then was the Vizier. With all alacrity he issued the Sultan's commands to the captains, who went forth with their soldiers to find and seize Aladdin. It was a difficult task for them, for they all loved him greatly; and, when they came upon him, they asked his forgiveness, yet took him and led him bound and manacled before the Sultan. But the Sultan, being filled with rage at the loss of his daughter, no sooner set eyes on Aladdin among his captors than he ordered him to the Executioner. Now when this came to the ears of the people, they surrounded the palace and barred its gates and doors, and raised a great clamour without, so that the Sultan sent his Grand Vizier to ascertain the cause.

Meanwhile on the scaffold the Executioner had spread the mat of death and Aladdin was kneeling thereon blindfolded, ready for the blow. The Executioner walked round him thrice and then turned towards the Sultan, who stood at a window, and waited his command to strike. At this moment the cries of the people grew louder and fiercer and the Sultan beheld them scaling the walls of the palace. Then fear got hold of him for the issue, and he signalled to the Executioner to stay his hand, and bade the Vizier proclaim to the people that Aladdin was pardoned.

As soon as Aladdin was freed from his chains he begged speech of the Sultan, and said to him, "O my lord, I thank thee for thy clemency, though I know not yet wherein my offence lay." So the Vizier took Aladdin to the window and bade him look forth. Utter amazement fell upon Aladdin when he saw that his palace had completely disappeared, leaving no vestige to mark the spot where it had stood. He was so dazed and bewildered that he turned in silence and walked back into the Sultan's presence like one in a dream. "Well," said the Sultan, "where is thy palace? And, what is more to me, where is my daughter?" And Aladdin shook his head sorrowfully and spread his hands in helpless despair; but made no other reply, for he was dumbfounded. Again the Sultan spoke: "It was my thought to set thee free so that thou mayest search for my daughter and restore her to me. For this purpose I grant thee a delay of forty days, and, if in that time thou canst not find her, then, by Allah! I will cut off thy head." And Aladdin answered him, "O King of the Age, if I find her not within forty days then I no longer wish to have a head left upon my body."

And Aladdin went forth sad and dejected. The cries of joy with which the people greeted him fell like lead on his aching heart. He escaped from their good will and wandered in the city like one distraught, greeting none, nor raising his eyes to any greeting. For two days he neither ate nor drank for grief at what had happened. Finally he wandered beyond the confines of the city into the desert. There, on the banks of a dark pool, he resolved to drown himself and so end his misery. But being devout and fearing God, he must first perform his ablutions. So he stooped and took water in his hands and rubbed them together, when lo! a strange thing happened; for as his hands came together, he chanced to rub the ring which was on one of his fingers. In a flash the Slave of the Ring appeared and, standing before him, said, "O my master, what is thy desire?" Aladdin then was seized with great joy, and he cried, "O Slave, I desire my palace and my wife." "Alas!" answered the Slave, "that I cannot bring about, for this matter is protected by the Slave of the Lamp who hath put a seal upon it." "Then," urged Aladdin, since thou canst not bring the palace and my wife to *me*, transport *me* to the palace wherever it may be upon the earth." "On the head and the eye," replied the Slave, and immediately Aladdin found himself borne swiftly through the air and set down by his palace in the land of the Moors. Although the night had fallen he could recognise it without difficulty, and close at hand was the window of his wife's chamber. Great joy at this exhausted what little strength remained to him—for he had neither eaten nor slept for many days—and, overcome with fatigue and weakness, he threw himself down beneath a tree hard by and slept.

Awakened at dawn by the singing of birds in the garden, Aladdin arose, and, having bathed in a stream, recited the morning prayer, after which he returned and sat beneath the window of Bedr-el-Budur's apartment. Now the Lady Bedr-el-Budur, filled with grief at her separation from her husband and her father, could neither sleep nor eat by reason of her keen distress. Each day when dawn leapt into the sky she would arise and sit at her window and weep. And on this morning she came as usual, but did not weep, for she saw Aladdin sitting on the ground outside. And they both cried out and flew to one another; and their greeting was full of joy. She opened a side door for him, bidding him enter, for she knew it was not the time for the accursed Dervish to come to see her as was his daily wont. Then, when they had embraced and kissed and shed tears of joy, Aladdin said to her, "O my beloved, before all else answer me one question: in my apartment there was an old copper Lamp which——" "Alas," broke in Bedr-el-Budur, "that Lamp was the cause of it all, for the man who obtained it by a stratagem told me of its virtues, and how he had achieved this thing by its aid." And immediately Aladdin heard this he knew that it was indeed the Dervish who had worked this woe upon him.

"Tell me, how doth this accursed man treat thee?" he

[169]

asked. "He cometh once a day," she replied, "and he would fain win my love and console me for thy loss, for he saith the Sultan, my father, hath struck off thy head, and at the best thou wert of poor family and stole thy wealth from him. But he gets no word from me, only tears and lamentations." And Aladdin embraced her again and comforted her for what she had suffered. "Tell me," he asked again presently, "where doth this accursed keep the Lamp?" "Always in his bosom," she replied, "where he guards it with the greatest care and none knows of it but me." Aladdin was overjoyed when he heard this, for he thought he saw a way to obtain the Lamp. "Listen, my beloved," he said, "I will leave thee now and return shortly in disguise. Bid thy maid stand by the side door to let me in. Then I will tell thee my plan to slay this accursed one and take the Lamp."

Then Aladdin went forth upon the road that led to the city, and he had not journeyed far before he met a poor peasant proceeding to his daily toil. Stopping him he offered to exchange his own costly garments for those the peasant was wearing. But the man demurred, whereat Aladdin set upon him and effected the exchange by force. Then, leaving the peasant battered and bruised but dressed like a prince, he went on into the city, and, coming to the market, purchased some powder of benj, which is called "the son of an instant," for it stupefies in a moment. With this he returned to the palace, and, when he came to the side door where the maid was waiting, she recognised him and opened immediately. Very soon he was exposing his plan to Bedr-el-Budur.

[170]

"O my beloved," he said, "I wish thee to attire thyself gaily, and adorn thyself with jewels in the sparkle of which no grief can live; and, when the accursed cometh, greet him with a smile and a look from thy lovely eyes. Then invite him to sup with thee, and, when thou hast aroused a blinding passion in his bosom, he will forget the Lamp which lieth there. See," he drew forth the powder, "this is benj, 'son of an instant.' It cannot be detected in red wine. Thou knowest the rest: pledge him in a cup, and see to it that the benj is in his and not in thine. Thou canst do this?"

"Yea," replied Bedr-el-Budur. "It is difficult, but I will dare all for thee; and well I know that this accursed wretch deserves not to live." And on this assurance Aladdin withdrew to a private chamber and sat him down to wait. He realised his extreme danger, for he knew that if the Dervish so much as suspected his existence in the flesh a rub of the Lamp and a word to the Slave would bring him instant death; but he did not know that Bedr-el-Budur, having learnt the virtues of the Lamp, had exacted a pledge from the Dervish that he would make no further use of it until she had given him her final decision as to whether she would come to him of her own free will and accord, which she maintained was a better thing than subsequently to be impelled by the abominable power of sorcery.

When the Dervish appeared, she sat weeping as usual, and it was not until, in his protestations of love, he said words that were suitable to her purpose that she paused and half dried her tears as if it needed little more to make her weigh his petition with care. Observing this he drew near and sat by her side, and now, though no longer weeping, she had not yet found words for him. He took her hand, but she snatched it way crying, "No, it cannot be! Never can I forget Aladdin!" He pleaded with her, and his passion made him eloquent. She pushed him away petulantly. "Nay, nay," she cried, "I cannot resign my heart to thee at will. Give me, I pray thee, a little space of time—two days; *one* day—I may decide in one, if weeping do not kill me." The Dervish smote his breast. "Think, O Lovely One, how I have waited to win thee as man wins woman, when in a moment I could call thee mine by other means." And his hand moved to his bosom where lay the Lamp. "Stay!" she cried, rising and standing before him. "Thy pledge! Abide thou in patience. I will come to thee in one hour."

So she went, leaving the Dervish in an ecstasy of doubt. At the expiration of the hour the door opened and she stood before him a vision of loveliness in resplendent attire bedecked with priceless jewels. A smile was on her face and her answer to him was in her eyes. She seated herself by his side and said boldly, "Thou seest how it is with me. My tears for Aladdin—who is dead—flowed till the hour was half spent; then, I know not why, they changed to tears of joy for thee, who art alive. Then I arose and arrayed myself gladly and came to thee. Yet even now I am not wholly thine, for tears—now grief now joy, I know not which—contend in mine eyes for him or thee. Wherefore come not too near me lest what thou hast won be forfeited. Perchance if we sup together with a jar of the red wine of thine own country—nay, go not thyself for the wine," said Bedr-el-Budur, bethinking her of the Lamp. "Do not leave me. One of my slave girls will go."

While she was gone Bedr-el-Budur pretended to busy herself issuing orders to the household about the preparation of supper. And under cover of this she sought and found Aladdin. "It is well," she said as he held her to his heart and pressed his lips to hers. "But, O my beloved," he replied, "art thou sure that the Lamp is in his bosom?" "I will go and see," she answered. And she returned to the Dervish and, approaching him shyly, began to doubt the truth of this great thing—his love for her. As she did this she placed her hands on his shoulders and looked into his eyes; whereat the Dervish drew her close to him and she felt the Lamp in his bosom. Immediately she wrenched herself free and left him with a glance in which disdain and love were kindly mixed. "It is so," she said on returning to Aladdin, "the Lamp is in his bosom, and, since he embraced me—I could not help it nor could I endure it, beloved—it is a wonder the Slave of the Lamp did not appear to see how I tore myself away, I was pressed so close."

Meanwhile the slave girl returned with the wine, and, supper being ready, Bedr-el-Budur invited the Dervish to sit by her at the table. And when they had eaten somewhat, she paused and questioned him with a glance. It was for him to call for wine, and he did so. Immediately a slave girl filled their goblets, and they drank; and another and another until the distance between them was melted,

[173]

and they became, so to speak, the best of boon companions.

At length, when the supper was drawing to an end, and the wits of the Dervish were well mastered by wine, Bedr-el-Budur leaned towards him in an unbending mood. "This wine of thine has set me on fire, beloved!" she said. "But one more cup and then, if I say thee nay, do not believe me, for thou hast kept thy pledge and hast won me as man wins woman. And this shall be a loving cup, for it is the fashion in my country for the lover to take the loved one's cup and drink it." "O lovely one of my eye," he replied, "I will honour thy custom, since thou hast so greatly honoured *me*."

At this Bedr-el-Budur took his cup and filled it for herself, while a slave girl, who knew what to do as well as she hated the Dervish, handed him the cup which, though it contained the benj, she had just filled as if for her mistress. She even had to be told twice that it was not for her mistress but for the guest. So the Dervish took it, and looked into the eyes of Bedr-el-Budur brimming with love. They drank, and immediately the Dervish fell senseless at her feet, while the cup, flung from his nerveless hand, clattered across the floor.

In the space of moments Aladdin was on the spot. Bedr-el-Budur's arms were round his neck, and she was sobbing on his breast, while the Dervish lay stretched helpless before them. And when he had comforted her she went, and the slave girls with her. Then Aladdin locked the door, and, approaching the Dervish, drew the Lamp from his bosom. This done, he stood over him and swore a fearful oath, then, without further shrift, he drew his sword and hewed off his head, after which he drove the point of the sword through his heart, for only in this way can a wizard be warned off the realm of mortals.

Once in possession of the Lamp Aladdin lost no time. He rubbed it and immediately the Slave appeared. "I am here, O my master, what is thy wish?" "Thou knowest," replied Aladdin. "Bear this palace and all that is in it to the Land of Cathay, and set it down on the spot from which thou didst take it at the command of that." He pointed to the dismembered wizard. "It is well," said the Slave, who served the living and not the dead; "I hear and obey, on the head and the eye." Then Aladdin returned to Bedr-el-Budur, and, in the space of one kiss of love, the palace with all therein was carried swiftly back to the original site from which it had been taken.

Now the Sultan was in grievous mood ever since the loss of his daughter—the apple of his eye. All night long he would weep, and, arising at dawn, would look forth on the empty space where once had stood Aladdin's palace. Then his tears would flow as from a woman's eyes, for Bedr-el-Budur was very dear to him. But, when he looked forth one morning and saw the palace standing as it had stood, he was rapt with joy. Instantly he ordered his horse, and, mounting, rode to the gates. Aladdin came out to greet him, and, taking him by the hand with never a word, led him towards the apartments of Bedr-el-Budur. She too, radiant with joy, was running to meet him. Like a bird of the air she flew to his arms, and for some moments neither of them could say a word for very happiness. Then in a torrent of words, she told him all about the accursed Dervish; how by his sorcery he had conveyed the palace to Africa, and how Aladdin had slain him, thus releasing the spell and restoring everything to its place. But not a word did she say about the Lamp and its virtues. Then they arose and went to the chamber which contained the trunk and severed head of the Dervish. And, by the Sultan's orders, these remains of the Sorcerer were burnt to ashes and scattered to the four winds of heaven.

And so Aladdin was restored to the Sultan's favour, and he and the Lady Bedr-el-Budur dwelt together in the utmost joy and happiness.

ONE night, in the City of Baghdad, the Khalifeh Harun-er-Rashid went forth with Ja'far, his Grand Vizier, and Mesrur, his Executioner, all three disguised as merchants, for it was the Khalifeh's whim to wander abroad in this way at times, in order to learn how his people fared among themselves.

Taking their way at random, they had not gone far before they noticed a brilliantly-lighted house whence came sounds of music and revelry. "O Vizier," the Khalifeh said to Ja'far, "it is in my mind to enter this house, and see what entertainment we might find. Wherefore, devise some excuse whereby we may gain admittance." So Ja'far knocked at the door, and it was opened presently by a beautiful lady, tall and graceful as a windflower.

"O my mistress," said Ja'far courteously, "we are merchants from Tiberias, and, knowing not this City well, we have lost our way. I perceive that thou art kind, as well as beautiful; and I am emboldened to ask thee for safe shelter in thy house."

The lady regarded the three lost merchants with an approving glance, for, though she knew not their high degree, the dignity of state cannot be well concealed from a woman's eyes. "Wait a little," she said; "I will consult my sisters,"

And with this she retired within the house. Presently she returned, and bade them enter; whereupon they followed her into a sumptuously furnished apartment, where they found two other ladies as beautiful as the first; and with them was a porter—an amusing fellow, as full of quips and cranks as he was of wine—who had been entertaining them with joke and song and dance. The ladies smiled upon the three merchants, and welcomed them graciously, setting food and wine before them, and bidding them join in their merriment.

And to entertain the three merchants the porter related how that day, whilst he had been reclining against his crate, waiting for custom, one of the three ladies had accosted him in the market-place, bidding him take up his crate and follow her. "She was wrapped in a long veil of gold-embroidered silk, with a border of gold lace at each end, and when she raised her face-veil she displayed a face of such exceeding beauty, that I gladly did as she had bidden me, exclaiming, 'This is indeed a fortunate day!'" After this beginning the porter went on to describe with much drollery how first the lady had knocked at the house of a Christian, from whom she had received a quantity of olives and two large vessels of wine. And after she had placed these in the crate she said, "Take it up and follow me." And he had taken up the crate and followed her. She next stopped at the stall of a fruiterer, from whom she bought Syrian apples, Othmanee quinces, peaches of Oman, and many other rare fruits and flowers. And these also she had placed in the porter's crate. "And when she had further bought ten pounds of meat, and many sweets and perfumes—all of which she commanded should be placed in my crate," continued the porter, "I said unto the lady, 'If thou hadst but informed me beforehand of the extent of your requirements, I would have brought a mule with me.' But so sweet was her smile that I would have followed her to the ends of the earth, instead of only to this street. And so am I come hither," concluded the porter.

And the Khalifeh, who was greatly entertained by the porter's ready wit, which kept the company in constant laughter, turned to Ja'far and said softly, "Verily, O Vizier, we should like this fellow's head and all it contains. Nay, O Mesrur," he added, turning to his Executioner, "I want not his head without the rest of him. He shall be my wag." "O King of the Age," answered the Grand Vizier, "I hear, and obey." Meanwhile, the porter continued to amuse them, but at length he became so intoxicated that his efforts to amuse were unsuccessful, whereat the entertainment flagged. "It seems to me," said the Khalifeh, "that these three ladies are no ordinary persons; perchance they have a history. Ask them to entertain us with their various stories." Accordingly the Vizier singled out the eldest and put the question to her. But she liked it not, and, with a clouded brow, led him to the door, on the lintel of which she pointed out an inscription: "Ask not what doth not concern thee, lest thou hear what may not please thee." Ja'far returned and informed the Khalifeh of this, which only served to increase his curiosity. While he was planning a way with the Vizier to induce them to tell their history, there came a knock at the door. One of the sisters went to open it, and presently returned, saying, "There are three Dervishes without, each of them clean shaven, and each lacking an eye."

"Ask them if they were born blind of an eye," said one of the sisters, "and if they are brothers." So the lady went and asked them these questions, and returned presently with the answer: "They were not born blind, but each lost his eye through an adventure; neither are they brothers, having met for the first time in this City, where they have lost their way. They are wandering Mendicants or Calenders."

At this, her sister turned to Ja'far. "Thou didst desire to hear our stories, O my master, but it seemeth that these Dervishes may have stories more interesting to hear. Shall we admit them?" The Khalifeh added his approval to that of Ja'far on this point, and the three Calenders were admitted. And strange looking men they were. Differing widely in feature and expression, they were all alike in the manner of their dress and general appearance. Each had lost one eye; and each had long black moustaches, twisted like silk, and drooping over a clean-shaven chin. Being of the order of mendicants, they bowed humbly, and stood silent. "Tell us how it is," said the eldest of the sisters, "that you three, being no relation one to another, and each lacking one eye, should be together." "In that," said one of the Calenders, "there is no more cause for wonder than that you three women, all unrelated one to another before birth, and all equally beautiful, should find yourselves sisters of one household."

STORY OF THE THREE CALENDERS

At this the Khalifeh whispered to Ja'far, "This man's speech and address are not those of a mendicant. If I mistake not he hath moved in Royal Courts."

"Yet, O my mistress," the First Calender continued, "it may be that it was decreed by Destiny that we three, coming from three widely separate kingdoms, should meet in this City, the Abode of Peace, for our conditions appear to be similar. Each of us having lost, not only an eye, but a throne—for know that we are kings, and the sons of kings —has been led hither by the same stars, to kneel at the feet of the Khalifeh Harun-er-Rashid and implore his aid in the restoration of our royal state."

On hearing this, the Khalifeh looked down his beard, saying within himself, "If they knew, they would kneel and implore here and now. But they know not." Then a stratagem within a stratagem got hold of him, and he arose and bowed low to the three ladies.

"O my mistresses," he said, "whose beauty is unequalled, save by that of each to each, I crave your permission. It seems there is an entertainment in this matter. Here we have Three Royal Calenders suppliant to the Khalifeh— on whom be peace! Now, it will be good for them to rehearse their parts for our amusement; for so, when at last they gain audience of the Khalifeh, they will be well versed. Grant me then the privilege, O fair ones, to play the part of the Khalifeh, for I am not unskilled in the art of such play. Indeed, I have appeared before the Khalifeh himself —("In a mirror," assented Ja'far, in thought),—and he was greatly pleased with my impersonation and my appearance."

"Verily," said one of the sisters, in approval, "thou art a kingly man, and thou wilt play the part well. What say you, O my sisters?" she added, turning to the other two. They agreed, laughing, and clapping their hands, for they liked the idea of real suppliants rehearsing to a stage Khalifeh.

"Good!" cried one, "and these Calenders will approach thee as if thou wert in sober truth the Khalifeh."

"And," rejoined Er-Rashid, "as if these two were indeed my Grand Vizier, Ja'far, and Mesrur, my Executioner."

Loudly the two laughed at the Khalifeh's happy conceit, and preened themselves for office, Ja'far assuming his old look of terrible solemnity, while Mesrur, drawing his great sword, with a grin, struck an attitude that many had beheld for the last time.

The Calenders unbent to the play; the ladies sprang into animation; even the porter was rolled from a couch to give place to the Khalifeh, who sat himself thereon in royal state.

"On pain of death, O Calenders," said the Khalifeh—and all except Ja'far and Mesrur marvelled at his royal dignity —"I command you to make known to me severally the stories of your lives, for I would fain learn how each of you came to lose a throne, and an eye."

On this the Royal Calenders, taking up the jest in a proper spirit, advanced and kissed the ground.

"Rise!" said the Khalifeh, imitating himself to perfection, "and see to it that your stories please not only me, but Mesrur, my Executioner; for his sword hath a cutting edge, and I observe that you have your heads with you." Singling out one of the three, he commanded the other two to stand aside. Then the first Royal Calender spoke as follows:—

THE STORY OF THE FIRST CALENDER

Know, O Prince of the Faithful, that I am a King, the son of a king, and one robbed of his heritage. My father's brother was also a King, and his son, my cousin, was born on the same day as myself. We two Princes were friends, and paid long visits to each other. On one occasion, when I was staying with him, he made much of me, honouring me with a rich banquet. When this was over, and we were alone, and the wine had made us genial, he drew near to me, and said: "O my cousin, I desire thine assistance in a matter that concerneth me greatly."

"I will serve thee without question, O son of my uncle," said I. But he made me swear by the holiest oath that I would assist him in his undertaking. Then, when he was satisfied, he left me for a little, and returned with a beautiful young woman, dressed in the manner of a queen. "Lead this woman before me," he said, "to the place of sepulture, which thou knowest. Enter that place, and await my coming."

Wondering greatly, but questioning nothing, I led the woman forth, and we waited for him among the tombs. Soon he came, bearing a bowl of water, some plaster, and a pointed bar of iron. Approaching a certain tomb, he dislodged the stones with the iron bar, and disclosed a vault with a stairway descending into it. Then, addressing the woman, he said: "Hast thou chosen?" And she replied, with a steady gaze, "Yea, I have chosen." And she descended the stairway into the vault. Then he said to me: "Cousin, farewell! for I too descend. Place the stones together above us, and cement them with the plaster moistened with the water, so that none can say, 'This vault is not as it should be.' Farewell! And may thy head long survive mine!" With this, he descended into the vault.

Bound by my oath, and like one compelled against his will, I did his bidding, ceasing not until I had closed up the tomb in such a way that none could tell it had been opened. But that night I was visited by terrible dreams, which magnified the enormity of what I had done. Repentance pricked me, and I rose, and went to the place of sepulture. There I searched for the tomb, but alas! so cleverly had I done my work that I could not trace it. All day long I sought it, but in vain; and, when evening fell, I returned to the palace burdened with grief and remorse. Again my sleep was disturbed with dreams of horror, so that at daybreak, repenting of my action still more keenly, I repaired a second time to the burial place. But again my search was unsuccessful. And so I continued for seven days, searching and calling out among the tombs, but never I could find the place of my quest, nor from any tomb came back an answer to my cry. At last, nearly mad with grief and remorse, I left my uncle's palace to return to my father. But there fresh trouble awaited me, for, no sooner had I entered the gates of the city, than a party of guards sprang upon me, and bound me, and cast me into a dungeon.

O Prince of the Faithful, imagine my despair. I was the son of the King, and his servants had treated me in this manner. With anger I inquired the cause of this, but none answered me. At last I saw one who had been my own servant, and had received many benefits at my hands. I put the question to him, and he replied: "O my master, thy father is no more, for the Grand Vizier hath killed him, and now sitteth in his place." At this I bowed my head in grief for my father, and despair for my own life. And they led me before the Grand Vizier who had slain my father.

Now this Vizier had never been my friend, especially after an accident in which I was made instrumental by fate in depriving him of one of his eyes. It happened in this way: One day I was using the cross-bow when I saw a rare bird alight on the parapet of one of the windows in the Vizier's palace. I shot at it, but the missile struck not the bird, which was protected by Providence. Passing it narrowly it sped in at the window, and, guided by Destiny, struck out the eye of the Vizier. My father being King the Vizier could do nothing against me, but the malice and hatred with which he had always regarded me from two eyes lost naught through being concentrated into one. No wonder then that now, my father being dead, and I standing before this regicide, bound and helpless, he fiercely commanded the Executioner to strike off my head.

"What is my offence?" I asked. "Offence!" he cried. "Is not this offence enough?" and he pointed to the socket where his eye had been. "That was done by accident," I said. "And this by design," he answered, advancing swiftly and thrusting out my left eye. He then commanded me to be bound, and placed in a chest, and when this was done, he said to the Executioner: "Take this carrion, and convey it beyond the confines of the city. There draw thy sword, and cut it in pieces, so that the wild beasts may the more readily devour it."

Accordingly, the Executioner carried me forth upon a mule into the desert, where he took me out of the chest, and was about to kill me, when I implored him to spare my life, reminding him of the many kind deeds my father and I had done to him and to others. He was moved by my supplications, but shook his head, saying: "O my master, if I slay not thee, the Vizier will slay me." "The Vizier is not here to see," I said. "There is none here but thee and me."

He was silent for a little. Then he said: "Depart with thy life, and return not to this country, lest both our lives be forfeit." When he had said this, I thanked him, and kissed his hands; then, lest he might change his mind, I fled from him, and ceased not to journey night and day until I reached my uncle's palace. There I related to my uncle all that had taken place, and he wept with excess of grief. "Woe cometh on woe," he said, "for know that thy cousin, my son, hath gone from me, and hath not returned for many days. None knoweth where he is, nor what fate hath overtaken him. Nephew, thou hast lost a father, and one of thine eyes; and now, woe is me! I have lost a brother, and an only son."

On witnessing his terrible grief I could no longer remain silent regarding the disappearance of my cousin. I told him all. "By Allah!" he cried, joyfully. "Where is this tomb of which thou speakest?" "Alas! O my uncle," I replied; "I know not. I searched for it for many days, but could not find it." On this my uncle commanded a company of workmen to proceed to the burial place, and there, in our presence, they opened tomb after tomb.

In this manner, on the evening of the second day, when a great number of tombs had been opened and closed again, we came upon what we soon discovered to be the right one. When the stones had been dislodged, my uncle descended the stairway, and I followed. On reaching the bottom, we were met by a blinding smoke. Enduring this, we found our way into an apartment wherein was a table bearing food of many kinds. At the far end of this apartment we found a curtain. My uncle drew this aside, and we looked within upon a sight of horror. There, side by side, upon a couch, were the forms of my cousin and the lady, charred by fire, as if they had been thrown into a furnace.

On seeing this terrible thing, my uncle uttered a loud cry, and spat upon his dead son's face. "Wretch!" he exclaimed. "Thou art come into thine own, and hast gone where worse awaits thee for this deed. May thou never find forgiveness!"

"Wherefore, O my uncle?" I said. "Is not his state already grievous enough that thou must invoke a worse fate upon him?"

"O Son of my brother," he replied, "thou knowest not the sin of this accursed. From his youth he was inflamed with love for his foster sister, who now lies there upon the couch, and, in defiance of my will, he persisted in and encouraged this passion. I took steps to separate them, but who can lock love out? For when he knew my will, he called the Devil to his purpose, and he entered and took possession of them both. And so it was that he made this secret place among the tombs wherein they met. But fire from Heaven consumed them, as thou hast seen, and now they are further punished in the fires of Iblis." Then he wept bitterly, and I covered my head and wept with him. And when at last he could speak, he said: "But his place shall be filled by thee. Thou art now my son in his stead."

Long time we wept together there in the tomb by the side of the charred bodies of the dead, for we had no lack of trouble upon our heads. Then we arose, and ascended the stairway, and my uncle ordered the workmen to replace the stones upon the tomb. Sadly we turned away, and retraced our steps to my uncle's palace. There we were about to dispose ourselves to rest when we heard unwonted sounds without—the tramp of an advancing host; the clank of armour, and loud cries of dismay from the populace. Drums beat and trumpets sounded; shrieks came out of riot, and groans issued from the wake of galloping hoofs. Then came a eunuch running, his face distorted, and his garb dishevelled.

"The City is lost!" he cried. "On a sudden, being taken

unawares, it is surrendered to the enemy. O King, thy brother's Vizier hath slain him, and he hath now come hither with his army, and none can stand against him."

At this my uncle arose, and hastened forth; but I, knowing full well what would happen to me if I fell into the Vizier's hands, remained, and took thought on how I might escape unobserved by any of my father's city. I could think of naught but to shave off my beard, and change my clothes, thus disguising myself. This I did in all haste, and so made my way through the turbulent crowds of people, and escaped.

Far, far to the North I knew was the City of Baghdad, the Abode of Peace; and I bent my steps hither, for I said within myself, "There abideth the Khalifeh, the Prince of the Faithful, and the King of the Age. I will go and kneel at his feet, and humbly entreat him to strike mine enemy, and restore to me my father's throne." And when I arrived in this City some few hours since, it was night. I stood at the cross roads, not knowing which way to turn, when one like myself, a mendicant, drew nigh, and I saluted him. "I am a stranger," I said. "Canst thou direct me to a khan for shelter?" And he replied, "I too am a stranger, and would put the same question to thee." But lo, as I looked at him, I saw that he was in like case with me, having lost his left eye. I was about to question him on this, when a third mendicant came out of the night, and accosted us. "By Allah!" cried the two of us in a breath, "and thou too hast lost an eye!" "Verily," said he, "we are all strangers one to another, but the stars have enmeshed us in their network, and so have drawn us together with one purpose." "And that is?" we asked. "To seek audience of the Khalifeh," he answered, "for the tables of the stars have told me that I, a King, and the son of a King, should meet in this City two others who, royal like myself, have planned to seek the Khalifeh of the Lord of all creatures, craving redress for wrongs."

And the three of us marvelled at this thing, and at the exact computation of time and space in the mind of Destiny. And thus, from strangers we speedily came to be friends, having a common object. Then, proceeding forth together, we came at length to this house, where, by the grace of these hospitable ladies, we relate our true stories as if to the——

"As if?" cried Mesrur, grasping his sword, and clanking it on the table before him.

"As if!" echoed Ja'far, springing from his seat with well-feigned indignation.

"Silence!" cried Er-Rashid, rising in stately wrath. "O Calender, thy story is good, but if thou wert about to say 'as if to the Khalifeh' thou wert out of order. When I play a part, I play a part. I *am* the Khalifeh! The Prince of the Faithful! The King of the Age!"

The ladies laughed, with beaming eyes. The three Royal Calenders yielded to the jest with winks and nods to one another; then, as the porter grovelled the floor in mock obeisance to the Lord of the Earth, the others followed in like spirit, and prostrated themselves in all humility.

"Peace be on you!" said Er-Rashid. "Rise, and be

seated!   As for thee, O Calender, thy case is extraordinary, and I will see to it that thou art restored to thy throne.   Now it is our royal will that ye proceed with this entertainment."

At this the second Calender advanced, and, having kissed the ground, rose, and spoke as follows:—

THE STORY OF THE SECOND CALENDER

O King of the Age, my story is such that none hearing it need lack a lesson or a warning.   I, a King, the son of a King, devoted my youth and early manhood to the study of the arts and sciences, so that I became proficient, and excelled greatly in all branches of learning.   My fame as a scribe spread far and wide, even to India, so that the King of that land sent a messenger with rich gifts to my father, requesting that I might be allowed to visit him.   This pleased my father, and he fitted out a fleet of ships laden with rich gifts, and set them at my disposal.

With a goodly company I sailed eastward, and after many days reached land.   Disembarking some splendid horses we had brought with us, we loaded them with gifts and set out for the King's capital, but we had not proceeded far when a cloud of dust arose in the distance and swept rapidly toward us, with a sound like thunder; and, not until it was near at hand did we observe, outstripping the cloud, a large body of horsemen.   Wild-eyed and fierce, and with lances poised, these rode down upon us.   We shouted to them that we were ambassadors to the King of India, but this was of no service to us, for it appeared that these men were robbers and recognised no king. This we learned from their cries and shouts as they swept upon us, slaying all within reach of their spears. Some of us fled. I was one of them, though I was wounded, and so closely were the robbers occupied with the treasure upon the horses, that they did not pursue.

Separated from the other survivors, and not knowing which way to search for them, I journeyed on and on, weak from loss of blood, and wretched from my change of state, until in the evening I discovered a cave at the foot of a mountain. Here I rested until the morning, when, after having journeyed on for some hours, I found I was approaching a great city. With joy I made my way towards its sunlit towers and spires, passing through gardens of ever-increasing luxuriance, until I came to the busy parts of the thoroughfares, where merchants thronged the market places, buying and selling.

Not knowing how to proceed in this city, I looked about for some one who might give ear to my tale, and advise me what to do. At last I espied a tailor sitting at work in his shop, and decided that I would speak with him. He received me kindly, and I told him my tale, acquainting him with all that had happened since I left my father's capital. When I had finished he shook his head gravely, and said: "My son, verily thou art in a hard case, though it is fortunate thou camest to me with thy story, and not to another. Knowest thou not that the King of this city is thy father's greatest enemy, having a blood-debt against him? Wherefore, tell not thy tale again to any, lest the King hear of it, and inflict an injury of vengeance upon thee." The tailor then treated me with hospitality, setting food and wine before me, and bade me remain in his house awhile.

When he had harboured me for some days, the tailor desired to know, if I had any trade by means of which I could earn my living. Whereat I informed him that I was learned in the arts and sciences, and a fine writer. "Alas!" he said, "there is no profit in such things. This is a city of commerce, where people devote themselves to getting money. Arise, therefore, O my son, and work for thy living."

He then fetched an axe and a coil of rope, and bade me go to the forest without the city and hew firewood, which, on my return in the evening, I might sell for a good price. So I followed his counsel, and, when I found that my day's work brought me half a gold piece, I continued to dwell with the tailor, and hewed wood for the space of a whole year, paying my way, and steadily setting by something of my earnings day by day. Then a strange thing happened to me.

One day, while I was clearing the earth from the roots of a tree in the forest, I came upon a ring of brass. This, I soon discovered, was attached to a trap door, which with some difficulty I removed. Then, seeing before me a staircase, I descended until I reached a door, by which, on opening it, I found admittance to a large underground palace, richly furnished. On wandering through the rooms of this place, I came at length to one more richly decorated than all the others; and here, reclining upon a couch, was a lady of surpassing loveliness. The rarity of her charms dazzled me and took my breath away, so that I stood speechless before her. "Art thou a man?" said the lady, regarding me intently, "or art thou an Efrite?" This loosened my tongue, and I replied, "I am a man, as thou art a woman." She answered, "Yea, I am a woman, and thou art the first man I have seen for a space of twenty-five years, every day and night of which I have spent in this place. How camest thou hither?"

Her voice was sweet as her face was fair, and my heart was melted at the thought of her long captivity. I resolved to tell her my story, for here at least was one who could not spread it abroad in the bazaars. Accordingly I seated myself on the couch at a little distance from her, and related my story from beginning to end; whereupon she wept at my hard lot, saying, "O my master, thy case is not unlike mine." And she proceeded to acquaint me with it.

"I am the daughter of the King of the Ebony Isles," she said. "My father married me to my cousin, but on the night of our wedding an Efrite—a true son of Iblis—appeared, and, snatching me from my husband, carried me through the air to this spot where he had built this palace and filled it with all things necessary to my comfort. And from that night, twenty-five years ago, to the present, I have never seen the outside world. On every tenth day he cometh to me, to leave me on the following morning, but if I desire his instant presence at any time, I have but to press this panel of the wall whereon are inscribed some magic characters, and immediately he appeareth before me. Four days have now passed since he was here, so that there remains six of the ten. Do thou therefore dwell here with me for five days, and depart one day before he cometh."

I agreed to this, and when I had bathed, and put on some garments which she gave me, I sat by her side, and we ate and drank, and conversed happily together. Presently she sang to me in a sweet low voice, and, being fatigued, as well as drowsy with wine, I slept.

When I awoke, she was bending over me, with joy on her face. "Allah hath been good to me in sending thee here," she said, "for I was nigh to death with loneliness." At this my heart swelled with love for her, and I could think of naught else but her wondrous charm and beauty. And when I told her this, she said nothing, but the light of her eyes told me all there was to tell. And I remained with her in the greatest joy and happiness. We feasted, and drank, and sang; and, while I played upon musical instruments, she danced with a grace and skill that I had never seen before. At length, on the third day, when I was drunk with love and wine, I said to her: "Let me take thee from this sumptuous dungeon, and free thee from this vile Efrite." But perchance she knew that this would be impossible, for she replied, laughing softly, "Hold thy peace, O man; thou hast nine days out of the ten." This inflamed me, and my passion made me valiant. "It is the tenth day I want," I cried, "and the other nine as well. Lo here! I am a slayer and a conqueror of Efrites. I will this instant break this panel with the magic signs, so that the Efrite may come and be slain." With a cry she sprang forward to stop me, but I escaped from her embrace, and, aiming a violent kick at the panel, broke it.

"Flee for thy life ere he cometh," she cried, pointing towards the door. I scarcely knew whether to flee or to remain and face the Efrite, but my feet settled the matter for me, and I gained the doorway in a bound. Then, turning my head, I saw the ground open, and there rose into the room an Efrite of terrible aspect, who looked threateningly at the woman, and demanded to know the cause of his being summoned in such a manner. "Nay it was naught," said she, "save that I tripped and fell against the panel, breaking it as thou seest." "Thou liest!" he cried, in a voice of rage, and, as he said it, his eyes, rolling round in his head, fell upon my sandals and my axe, which in my haste I had left. "Ha!" he exclaimed, snatching them up, "some man hath visited thee, and hath left his axe and his sandals. Confess, vile woman!"

But she denied it, saying, "No man hath visited me, and thou must have brought these things with thee, for I have never set eyes on them until this instant." "Again thou liest!" he roared, "and unless thou tell me his name, I will beat thy body black and blue." With this he turned to look for the wherewithal to beat her, and, at the sight of his fierce face and huge bulk, my heart turned to water within me, and I fled up the stairway. Before I reached the top I heard the sound of blows, followed by loud cries and shrieks from the woman. Full of bitter repentance that she should suffer thus on my account, and unable to endure the sounds of torture, I hastened through the trap door and fastened it behind me. Then, when I had covered it with earth, I fled through the forest and paused not till I had gained the house of the tailor.

I found him in a state of great anxiety on my account, for I had been absent three days and three nights. "I feared thou hadst fallen a prey to some wild beast," he cried, "but praise be to God that thou art safe!" I thanked him, and, saying that I was fatigued and would tell him all later, went to my own apartments to weep over what had come to that poor woman through my rash action. But I had not been there many minutes when the tailor came to me, saying, "There is one, a foreigner, in the shop, who desires to speak with thee. He hath an axe and a pair of sandals, which he thinks are thine, and the other woodcutters have directed him to thee; so come forth to receive them, and to thank him." With this, he returned to the shop, leaving me pale with fear, for well I knew the meaning of this thing. While I was planning what to do—whether to go into the shop, or escape by some other way—the floor was rent asunder, and there rose from it the Efrite. In a loud voice he told me that he had tortured the lady nigh to death, but without avail, for she would tell him nothing; whereat he had taken the axe and the sandals, and, by inquiries, had traced me to the tailor's abode. With this, he seized me and bore me aloft through the roof of the house, and thence rapidly through the air into the forest, where he descended through the earth and placed me within the chamber of the palace from which I had fled. There, on the floor, laid the lady, bleeding from the wounds inflicted by the Efrite's torture. "Shameless woman!" cried he, standing over her; "here is thy lover. deny it not." She glanced at me, and answered him: "I have never set eyes on this man before." He appeared to take thought for a moment, and then he said: "Thou wilt swear that thou lovest not this man?" She answered him: "I know him not; I love him not." The Efrite drew his sword. "If thou lovest him not," said he, "take this sword and strike off his head."

She took the sword from him, and, coming towards me, raised it to strike; but I made a sign with my eye, imploring her pity. She replied also with a sign, as if to say, "I have suffered all this through thee." But I still implored her with the speech of the eye, for, as the poet saith:

The language of the eye like the kisses of the mouth is sweet as honey, and only lovers understand it.
When the lips are closed, love openeth the windows of the soul, and conveyeth its meaning by soft glances.

And when my meaning was thus conveyed to her, she flung away the sword and faced the Efrite, crying, "I cannot slay him, for he hath done me no injury." The Efrite answered her not, but, taking up the sword, handed it to me. "Strike off her head," he said, "and I will set thee free." I took the sword, and arose to do the deed; but, while my arm was raised to strike, love spoke again from her eyes. My hand trembled, my heart melted. I flung my sword from me. "Wherefore should I slay this woman, who hath done me no injury, and whom I have never seen before?" I said to the Efrite. "Never before God can I commit this crime." The

Efrite took the sword, and saying, "It is clear there is love between you," he cut off one of the lady's hands, then the other, and then both her feet. And, in her pain, her eyes were turned on me, and the words of love were in them. The Efrite saw her look, and cried, "Is it not enough? Wilt thou still commit the crime of unfaithfulness with thine eye?" And raising his sword again, he cut off her head.

"O man," he said, turning to me, "is it lawful for one, having known his wife for twenty-five years, to kill her for the crime of unfaithfulness. As for thee, I will not permit thee to join her. I will not take thy life, but, as I am minded to punish thee, I will give thee thy choice as to whether thou wilt be changed into the form of a dog, or an ass, or an ape." Since he had shown me this clemency, I thought by pleading to melt him further, so that perchance he would pardon me altogether. Therefore, I recited many instances of kindness and generosity shown by Efrites to mortals, some of which I had gleaned from books, while others I invented then and there, with a ready wit. But, though the Efrite listened, his bearing changed not towards me one hair's-breadth. "Thou hast been misinformed," he said at last. "The Efrite knows neither kindness nor generosity: he is only constrained by the justice of those who have sovereignty over him. Wherefore, hold thy peace, and neither fear that I shall slay thee, nor hope that I shall pardon thee. Thou shalt be punished by the power of enchantment, and thou knowest not how to prevent it."

Immediately on these words, he stamped the floor with his foot, and the sides of the palace rocked on their foundations, and fell together; but seizing me, he clove a way through the falling structure, and bore me aloft to a great height. Presently he set me down upon the summit of a high mountain, where he took up a handful of dust, and having chanted some strange words over it, cast it upon me, crying, "Change thy form, O Man! Retain thy form, O Ape!" And immediately I suffered a rending pang in my bones and flesh, and behold, I was a man ape, old and ugly, and clothed only with hair. When I looked up from examining my ungainly limbs, the Efrite had disappeared.

Long I remained, crouching on the summit of that mountain, realising my punishment, the keenness of which lay in the fact that it was only my form that was changed. My memory, my mental powers, and my likes and dislikes all remained to me, though I was bereft of the power of articulate speech. At last, rousing myself, I descended the mountain, subdued and resigned, to meet whatever further fate awaited me. I journeyed on through strange places, meeting no human being nor any of my present kind in the forests and deserts through which I passed, and subsisting on berries which I gathered from the trees. Finally, I came to the seashore, and lo, there was a vessel making towards the land. Presently the ship cast anchor, and some sailors landed in a small boat with some barrels, by which I knew that they were seeking water. There were six of these barrels, and when they had filled three of them from a spring some little distance inland, and had gone again with the other three to fill them also, I jumped into the boat, and secreted myself behind the three barrels, saying within myself, "If

I can get on to the ship unobserved, and hide, I may reach a better land than this."

Presently the sailors returned with the remaining barrels, and placed them in the boat. I remained undiscovered, and when we reached the vessel's side, I leapt on board, and hid myself! But alas! I was soon observed, and not being able to explain my position there, knew not what my end would be. Moreover, the merchants who found me clamoured that I should be cast into the sea to drown, for they said, "This ugly brute will be unlucky to us, and, if he remain on the ship, we shall meet with some grievous misfortune." While they were discussing among themselves whether to slay me with the sword, or cast me overboard to drown, the master of the ship chanced to spy me, and as soon as I saw him, and knew him for the master, I ran forward and threw myself at his feet, clutching and tugging his garment in the endeavour to excite his compassion. And in this I was successful, for he looked down at me with interest, saying: "In truth, this is an intelligent ape; see how he claims my protection! By Allah! he shall have it! Know, O ye merchants, that this is *my* ape, wherefore harm him not, nor hinder him in his coming and going." He then took me, and treated me henceforth with the greatest kindness; and, in return for this, I proved myself still more intelligent by serving him in every way I could. When he discovered that I could understand everything he said to me, although I could not speak myself, his astonishment was great. "By the Prophet!" he cried, with a great laugh, "methinks this ape hath already forgotten much that I have yet to learn."

Meanwhile, we sailed many days upon the sea, until at last we reached a great city built upon the side of a mountain. The houses of this city were numberless, and the inhabitants thereof beyond all reckoning. Scarcely had we cast anchor, and set foot on land, when there came to us some high officials of the King of that city, with many greetings and congratulations on our fortunate journey. "Our King hath seen thy vessel drawing near," said one of them to the master, "and he bade me say to thee: "Thine is a large vessel, and no doubt there are many passengers on board. Is there, perchance, one amongst them who is a skilled caligraphist?" For thou must know, O my master, that since the death of one of the King's Viziers,—a marvellous writer,—he hath searched the city in vain to find his equal. Wherefore he hath sent thee this roll of parchment whereon he desireth that each of thy company write a line as candidate for the high office left vacant."

Immediately on hearing this, I sprang past the master, and seized the parchment, whereat there was great consternation lest I should tear it to pieces. But when I ran to a bale of goods near by, and, seating myself upon it, held the paper correctly with one hand, while making the motions of writing with the other, the master said, "Let him write. He is a most marvellous ape, and I have yet to discover the full extent of his intelligence." Out of curiosity, the officials, who were incredulous in the matter, agreed, and I was supplied with pen and ink. Then I wrote in a large formal hand:

STORY OF THE THREE CALENDERS

He who writes will perish, though his writing live after him;

Let him write, therefore, only what will stand to the end of time.

Then in the epistolary hand I wrote:

O King, thy virtues are so many and so great,
Fame has not space to set them on her page.
Ten thousand writers, writing for an age,
One half thine excellence alone could indicate.

To these I added, in several smaller and different hands, other quatrains in praise of the King; and, having finished, I gave the parchment to the official. When he saw my writing he could not contain his astonishment. He passed it round among the merchants, all of whom marvelled greatly, while some, thinking they could outwrite what I had written, took pen and ink, and wrote. Finally, the official and his party returned with the parchment to the King.

Now, it seems that when the King had read all that was inscribed upon the parchment, he liked none of it but mine; and, having summoned his attendants, he said to them: "Take this parchment and find the author of this handwriting. Clothe him in a splendid robe, and mount him upon the best of my horses, and bring him hither." On this, the officials who stood by could not restrain their laughter, so that the King was incensed at their behaviour, and was about to mark his displeasure by swift punishment when their chief advanced and explained the matter. "O King,

[203]

didst thou only know why we laugh, thou wouldst laugh
louder than any of us.   We crave thy Felicity to pardon us,
but this writing was done, not by any son of Adam, but by
an ape, which belongeth to the master of the ship."
"What?" said the King, "this excellent work done by an
ape?"   "Yea, your Majesty, it is even so, on the head and
the eye.   This ape, which is at least a hundred years old,
and proportionately ugly, wrote those quatrains in our
presence."   The King laughed heartily and said, "Make
haste, and bring this ape before me in the manner I commanded, for I have never heard of anything so wonderful."
And he gave them a written and sealed order to the master
of the vessel.

O Prince of the Faithful, I learnt all this that I have told
thee from their narration to the master on their arrival.
On seeing the King's order the master handed me over to
them, and they clothed me with the splendid robe, and placed
me upon the King's horse.   Great was the wonder of the
people when the procession started for the palace.   Seeing
an ugly ape, dressed in a royal robe and mounted upon the
King's most splendid steed, their laughter died a sudden
death in their throats, and they gaped and wondered.   The
rumour of my progress went before, and the way was soon
thronged with people of high degree and low, while from the
windows of houses and palaces looked forth a multitude of
citizens to witness this strangest of all spectacles.   Then,
gradually, arose a great cry of wonder and astonishment,
which spread throughout the city: Had the King chosen an
ape for his Grand Vizier?   What marvellous thing was this?

But the King was the King, and the people was the people, and none among them could doubt his doings. And so I rode on in dignified procession.

. . . .

[At this point in the story, the Khalifeh, set off by the three ladies, could not forbear laughing. "Verily," he said, slapping his hand on his knee, and rocking with mirth, "were I in reality the Prince of the Faithful, and not a poor impersonator, so would I laugh at the thought of this solemn ape, clad in a royal robe, and mounted on the King's horse, proceeding in stately dignity through the city." Then, mastering his laughter, he added, to Ja'far, "O Vizier, I play my part badly when I say "were I in reality the Prince of the Faithful," for thou knowest, and my Executioner knows, that I *am* the Khalifeh!" Loudly did Ja'far and Mesrur laugh at this, and the others joined them, and clapped their hands, saying it was an excellent piece of play acting. "Proceed, O Royal Brother!" said the Khalifeh with grave dignity; and the story was resumed.]

Arriving at the palace I soon found myself before the King seated on his throne in a vast chamber, where were assembled the great ones of the earth. I made my obeisance three times to the King, and then, when he motioned me to be seated, I sat down, in the fashion of an ape, upon my haunches. So far, my intelligent respect to royalty commanded the admiration at once of the King and his subjects, for my performance required only the gift of speech to render it perfect. The King then ordered his Court to withdraw, saving only his chief Memluk, a young slave, and myself.

He then bade us follow him into his private apartment, where he ordered food to be served. When it was ready, he beckoned me to approach and eat. At this I advanced and kissed the ground before him seven times, after which I sat down at the table and ate. When the repast was over I took a broad leaf from the flower-pod of a palm near at hand, and having signed to the slave to bring me pen and ink, wrote upon it the following verse:

> Know, O blade that enclosed the flower of the palm!
> That what thou protectedst less beautiful seems,
> Being now thus revealed, than the favour of Kings
> Unbladed to me by the finger of fate.

Having written this, I placed it before the King and arose, and seated myself at a little distance. But when he had read it, his face was distressed with wonder. "This surpasseth all," said he. "How can an ape possess such skill in the writing and rounding of a verse?" And he was overcome with astonishment. He motioned me to approach him, and said, "Thou art a wonderful ape: drink to me in this my favourite liquor!" And he handed me his cup. I took it and drank, and as soon as I felt the warm impulse of the liquor I was quickened in my inspiration, and wrote upon the cup:

> Stronger than the blood of heroes,
> Sweeter than a woman's kiss;
> Rare and royal though its savour,
> Joy less fine than Kingly favour
> Lies in this.

STORY OF THE THREE CALENDERS

The King took the cup, and read what I had written. "By Allah!" he exclaimed. "Find me the man who hath the skill of this ape!"

Still wondering greatly as to the extent of my learning and intelligence, the King called for a chessboard; and, setting it before me, questioned me by signs as to whether I understood the game. By way of assent, I kissed the ground, and humbly seated myself before the board. Now my name, as a chess player, had gone forth through all lands, but it still remained for me, as an ape, to justify that name. Solemn and silent we sat at the board—the King of a vast territory matching his skill (of which I had heard, as he had heard of mine, from afar) against that of an ape. Knowing all the science of the game, much of which I had myself discovered, I tested his skill by various openings, saying within myself, "This game I will not win, provided that I learn his measure." It so fell out that I lost, and the King, noting the character of my play, was pleased at his success. "Another game," said he, resetting the pieces.

This time, knowing his play, I held back in my moves, and awaited his openings. At length he made one which I knew, for I myself had invented it. "That," said he, "is the opening of Prince Eymar, whose treatise I have studied. I will allow thee a space to study it, and reply." What was his surprise when I replied immediately with the counter move! At that, from excess of wonder, he was unstrung, and, knowing not the following moves as well as I, he lost. Again we played, a third time, and I, seeing from his eagerness that he had still something to spring upon me, fell in with his moves until we reached the position which was the crowning point of my treatise. At length it came to a pass which I knew well. There was only one way out—a pawn in a distant corner of the board. I moved it readily. "By Allah!" he cried, upsetting the board with all that was on it, "thou art the most intelligent—as well as the ugliest—ape I ever saw." Then, to appease him, I bethought myself of the battlefield of sixty-four squares, and wrote the following stanza on the edge of the board:

> Two armies met and fought, and in the fight
>> Were many slain;
> Yet peace succeeded; and that night
> Each drank success to each,
>>> And drank again.

During all this, the perplexity of the King had waxed greater and greater. At length, in order that his wonder might be shared by another, he sent for his only daughter—the Lady of Beauty—in order that she might witness these unheard of doings of an ape. No sooner had she entered the apartment than she hastily adjusted her veil. "Sire," said she, "why dost thou summon me thus into the presence of men?" "Nay, O my daughter," answered the King, "there is none here but myself, a eunuch, a slave, and this ape." Her fingers fastened her veil more closely as she replied, "O my father, this that thou callest an ape is no ape at all. Thou knowest I have the gift against enchantment, and I tell thee this is a man, the son of a king, and his name is Prince Eymar. He hath been transformed into this shape by a son of Iblis. Sire, I know this from the teaching of my old nurse, who instructed me in the seventy rules of magic."

The King was amazed at his daughter's words, and, looking towards me, said, "I can readily believe that thou art Eymar, for none other could beat me twice at chess. What sayest thou?" And I bowed my head, signifying that what had been said was true, and I wept bitterly. Then said the King to the Lady of Beauty, "O my daughter, if thou hast this power of discernment, which I knew not, perchance thou hast the power also to undo the enchantment wrought upon this Prince. If thou canst, I am minded to make him my Grand Vizier, for there is none like him." And she replied, "O my father, I know, and I am able. Witness what I shall do."

The King's daughter then brought forth a large knife, on the blade of which were strange characters engraven. With this she drew a wide circle upon the floor before us, and inscribed within it many magic signs. This done, she stood within the circle, and sang a wild barbaric chant, at which the place began to grow dark, while the roof and walls and floor creaked and groaned with ominous sounds. Suddenly, while fear got hold on us, there was a blinding flash, and the Efrite appeared within the circle, immense and hideous, his teeth gnashing, and his eyes flashing fire.

"Traitress!" he cried; "did we not swear never to cross one another's path?" "Wretch!" she replied, "I took no oath with thee." At this, the Efrite quickly assumed the form of a lion, and sprang upon her to rend her; but she, being wary, plucked a hair from her head, and breathed upon it, whereupon it was instantly changed into a sharp sword. With this she severed the lion's head from his body, but the head at once became a scorpion. On this the lady became a serpent, and pursued the scorpion, which then took the form of an eagle. But the lady was now a vulture, and the two fought, screaming, in the air. Anon, the eagle changed to a huge black cat, and the vulture, changing to a wolf, fought with it, until at last the cat, finding itself well-nigh vanquished, assumed the form of a pomegranate, and rolled into a pool at one side of the circle. When the wolf dashed in after it, the pomegranate rose up into the air and burst, its grains being scattered over the floor. Quick as lightning, the wolf changed into a cock, which began picking up the grains. And when it had picked up what we thought were all, it began to flap its wings, and run to and fro, looking, as it were, for the last seed. It ran to us with a terrible cry, then, turning, it espied a seed on the brink of the pool, but ere it could reach it, that seed had rolled into the water, and changed itself into a fish. The cock flew screaming to the pool and, assuming the shape of a pike, dived in. Then there was a terrible commotion in the depths. The water foamed and boiled, and the whole place shook as if monsters of the deep were in conflict. Suddenly there was a mighty cry, as the Efrite rose from the pool, encircled with a flame of fire, which continued to issue from his mouth, his nostrils, and eyes. But beside him, in an instant, was the King's daughter, also emitting fire. Then began the most deadly contest between them. From their eyes and mouths darted shafts of fire at one another, until they were enshrouded in a dense smoke. Long the battle raged within this murky canopy, until at last the Efrite was driven forth from it. Pursued by the King's daughter, he rushed at us, and blew fire in our faces, scorching the King's beard, destroying one of my eyes, and killing the eunuch and the slave outright. But, in a moment, the King's daughter was upon him. There was a blinding flash, a cry of victory from her, and we looked and saw the Efrite reduced to a heap of ashes on the floor at her feet.

"It is done!" she said, panting. "He forced me to the last test of fire, and I conquered. Yet I die, for this fire cannot be quenched, except by my life. Quick! bring me here a bowl of water." I snatched a bowl that stood near by, and ran and dipped some water from the pool. She took it, and having chanted some strange words over the water, sprinkled it upon me, saying: "In the name of Truth return to thine original form." At this the pang of change rent my flesh and bones, and I became a man again, as I was before, saving the loss of an eye. But lo! as I looked at the King's daughter, to thank her, I saw a fire come out of her breast, and envelop her head and face. Moans came from within the flame, and she staggered to and fro with muffled cries: "There is no God but Allah! No God but Allah! and Mohammed is——" Suddenly, there was a flash of fire, and when the flames had disappeared, there, at our feet, lay a second heap of ashes.

I mingled my tears with those of the King, and remorse and bitterness took possession of my soul, for, I reflected, this sweet-faced lady had met her death through me. Yet all is as Allah wills it.   The whole realm was cast into mourning over this sad event.   The King enshrined his daughter's ashes in a magnificent tomb, and commanded the ashes of the Efrite to be scattered to the four winds.   Me he summoned to his presence, and spoke these words: "Would that I had never seen thee, for so I had not lost my daughter. Yet the ways of God are inscrutable, and his will is fulfilled with thee and me.   Depart, therefore, O my son, in peace; and think not that I bear thee malice."

So I went out from his presence, and shaved my beard, and left the city.   And thus through many regions have I travelled to gain the Abode of Peace, and lay my case before thee, O Prince of the Faithful.

.   .   .   .

His story being finished, the Khalifeh spoke.   "Thy case is extraordinary," he said, "and thou hast done well to bring it before me."   And yet, none but Ja'far and Mesrur knew, or even suspected, that he was the Khalifeh.   Then, after an interval, the Third Royal Calender rose, and related his story as follows:—

THE STORY OF THE THIRD CALENDER

O KING of the Age, my history is more wonderful than those of my two associates. Their misfortunes were fashioned by the finger of Fate, while mine were the outcome of my own self-will.   Yet in the event we are equal, since we each account to thee for the loss of an eye.

STORY OF THE THREE CALENDERS

Know then, O King, that I, who stand before thee, am a King, and the son of a King. At my father's death, I ascended the throne, and ruled my subjects wisely, as he had done. Yet, unlike him, I was by nature a seafarer, and would often absent myself for the space of a month or more on voyages to parts beyond my kingdom. And it so chanced that from one of these I never returned to my city. And the cause of this I will set before thee.

I had been voyaging for some twenty days with a fleet of ten ships, when we were suddenly becalmed. A few hours later, the master of the vessel I was in came to me in a state of consternation, and told me we were drifting in a rapid current, so wide as to include all the ten ships of the fleet. At this we signalled to the other ships, and all tried with oars to escape this current; but its width was beyond us; it seemed to flow from all sides to a centre. Then, on a closer scrutiny, we saw that our ships were out-stripping the current, propelled, or attracted, by we knew not what. At this, the master gave a great cry, and plucked his beard, and flung his turban on the deck. "O Sire," he said, "we are doomed! I know now the fate that awaits us. We are speeding towards a great mountain of loadstone, of which I have heard—a great black mountain, which attracteth everything that cometh near it. Soon the very nails of all these ships will be drawn to this mountain, and the ships themselves will fall to pieces."

At this I was dumbfounded. I could not believe that such a thing was possible; and yet there was no denying that we were being drawn by some unseen influence ever more and more rapidly through the water. "Tell me," I said, "what is the history of this mountain?"

"It is black, steep, and inaccessible," he replied. "On its summit is a dome of brass, supported by ten pillars of brass; and on this dome is a brazen horseman, mounted on a brazen horse, bearing in his hand a spear of brass, and on his breast a plate of lead, engraven with mystic signs. Sire, while that horseman sits upon his horse, the spell of the loadstone spares no ship in the surrounding sea, for without iron no ship is built."

The master's words were only too true, for soon the ships were rushing more swiftly through the sea, and it was not long before we sighted the black mountain, of which he had spoken. Our velocity increased. The cleavage of the water rose from our bows. Our ships groaned with the strain, which every moment grew more and more intense. Swifter and swifter we sped on, as nearer loomed the mountain; and we all knew what was before us, and cried out to God for help. At last, our speed was so excessive that no ship could any longer endure the strain. With a creaking and groaning and rending of planks, the nails and ironwork were wrenched away; and every ship fell asunder, and spread itself in wreckage on the sea.

Many were drowned immediately, while some few clung to floating spars. I was one of these, and I know not if others, beside myself, survived, for I could only cling to my plank, and call on God, so great and boisterous were the waves. Hours later I found myself cast up on the strip of shore at the foot of the great black mountain. I praised

God for my deliverance, and then, being both hungry and thirsty, I searched for fruit among some trees growing upon the slopes. I soon found some hard by a small stream, and, when I had eaten and drunk, I noticed a pathway by the stream, and followed it. Presently I came to the steep ascent of the hill where the path took the form of rugged steps. Recalling the legend of the horseman, and praying devoutly that I might overthrow him, I toiled up and up the mountain side by this roughest of paths. By the grace of God I at length reached the summit, and found there the great dome surmounted by the horseman. Too fatigued to do more than climb into the dome, I flung myself down there and slept. And, as I slept, a voice spake to me in a dream: "O valiant one, know that in the ground beneath thy feet lie a bow of brass and three arrows of lead, all engraven with talismanic signs. Search for these, and, having found them, shoot the three arrows at the horseman, whereupon thy bow will fall from thy hand, and he and his horse will be hurled down into the midst of the sea. Take thy bow, and bury it again; and, as soon as thou shalt have done this, the sea will rise swiftly up the mountain sides, until it reaches the foot of the dome. Then, before thee, thou wilt perceive a man in a boat, with an oar in each hand—he being of metal also, but different from the horseman. Embark with him in his boat, and within ten days he will convey thee to a calm sea, and to a ship which will bear thee to thine own land. But beware, O Prince, lest in all these things thou utter the name of God, for, by so doing, thou wilt be in extreme peril."

When I awoke, I marvelled at the vividness of this dream,

and, remembering all the voice had said, I dug in the ground where my feet had lain. There I discovered the bow and the three arrows, and, taking them forth, I shot at the horseman. Twice my aim failed, but the third arrow struck him, and lo, he and his horse fell headlong down the mountain into the sea. Then, the bow having fallen from my hand, I took it and buried it within the dome. As soon as I had done this, I perceived the sea surging rapidly up the mountain sides. Up and up it came, boiling and seething, until at last it reached the foot of the dome, than which it rose no further. Presently a boat drew near from the midst of the sea, rowed by a man of gleaming metal. Remembering the warning not to utter the name of God, I entered the boat, and the man rowed me away over the sea for many days, until we came in sight of some beautiful islands. When I set eyes on these habitable spots of safety then my heart leapt for joy, and, forgetting the warning of my dream, I cried in my delight, "God be praised!" No sooner had the words escaped my lips than the boat and the man sank into the sea, leaving me upon the surface. My peril was now extreme, for unless I could gain the land I must surely drown. The islands were distant, but they were my only hope, so I swam them hour after hour, until night fell. Still I swam on and on in the dark, and at last, when I was spent, and about to sink, I felt a great wave rise beneath me, and hurl me forward. It carried me high up on the shore of an island, where it left me utterly exhausted, but safe from the sea.

The next day, as I was walking along the shore in search

of food, I heard voices coming from behind a bend. Thinking not to lose a chance of being taken on board some vessel, I looked round the bend, and saw ten black slaves of evil aspect, landing from a vessel and bearing spades and axes. I liked not the faces of these men, and feared to expose myself to their view; moreover, being curious as to their mission, I resolved to watch them. Noting the direction they were taking, I ran along the shore for some distance, and then, turning inland, I proceeded until I came to a high tree, into the topmost branches of which I climbed. Presently I saw the slaves pass by and stop at a spot in the middle of the island, where they dug up the ground, until at length they came upon a trap door, which they lifted and set on one side. Then they returned to the vessel, and brought from it loads of provisions, necessaries and even luxuries of every kind. Many times they went and came, and by their loads it was evident they were preparing some underground dwelling for habitation. At length, after many journeys to and fro, they returned from the vessel laden with beautiful garments of every kind; and with them came an aged sheik, leading by the hand a young man, whose grace and beauty could scarce be expressed in poems. They and the slaves entered the underground abode, and when, two hours later, I counted those who came forth, the young man was not of the number. When they had closed the trap door, and replaced the earth upon it, the slaves conducted the sheik back to the vessel, and sailed away.

These doings caused me great wonder in my tree, and I resolved to see what they meant. I made haste to descend,

[217]

and, having reached the spot, I ceased not to scrape away the earth until I had found the trap door. I removed this, and descended a flight of wooden steps, which led me to a large apartment, luxuriously furnished; and there, reclining upon a couch, with flowers and fruits before him, was the handsome youth. "Fear me not," I said, when I saw that he had turned pale on observing my sudden intrusion; "I am a man, like thyself. Destiny hath led me hither, to relieve thy solitude." Then, seeing that he greeted me with delight, I said to him: "O, my brother, tell me how it is that thou art here in this secret place." And he complied with my request, and related to me his history.

"O brother," he said, "my fate has been exceeding strange. My father is a rich dealer in jewels, and his business lies with kings. Many years ago he was wont to grieve that, though God had given him wealth, He had not blest him with a son. Shortly after, he dreamed that a male child would be born to him, but that its life would be cut off at the age of sixteen, and he awoke weeping. His dream was fulfilled, in so far that within a year my mother gave birth to me. Great was his joy at this, but, remembering the further prophecy of his dream, he called in the astrologers, who, by their calculations, confirmed it. 'Thy son's fate,' they said, 'is connected with a great mountain in the sea, called the Mountain of Loadstone, on the summit of which is a horseman of brass, bearing on his breast a tablet of lead, with mystic signs engraven. Sixteen years hence a king, the son of a king will arise, and hurl that horseman down into the sea, shortly after which he will slay thy son.'

STORY OF THE THREE CALENDERS

"My father grieved very greatly at this, and ceased not to love me the more throughout my youth. When I was nearing the age of sixteen, he again summoned the astrologers, who told him that the horseman had already been cast down into the sea, and there remained now only ten days of my life. Then my father arose and prepared this place for me, so that I might dwell here in secret until the completion of the days, for the astrologers had said that if, by the will of God, I passed safely out of my sixteenth year, I should live to a great age. And thus it is that I am here, O my brother."

"What strange thing is this?" said I within myself on hearing his words. "It was I who cast down the horseman, but, by Allah! it will not be I who will slay this gracious youth." Then, turning to him, I said: "Fear nothing, sweet youth! Here, at least, thou art safe. I myself will protect thee, and, when the term is expired, I will go forth with thee to thy father, and he shall restore me to my country, and so reap a great reward." He rejoiced at my words, and was comforted, and so far was I from wishing him harm that I waited upon him, and during the night slept by his side. Once he awoke from dreams, crying: "The horseman is down! He hath fallen into the sea! Whither, oh! whither shall I flee for safety?" But I quieted him, and comforted him, saying: "Never will such a calamity as thou fearest come to thee while I am by thy side."

For nine days I served him, sparing no trouble for his comfort; and on the tenth I could not conceal my joy, for I knew that, if it rested with me to slay him, he would be alive on the morrow. My happiness infected him, and he begged me to heat some water that he might bathe and array himself in bright garments, and then, with me, celebrate the hour of his release. I prepared all he required, and he bathed, and arrayed himself in costly robes, and reclined upon the couch to rest. It was the hour of sunset: a little while remained till the term expired. "O brother," he said to me, 'wilt thou in thy kindness cut me up a watermelon, and sprinkle it with sugar?" "O brother mine," I replied, "I see here a melon, but where is the knife?" He pointed to the shelf above his head, saying, "Thou wilt find one there, O my creditor." Then I stepped up on one side of the couch, and found the knife, and drew it from its sheath; but, having done this, my foot slipped, and I fell headlong. The next thing I knew was that the knife was buried in the youth's breast, with my hand upon the haft. I uttered a loud cry, and beat my bosom. Oh! the grief of it! Dead! And by my hand! O God! by what cruel misfortunes dost thou convince mortals that Fate and Destiny are thine instruments!

Long I wept by the side of the youth, imploring pardon from those cold lips; one glance of forgiveness from those glazed eyes. Then, sad and sorrowful, I arose and ascended the steps; and, having replaced and covered the trap door, departed from that place. I remained upon the island, nursing a heavy weight of grief. From a place of hiding I saw them come and take the youth's dead body away. I saw his aged father's sorrow, as he followed weeping, and watched the vessel sail away out of sight. But great as was this calamity, I was destined to further trouble.

In my daily wanderings about the island, I discovered that on one side of it the sea had been gradually receding. When another week had passed, there was a considerable extent of land that had risen above the water. I watched this day by day for a space of some months, at the end of which time dry land stretched into the distance so far that I resolved to set forth upon it, hoping to come at length to an inhabited region. I had proceeded some leagues when I saw before me, in the distance, an upland with a splendid palace upon it, shining all golden in the rays of the sun. When I drew near, almost dazzled at the sight of it, an old man came out to meet me; and following him were ten young men, each lacking an eye—a thing which caused me great astonishment. They and the old man saluted me, and asked me whence I came, whereupon I told them my story, which they listened to with looks of wonder. Then they invited me into the palace, and one of them said: "Be welcome, O brother, but see to it that thou ask us not respecting our condition, nor yet how it is we each lack an eye." Presently the old man brought food and wine, and we ate and drank together, conversing on many things until it was time to sleep. Then one of them called to the old man to bring the materials for penance, and he arose and placed before each a basin full of ashes and powdered charcoal. One and all then bared their arms and blackened their faces with the mixture, crying continually, "Once we were dwelling in happiness, but now we are wretched; and this is the result of our idle curiosity." This they kept up till daybreak, when they washed their faces and changed their clothes and slept.

Next day, being unable to cast off my curiosity regarding his strange behaviour, I beseeched them to tell me the reason thereof, and one of them replied: "O young man, ask not what doth not concern thee, lest thou hear what may not please thee." But I was not content with this answer, and continued to entreat them to tell me the reason of their actions, and also the cause of each having lost an eye. "Nay, be silent," said another; "what the mind doth not know, the heart doth not grieve." Yet I still pestered them with my questions, giving them no peace. At length they lost patience, and, after conversing together awhile, one of them said to me: "O young man, if thou dost above all things desire to know the cause of these things, submit thyself to our hands, and thou shalt learn." And I answered, "I desire nothing more than to know"; for my curiosity had become a fever.

Then they slaughtered a ram and flayed it, and, placing a knife in my hand, sewed me up in the skin and carried me to a hilltop at a little distance, where they left me. Presently I heard the flapping of giant wings, and then the ram's skin, with me inside it, was seized by the talons of a great bird and borne up and away. After a long flight, the bird set me down upon a high plateau. Remembering the knife they had placed in my hand, I ripped open the skin, and emerged. The gigantic bird, on seeing me, flew off screaming.

Far in the distance, at the side of a hill, I saw a splendid palace, sparkling in the sunlight. It was the only habitation that I could discern, so I made my way towards it. After some hours' journey, I reached its gates, and seeing them open, entered, and soon found myself in a great chamber of indescribable splendour, where forty beautiful damsels, each one like a goddess, welcomed me with cries of joy. "O our Master and Prince," they said, "why hast thou tarried so long? We, thy handmaids, have waited many weeks for thy coming." And they set food and wine before me, and I ate and drank, some sang and others danced; and they were so wildly beautiful that any one of them would have melted the heart of an anchorite.

Thus suddenly was I launched into a life of pure delight, and I dwelt among these rare and radiant damsels, their sole Lord and Master, in luxury, and joy. Thus it continued for a whole year, with never a shadow of dullness in our days; but, on the first morning of the new year, they all came to me weeping, and bidding me farewell, as each in turn clung to me with the sadness of parting. "Wherefore this?" I cried. "Ye will break my heart if ye leave me." And one replied, "Nay, O master; we love thee most of any on earth, but we must leave thee for a time, and we fear to lose thee." And she fell to weeping afresh, and the others added their tears to hers. "Tell me what this means," I said to her. "O my master, if thou wouldst know," she replied, "we are the daughters of kings, and for many years it has been our practice to dwell in this palace, returning only to our fathers for forty days at the beginning of each year. To-day we must go, and we fear that, before we return, thou wilt disregard our directions, in which case thou wilt be lost to us. Here are the keys, a hundred in number, which will unlock a hundred doors for thee, admitting to gardens of various kinds, in which thou wilt find a hundred different delights; but we do entreat thee, open not the door which is fashioned of pure gold, for if thou dost, we shall never see thee again, and that is what we fear."

I took the keys, greatly wondering, and when I had embraced them all, and said farewell, they departed, with sad looks, leaving me alone in the palace. Many times I swore to myself that I would never open the golden door, and even as I swore, the wish to do it came uppermost. But I forced it down, saying: "There are ninety-nine doors without this one: surely it is enough!" And that evening, feeling sad and lonely, and longing for entertainment, I took the keys, and, selecting one engraven with a character corresponding to that on the first door, I opened and entered.

Within lay a garden like paradise, with running streams, and hanging fruits, and birds that sang the praises of their Creator. Every kind of delicate perfume breathed from the rarest of flowers, and the bosom of the dreamy trees moved in the soft wind as if languorous with love. Seeing this wonderful place, I was impelled by curiosity to explore what lay behind the second door. Accordingly, I opened it and entered. Here was a large domain of forest and meadow, watered by a crystal river. Uplands on which the sunlight slept led up to mountain peaks towering against the sides of heaven. I noted all this with wonder, saying, "I will return, and enjoy this at my leisure; meanwhile, I die to know what fresh joy is concealed by the third door."

STORY OF THE THREE CALENDERS

When I entered the third place of delight, I found it to be a spacious aviary, containing all the birds of song and of rare plumage that could be found on earth. This vast place was paven with many-coloured marble, and graced with patches of forest and greensward. The birds drank from crystal fountains, and, flying off, sang gloriously. The streams of these fountains were of different colours, and when I drank of one, I found it was pure wine. So I wandered from one to another sipping the rarest vintages I had ever known, until, coming to a soft couch of moss, I reclined, and was lulled to sleep by the songs of countless nightingales.

When I awoke next morning, I opened the fourth door and found beyond it a treasury passing the imagination of kings. Jewels and precious stones there were beyond reckoning. "These," I said, "are mine, and forty priceless damsels are also mine: what Sultan can compare with me?" That day, and on the following days, I opened one door after another, finding within each the strangest and most wonderful things man ever beheld; until, on the thirty-ninth day, I had opened every door except the last,—the one fashioned of pure gold. Long I looked at it, recalling my oath, and fortifying myself against temptation. Many times I turned away from it, with the key in my hand, but always the Devil drove me back again. Then, at last, my curiosity became acute, and I could not refrain.

I opened the door, and passed within. I was met by an odour fragrant beyond conception, which mastered my brain so that I fell in a faint. But I soon recovered, and, rising to my feet, went on, treading on golden tiles spread with saffron, and lighted on my way by golden lamps, from which were wafted the odours of musk and ambergris. I soon saw that the place was, in effect, a stable, though words fail to describe its splendour. There, standing at a crystal manger, full of choice sesame, with a trough adjoining filled with rose-water, stood a magnificent steed, as black as night. Never had I seen his equal. He was saddled and bridled, and his trappings were of gold and thread-of-gold, sparkling with gems. "This is the steed of my desire," I said, and then, as I approached him, he turned his head towards me, and neighed. Urged by the Devil, I led him forth and mounted him. But when I jerked the reins, he stood stock still. I persuaded him with my heels, but he did not move. Then I espied a whip deposited in the saddle. I took this and struck him a violent blow. With a neigh like thunder, he rose in the air, and soared up and up to a great height. Then he flew with me over hills and valleys, until at last he alighted on the roof of another palace. There he plunged and reared, and finally shook me off behind him; and, as I fell, a blow from his tail struck out my eye. Leaving me thus, he soared up and away, and was soon lost to sight.

When I descended from the roof, I found I was back in the palace of the ten young men. When they beheld me, and saw that my eye was gone, they cried with one voice, "No welcome to thee, O curious one! Thou art now in like case with us, having been chastised for thine impertinent curiosity. For know that we have all opened that golden door and ridden that black horse, and that is why we do nightly penance for our foolishness." I then begged them to receive me into their company, but they refused, saying their number was complete. So I went my way dejected, and wandered as a mendicant, ever on and on towards Baghdad, the Abode of Peace, resolved to seek the Khalifeh of the Lord of all Creatures and set my case before him.

· · · · · · · · ·

"Verily," exclaimed Harun-er-Rashid as the Third Royal Calender retired to his place, "this is the most astounding tale of all. Hear me now, all of you. These men have suffered greatly, but Fate hath no further trouble in store for them. By Allah, my armies are great, and I will restore each to his throne. As for you, O ladies," he continued, turning to the three sisters, "my Seraglio is dull and lifeless without you. Will you grace it with your presence?" "Yes, O Commander of the Faithful," cried they all, laughing merrily and clapping their hands, for they thought him a perfect impersonator; "we will come to thee." "On the head and the eye?" "Yea, O King, on the head and the eye is our promise given." At this the Khalifeh turned to his two officials. "O Vizier," he said, "I call thee to witness; and thee also, O Mesrur." And they answered smiling, for they liked the pretence of his pretence, "King of the Age, we hear and obey."

Then the Khalifeh approached the porter, who was asleep upon the floor, and stirred him with his foot so that he awoke and sat up. "O thou carrier of goods and vast quantities of wine," said the Khalifeh, "wouldst thou be the Wag of Harun-er-Rashid, Fifth Khalifeh of the House of Abbas?" The porter grinned. "O Prince of the Faithful," said he,

"I was born with that ambition, for they say that when the Khalifeh's Wag waggeth his tongue no other tongue may wag." And with this he kissed the ground seven times in mock obeisance. "It is well," said the Khalifeh, "for verily thou art a wag." And they all applauded his seeming royalty and said one among another, "Never have we seen such an excellent impersonation of a king."

The Khalifeh then pointed to the first signs of day in the east, saying, "There was never so pleasant a night but morning ended it." And then, with Ja'far and Mesrur, he set about taking his departure, thanking the ladies for their kind hospitality and bidding them remember the promise they had given. The Three Royal Calenders and the porter also bade the sisters farewell, and, when they were outside the house, the Calenders were directed to a Khan, while the porter took his own way home and the Khalifeh and his two officials returned to the palace.

On the following morning the Khalifeh of Baghdad sat on his throne, and his first thought was to send for the Three Royal Calenders, the three ladies, and the porter. "Lose no time in bringing them hither, O Vizier," said the Khalifeh to Ja'far. The Vizier sent in great haste, and, when the messengers returned with all of them, Er-Rashid received them in private audience.

Not one of them recognised the three merchants of the former evening, and their faces showed fear and surprise, for they knew not why they had been thus summoned. The Khalifeh spoke. "Know, O ye people, that I, Harun-er-Rashid, of the House of Abbas, do not forget my promises.

STORY OF THE THREE CALENDERS

I promised Three Royal Calenders that I would restore them to their thrones, and, by Allah! this shall be done. Three beautiful ladies of Baghdad promised me that they would come into my Seraglio, which thou didst witness, O Ja'far; and thou, too, O Mesrur." The two officials bowed low, confirming this. "But," continued the Khalifeh, "I have since decided to make them queens by bestowing them in marriage upon these three kings." And he indicated the Calenders. Then, turning towards the porter, he continued: "I also promised that a carrier of goods,—a merry fellow,—should be my Wag. This shall be, and his first duty will be to solve this riddle. Which is easier: for the Khalifeh to play the merchant, or the merchant to play the Khalifeh? Meanwhile, do you all agree to what I have proposed?"

They were all dumbfounded as they realised that their actor of the previous night had played his part so well, because he was indeed the Khalifeh himself. For some moments no one spoke; then they all made obeisance to him and kissed the ground. "O King of the Age," said one of the ladies, "I answer for my sisters and myself. We will obey thy commands willingly and with joy." Then one of the Calenders added, "O Prince of the Faithful, we also hear and obey, with equal willingness and equal joy." "And as for me, O King," said the porter. "I, being a wag, and also a liar of some excellence, knew that indeed thou wert the Khalifeh of the Lord of All Creatures, but I was compelled to dissemble for fear of thine Executioner's sword. Thus I solve thy riddle, O King: The Khalifeh played better than the merchant, whose play was equally good." The Khalifeh smiled and, turning to Ja'far, said, "O Vizier, bestow upon him the Robe of the Wag."

Then the Khalifeh arose, and, descending from his throne, placed the hands of the three ladies in those of the Three Royal Calenders. The Kadi and witnesses were summoned and the marriage contracts were signed and sealed. He then bestowed upon each of the three wedded pairs a splendid palace and sufficient money for their needs until such time as he had succeeded in restoring them to their thrones. And so did Harun-er-Rashid draw upon himself ten thousand blessings.

The Story of the King of the Ebony Isles.

A SULTAN of a far-away kingdom once journeyed into a distant country. One day, wandering without aim among innumerable treasures unguarded and left to waste, the Sultan grew weary and sat down in an embrasure to rest. Then it seemed to him that not far off he could hear a sorrowful voice chant verses of lamentation. Following the sounds with wonder he came to a curtained doorway, and passing through found himself in the presence of a fair youth richly dressed, seated upon a couch and bearing upon his countenance tokens of extreme grief and despondency. To the Sultan's proffered greeting the youth returned salutation, but did not stir from his seat. "Pardon me," he said, "for not rising; but my miserable condition makes it impossible." Having said this he again broke into doleful lamentation; and when the Sultan inquired as to the cause of so many tears, "See for yourself," he cried, "what I am now made into!" And lifting the skirt of his robe he revealed himself all stone from his waist to the soles of his feet, while from the waist upwards he was as other men. Then as he observed upon his visitor's countenance the expression of a lively curiosity and astonishment, "Doubtless," he went on, "as you now know the secret of my

miserable condition you will wish also to hear my story."
And he related it as follows:

"My father was King of the city which once stood about
this palace. He was lord also of the Ebony Isles that are
now the four hills which you passed on your way hither.
When I succeeded to the throne upon his death, I took to wife
my own cousin, the daughter of my uncle, with whom I lived
for five years in the utmost confidence and felicity, continually entertained by the charm of her conversation and the
beauty of her person, and happy in the persuasion that she
found in me an equal satisfaction.

"One day, however, it chanced, in the hour before dinner
when the Queen was gone to bathe and adorn herself, that
I lay upon a couch beside which two female slaves sat fanning
me; and they, supposing me to be asleep, began to talk
concerning me and their mistress. 'Ah!' said one, 'how
little our lord knows where our mistress goes to amuse herself
every night while he lies dreaming!' 'How should he
know?' returned the other, 'seeing that the cup of wine
which she gives him each night contains a sleeping draught,
that causes him to sleep sound however long she is absent.
Then at daybreak when she returns she burns perfumes
under his nostrils, and he waking and finding her there
guesses nothing. Pity it is that he cannot know of her
treacherous ways, for surely it is a shame that a king's wife
should go abroad and mix with base people.'

"Now when I heard this the light of day grew dark before
my eyes; but I lay on and made no sign, awaiting my wife's
return. And she coming in presently, we sat down and ate

and drank together according to custom; and afterwards, when I had retired and lain down, she brought me with her own hands the cup of spiced wine, inviting me to drink. Then I, averting myself, raised it to my lips, but instead of drinking, poured it by stealth into my bosom, and immediately sank down as though overcome by its potency, feigning slumber. Straightway the Queen rose up from my side, and having clothed herself in gorgeous apparel and anointed herself with perfumes, she made her way secretly from the palace, and I with equal secrecy followed her.

"Soon passing by way of the narrower streets, we arrived before the city gates; and immediately at a word from her the chains fell and the gates opened of their own accord, closing again behind us as soon as we had passed. At last she came to a ruined hut, and there entering I saw her presently with her veil laid aside, seated in familiar converse with a monstrous negro, the meanest and most vile of slaves, offering to him in abject servility dainties which she had carried from the royal table, and bestowing upon him every imaginable token of affection and regard.

"At this discovery I fell into a blind rage, and drawing my sword I rushed in and struck the slave from behind a blow upon the neck that should have killed him. Then believing that I had verily slain him, and before the Queen found eyes to realise what had befallen, I departed under cover of night as quickly as I had come, and returned to the palace and my own chamber.

"On awaking the next morning I found the Queen lying beside me as though nothing had happened, and at first I was ready to believe it had all been an evil dream; but presently I perceived her eyes red with weeping, her hair dishevelled, and her face torn by a passion of grief which she strove to conceal. Having thus every reason to believe that my act of vengeance had not fallen short of its purpose, I held my tongue and made no sign.

"But the same day at noon, while I sat in council, the Queen appeared before me clad in deep mourning, and with many tears informed me how she had received sudden news of the death of her father and mother and two brothers, giving full and harrowing details of each event. Without any show of incredulity I heard her tale; and when she besought my permisson to go into retirement and mourn in a manner befitting so great a calamity, I bade her do as she desired.

"So for a whole year she continued to mourn in a privacy which I left undisturbed; and during that time she caused to be built a mausoleum or Temple of Lamentation—the same whose dome you see yonder—into which she withdrew herself from all society; while I, believing the cause of my anger removed and willing to humour the grief which my act had caused her, waited patiently for her return to a sane and reasonable state of mind.

"But, as I learned too late, matters had not so fallen: for though in truth the negro was grievously wounded, being cut through the gullet and speechless, it was not the will of Heaven that he should die; and the Queen having by her enchantments kept him in a sort of life, no sooner was the mausoleum finished than she caused him to be secretly conveyed thither, and there night and day te. ded him, awaiting his full recovery.

"At length, when two years were over and her mourning in no wise abated, my curiosity became aroused; so going one day to the Temple of Lamentation I entered unannounced, and placing myself where I might see and not be seen, there I discovered her in an abandonment of fond weeping over her miserable treasure whose very life was a dishonour to us both. But no sooner in my just resentment had I started to upbraid her, than she—as now for the first time realising the cause of her companion's misfortune—began to heap upon me terms of the most violent and shameful abuse; and when, carried beyond myself, I threatened her with my sword, she stood up before me, and having first uttered words of unknown meaning, she cried:

> Be thou changed in a moment's span;
> Half be marble, and half be man!

And at the word I become even as you see me now—dead to the waist, and above living yet bound. Yet even so her vengeance was not satisfied. Having reduced me to this state, she went on to vent her malice upon the city and islands over which I ruled, and the unfortunate people who were my subjects. Thus by her wicked machinations the city became a lake and the islands about it the four hills which you have seen; as for the inhabitants, who were of four classes and creeds, Moslems, Christians, Jews, and Persians, she turned them into fish of four different colours: the white are the Moslems, the red are Persian fire-worshippers, the yellow are Jews, and the blue Christians. And now having done all this she fails not every day to inflict upon me a hundred lashes with a whip which draws blood at every stroke: and when these are accomplished she covers my torn flesh with haircloth and lays over it these rich robes in mockery. Of a surety it is the will of Heaven that I should be the most miserable and despised of mortals!"

Thus the youth finished his story, nor when he had ended could he refrain from tears. The Sultan also was greatly moved when he heard it, and his heart became full of a desire to avenge such injuries upon the doer of them. "Tell me," he said, "where is now the monster of iniquity?" "Sir," answered the youth, "I doubt not she is yonder in the mausoleum with her companion, for thither she goes daily so soon as she has measured out to me my full meed of chastisement: and as for this day my portion has been served to me, I am quit of her till to-morrow brings the hour of fresh scourgings."

Now when this was told him the Sultan saw his way plain. "Be of good cheer," he said to the youth, "and endure with a quiet spirit yet once more the affliction she causes thee; for at the price of that single scourging I trust, by the will of Heaven, to set thee free."

So on the morrow the Sultan lay in close hiding until sounds reached him which told him that the whippings had begun; then he arose and went in haste to the mausoleum, where amid rich hangings and perfumes and the illumination of a thousand candles, he found the black slave stretched mute upon a bed, awaiting in great feebleness the recovered use of his sawn gullet.   Quickly, with a single sword-stroke, the avenger took from him that poor remnant of life which enchantment alone had made possible: then having thrown the body into a well in the courtyard below, he lay down in the dead man's place, drawing the coverlet well over him. Soon after, fresh from her accustomed task of cruelty, the enchantress entered, and falling upon her knees beside the bed she cried, "Has my lord still no voice wherewith to speak to his servant?   Surely, for lack of that sound, hearing lies withered within me!"   Then the Sultan, taking to himself the thick speech of a negro, said, "There is no strength or power but in God alone!"

On hearing those words, believing that her companion's speech was at last restored to him, the Queen uttered a cry of joy.   But scarcely had she begun to lavish upon him the tokens of her affection when the pretended negro broke out against her in violent abuse.   "What!" he cried, "dost thou expect favour at my hands, when it is because of thee that for two years I have lain dumb and prostrate?   How darest thou speak to me or look for any recompense save death!   Nay!" he went on in answer to her astonished protests, "have not the cries and tears and groans of thy husband kept me continually from rest: and has not Heaven smitten me for no other reason than because thou wouldst not cease from smiting him?   So has the curse which thou didst seek to lay upon him fallen doubly upon me."

"Alas!" cried the enchantress, "have I unknowingly caused thee so great an ill?   If it be so, then let my lord give command, and whatever be his desire it shall be satisfied."

[237]

Then said the Sultan, "Go instantly and release thy husband from spell and torment: and when it is done, return hither with all speed."

Thus compelled, in great fear and bewilderment and sorely against her will, the Queen sped to the chamber in the palace where her husband lay spellbound. Taking a vessel of water she pronounced over it certain words which caused it instantly to boil as though it had been set on a fire; then throwing the water over him, she cried:

> Spell be loosed, and stone grow warm,
> Yield back flesh to the human form.

And immediately on the word his nature came to him again, and he leaped and stood upon his feet. But the Queen's hatred towards him was by no means abated. "Go hence quickly," she cried, "since a better will than mine releases thee! But if thou tarry or if thou return thou shalt surely die!" Thankful for his deliverance the youth stayed not to question, but departing went and hid himself without, while the Queen returned in haste to the mausoleum where her supposed lover awaited her. There, eager for restoration to favour, she informed him of what she had done, supposing that to be all.

"Nay," said the other, still speaking with the thick voice of a negro; "though thou hast lopped the branch of the evil thou hast not destroyed the root. For every night I hear a jumping of fishes in the lake that is between the four hills, and the sound of their curses on thee and me comes to disturb my rest. Go instantly and restore all things to their former state, then come back and give me thy hand and I shall rise up a sound man once more."

Rejoicing in that promise and the expectations it held out to her of future happiness, the Queen went with all speed to the border of the lake. There, taking a little water into her hand, and uttering strange words over it, she sprinkled it this way and that upon the surface of the lake and the roots of the four hills, and immediately where had been the lake a city appeared, and instead of fishes inhabitants, and in place of the four hills four islands. As for the palace, it stood no longer removed far away into the desert but upon a hill overlooking the city.

Great was the astonishment of the Vizier and the Sultan's escort which had lain encamped beside the lake to find themselves suddenly transported to the heart of a populous city, with streets and walls and the hum of reawakened life around them; but a greater and more terrible shock than this awaited the Queen upon her return to the mausoleum to enjoy the reward of her labours. "Now," she cried, "let my lord arise, since all that he willed is accomplished!"

"Give me thy hand!" said the Sultan, still in a voice of disguise; "come nearer that I may lean on thee!" And as she approached he drew forth his sword which had lain concealed beside him in the bed, and with a single blow cleft her wicked body in twain.

Then he arose and went quickly to where in hiding lay the young King her husband, who learned with joy of the death of his cruel enemy. He thanked the Sultan with tears of gratitude for his deliverance, and invoked the blessings of Heaven upon him and his kingdom. "On yours too," said the Sultan, "let peace and prosperity now reign! And since your city is so near to mine, come with me and be my guest that we may rejoice together in the bonds of friendship."

"Nay," answered the young King, "that would I do willingly, but your country lies many a day's journey from my own. I fear the breaking of the spell which held me and my subjects has brought you farther than you wished."

It was in fact true that the Ebony Isles had now returned to the place from which they had originally come. The Sultan put a smiling face upon the matter: "I can well put up with the tedium of my journey," said he, "if only you will be my companion. Nay, let me speak frankly to one whose demeanour in affliction has won my heart; I am childless and have no heir. Come with me and be my son, and when I am dead unite our two kingdoms under a single ruler." The young King, who had conceived for his deliverer an equal affection, could not withstand so noble and generous an offer; and so with a free exchange of hearts on both sides the matter was arranged.

After a journey of some months the Sultan arrived again at his own capital, where he was welcomed with great rejoicings by the people, who had long mourned over his strange and unexplained absence.

As for the old fisherman who had been the immediate cause of the young King's deliverance, the Sultan loaded him with honours and gave his daughters in marriage to sons of the blood royal, so that they all continued in perfect happiness and contentment to the end of their days.

The Story of Prince Assad & the Fairy Perie Nashara

THERE once lived a Sultan of India, who had three sons and one niece, all of whom he loved very dearly. The niece, who was as lovely as the dawn and slender as the crescent moon, was called Meliha, and having reached her twelfth year the Sultan proposed to wed her to a neighbouring Prince. But as soon as he revealed his intention to Heddar, Kadi, and Assad, the Sultan's three sons, they all made known to their father each one his own intention of marrying his cousin. Seeing what grievous unhappiness might result from this strife the Sultan, who could come to no decision, called his three sons to him.

"This matter admitting of no solution, and seeing that you cannot agree among yourselves as to who shall wed Meliha," he said to them, "I have decided upon a plan which gives each one of you an equal chance of winning her. To each one of you I will give an equal sum of money, after which you shall go your separate ways into different countries, and he who shall bring back with him at the end of a year the most wonderful object, shall receive the hand of our dear Meliha as reward."

With this decision the Sultan's sons were obliged to be content, though secretly each one held himself to be the

Adapted from "The Story of Prince Ahmed and the Fairy Perie Banou."— (*Townsend Edition.*)

best beloved of his cousin. But in reality more tender glances had passed between Prince Kadi and Meliha than any in the Sultan's household suspected. And the Sultan did as he had suggested; and after Heddar, Kadi, and Assad had received each a purse of money, they gladly started out on their several quests for the most wonderful object that might be found, first having decided among themselves to meet together at the close of the twelve months, at a place to be appointed, before preceeding to their father's Court.

Now Prince Heddar had long heard of all the splendours of the kingdom of Nariampur, which was ruled over by a friendly Maharajah, and without saying anything of his intention to his brothers he straightway wended his steps thitherwards; and after he had gained audience of the Maharajah, and had made most respectful obeisance, he requested permission to search the bazaars for the most wonderful object that they contained. This the Maharajah granted willingly; for Prince Heddar had informed him of his desire to marry his cousin, and above all the Maharajah was possessed of a sentimental disposition. "I will assist you in whatsoever manner I may," he said; "but if you should fail to return home with the most wonderful object of all, then return to Nariampur, behind whose harem walls glisten eyes more wonderful than the most wonderful object in all the world."

And the Maharajah sent forth a proclamation that any who believed themselves possessed of a great rarity should bring it before Prince Heddar. And Prince Heddar saw more wonderful things than even he had believed were to be found in Nariampur; but he remained unsatisfied until the rope merchant appeared in the bazaar.

Now the merchant who owned this rope claimed for it the most wonderful properties of any; nothing less than the power of drawing through the air at incredible speed any who should grip it in his hand and say whither he desired to be borne. But as Prince Heddar expressed disbelief in the powers of the rope, the merchant bade him lay hold of it, which he likewise having done, the merchant uttered the word "Baghdad," and the next instant the rope was being drawn through the air at a great speed, the merchant and the Prince clinging to it. And in the twinkling of an eye the rope set its passengers down in the streets of Baghdad; whereupon the Prince was so delighted that he at once agreed to purchase it of the merchant, and once more having grasped the rope, and having uttered the word "Nariampur," the merchant and Prince Heddar were borne swiftly to the kingdom of the Maharajah, who expressed delight at the successful outcome of the quest. And after the Prince had passed many happy days at the Court of the Maharajah, he again grasped the rope firmly in both hands, and uttered the name of the town in which he had arranged to meet his brothers.

Meanwhile Prince Kadi had not been without his own adventures, for having joined a caravan of merchants travelling into Persia, he soon made known upon his arrival at Shiraz, the capital, his desire to secure the most wonderful object the country could produce. And one thing and another, for which their owners claimed most marvellous properties, was brought before him. But he greatly feared that whatever he should choose, his brothers would choose some object more wonderful still. So he journeyed on and on, staying at the khans, or inns, of many outlying towns, until he came at last to Ashurada, which is on the seacoast. And here he heard speak of a wonderful shell, which when held to the ear permitted the listener to overhear any conversation in whatsoever part of the world he desired. And Prince Kadi desired that the owner of the shell should be brought before him. And he took the shell and held it to his ear, and said within himself: "Now let me overhear the conversation with which my beloved Meliha passes the hours away." And at once the laughter of Meliha fell deliciously upon his ears, as she played with her maidens; but though great was his longing, Meliha spoke no word of her absent lover.

And the merchant said: "O Prince! Have I then claimed too great a thing for my shell?" And Prince Kadi replied: "It is indeed the most wonderful object in all the world, and I cannot conceive of anything more wonderful."

And after he had given much money to the merchant in exchange for the shell, he again joined a caravan and made his way back to Shiraz where he sojourned many happy days among the wonderful gardens, mosques and temples, where the veiled eyes of damsels, more beautiful than any Prince Kadi had hitherto met, challenged his glances. But Prince Kadi had only thought for his cousin Meliha, whose voice called to him from the temple bells; whose breath

THE STORY OF PRINCE ASSAD

came to him from the scent of the flowers, and whose step followed him in the drifting leaves. And at the end of the twelve months, laden with jewels from the bazaars, spices, wines, silks and precious scents, he slowly made his way to the meeting-place appointed by his brothers.

Now Prince Assad had likewise been very active in his search for the most wonderful object in all the world, and his quest had carried him to Samaracand and far into Arabia, where he was greatly pleased with the rich and fertile valleys, and the fields and gardens teeming with fruit and blossom, after which he went to the Valley of Sogd, which is not only one of the most wonderful valleys in all the world, but also one of the richest. Nor had he journeyed to the valley without a purpose, for whilst yet in Samaracand he had been told of a magical spring, which rose in the valley from beneath the roots of a tree inhabited by a Good Genie. After long search, during which he had been directed this way and that way, he at length arrived at the tree of the Genie, and lo, from beneath its roots sprouted a spring so clear as to dazzle the sight. And Prince Assad took a switch and struck the tree three times, whereupon a voice cried out from within: "What would you have of me?"

And Prince Assad replied: "Good Genie, give me, I pray you, some of the crystal water which wells from beneath the roots of your dwelling—if indeed it shall restore the sick and dying as has been stated of it."

And the Genie replied from within the tree: "Take of it. It cures the ills of those who believe, and gives strength to all who drink of it. Do you believe?"

And Prince Assad replied: "I believe." And he filled the flagon which he had with him, and after thanking the genie many times, he set out once again for Samaracand, and from thence to the Indies, where at an inn, at the place appointed, his two brothers Heddar and Kadi already awaited him.

And great was the rejoicing of the three brothers to meet again, and neither was the pleasure of either marred by the fear that any than himself was possessed of the most wonderful object in all the world. And after they had feasted of the very best that the caravansery could provide, and had drunk until they were merry, Kadi and Assad called upon the eldest brother Heddar to bring forth the object of his quest. And without more ado Prince Heddar produced the wonderful rope which he had bound around his waist. And when they observed nothing other than a piece of rope it was all that Prince Kadi and Prince Assad could do to keep from laughing, perceiving which Prince Heddar cried:

"Nay, but I understand your merriment. Nevertheless this is indeed the most wonderful object that can be produced in all the world. For if you but lay hold of it with both your hands, you may be carried to any part of the earth, wheresoever you will." And he took his brothers into the yard of the inn, and after they had all laid hands upon the rope Prince Heddar uttered the word "Damascus"; whereupon they were all instantly raised from the ground and were drawn through the air at an inconceivable speed.

And when they had once again returned to the caravansery Prince Kadi and Prince Assad marvelled greatly at the wonderful rope, while each was yet hopeful that his own discovery would be pronounced the most wonderful by the Sultan.

After they were once more seated before their wine at the inn, Prince Heddar called upon Prince Kadi to produce his discovery, whereupon Prince Kadi said:

"I am amazed greatly, dear Heddar, at your wonderful discovery, yet am convinced that I have brought back that which is still more wonderful." And he placed the shell, whereby might be heard any conversation in any part of the world, in the hands of Prince Heddar, saying: "Place this shell to your ear." And Prince Heddar placed it to his ear.

And Prince Kadi said: "Whatsoever voice you would hear, wish that it may be so."

But suddenly the brothers were affrighted to see an expression of unutterable sadness steal over the face of Prince Heddar; and with one voice they cried: "What hear you, my brother," And Prince Heddar cried out in anguish, "There is sorrow and wailing; and in all the palace of our father the Sultan there is but one cry: 'Meliha is nigh unto death! Depart not from us, beloved Meliha! Depart not from us!'"

And the brothers all cried together in anguish: "Meliha! Meliha!"

But suddenly the light of a great joy returned to the eyes of Prince Assad, as he remembered the gift of the Good Genie, and he cried: "Be comforted my brothers. For I have brought back not only the most wonderful object in all the world; but that which shall restore to perfect health our beloved cousin Meliha! Within this flagon is magical water from the Valley of Sogd, and whosoever shall drink of it, however sick he be, shall straightway recover."

As Assad made an end of speaking a great lamentation arose in the inn; and inquiring hurriedly as to the cause, they were told that the wife of the innkeeper, who was sorely ill, was passing away. And Assad demanded that he should be brought to her. And he and his brothers went and stood beside the pallet upon which the woman was lying, and taking a drinking cup Assad filled it with the magical water and placed it to the woman's lips. And having drunk she at once stood up and scolded her husband right vigorously for having brought strange guests into her room. And the brothers were delighted, and paid their reckoning and made haste to depart from the inn.

But when they would have inquired of any passing caravan, Prince Heddar laughed, and producing the rope bade his two brothers once again to lay hold of it. And they laid hold of it, and, after they had pronounced the name of the Sultan's kingdom, to the great amazement of the innkeeper and his wife, they were instantly raised from the ground and were drawn rapidly through the air; and in the twinkling of an eye they were transported into the bedchamber of Princess Meliha, who lay very sick surrounded by her weeping women.

And after the brothers had been warmly embraced by the weeping Sultan, Prince Assad knelt beside the couch of Princess Meliha. And he took a cup from the hand of an attendant and poured into it some of the water from the spring of the Good Genie. And he raised the head of the Princess Meliha and placed the cup to her lips. And she drank of the water, and, because Prince Assad believed that she would recover, straightway the Princess Meliha opened her eyes, after which she sat up as well as ever she had been. And after she had given thanks to Prince Assad, her eyes straightway sought those of Prince Kadi. And the Sultan observed it, and was sorely troubled. For by this time he had heard of the other wonderful objects, and though he dearly loved the Princess, he feared that no decision might yet be reached by this means. And after he himself had journeyed by the wonderful rope, and had hearkened to a conversation in a far-away kingdom, he called his sons once more to him and, embracing Prince Assad, pronounced as follows:

"The magical water which you have brought hither has indeed saved the life of our beloved Meliha; but without the shell of Kadi you would not have known of her sickness; and without the rope of Heddar you would not have been able to reach her bedside in time to save her. Therefore, my beloved sons," he continued, turning towards them all, "I am still unable to arrive at a decision, and I have decided upon yet another test, whereby one of you may hope to gain the hand of your cousin. Some moons ago in our forests three deer were born of one mother. These I have ordered to be brought hither. To-morrow each of you shall be set upon his horse, and after the deer shall have been freed, you shall follow after; and the one who shall bring back his deer the first shall receive the hand of the Princess in marriage as reward." And the three Princes promised to abide by the Sultan's decision.

And that same evening the three deer were brought to the palace of the Sultan. And with her own hands Princess Meliha tied on to the neck of each a riband: a red riband on to the neck of the deer drawn by Prince Heddar; a gold riband on to the neck of the one drawn by Prince Assad; and a blue riband on to the neck of the deer which had fallen to the lot of Prince Kadi. And none but the Sultan noticed how that the Princess Meliha bent her head and whispered into the ear of the deer which wore the blue riband. And the Sultan ordered a great feast to be prepared, and that night the palace made merry.

But early in the morning Prince Kadi rose early, and he stripped some strands from the rope of Prince Heddar, and bound them round the hooves of the deer wearing the gold riband, after which he took of the water of the magic spring, and gave it as drink to the deer which bore the red riband. Prince Kadi then returned to his chamber and prayed long and earnestly.

Great excitement prevailed in the palace the following morning; and soon the doors of the Sultan's stable were thrown open and the deer driven forth. And as soon as they were well away the three Princes mounted their horses and followed after. And the Princess and her women retired to the look-out in the palace tower; and the heart of Princess Meliha rejoiced to see how the deer wearing the blue riband was quickly overtaken by Prince Kadi, and how soon the deer which were pursued by Prince Heddar and Prince Assad disappeared out of sight. And that same day Prince Kadi returned, and the deer wearing the blue riband was fastened to the saddle of his horse.

Now the deer around the neck of which was tied the red riband was so vigorous after drinking of the water of the magical spring that Prince Heddar, who was pursuing it, had no time to notice how the deer of Prince Kadi had lagged behind. And it was fully two days before he came up with the deer, and yet another two before he returned rejoicing to the palace of the Sultan. But his joy was quickly turned to chagrin upon finding Prince Kadi already returned and the wedding preparations proceeding apace. For the Sultan had now fully decided that the right to Meliha's hand had been fairly won by Prince Kadi. Nor did Prince Heddar ever suspect the trick that had been played upon him by his brother. But remembering the words of the Maharajah of Nariampur, that behind his harem walls glistened eyes more wonderful than the most wonderful object in all the world, Prince Heddar immediately set forth again, nor even waited to be present at the nuptials of his brother.

As for Prince Assad, who followed after the deer which bore the gold band, there are those in the Sultan's kingdom, who to this day still talk of the deer of the gold band the feet of which scarcely seemed to touch the ground—so swift was its pace. Nor was the speed of the horse which Prince Assad rode any the less. For if there were any that Prince Kadi feared in the affections of the Princess, it was his brother Assad, and, perhaps in answer to his prayers, he had later bethought him to entwine a strand of Prince Heddar's rope in the hoofs of the horse which Prince Assad was to ride. But though Prince Assad was so quickly out of sight of both of his brothers, that he had not time to notice how the deer of Prince Kadi had lagged behind, yet he never suspected the trick which his brother had played upon him. So on and on went the deer; and on and on went Prince Assad after it, and it was not until the third day, when they were approaching a high mountain, that Prince Assad noticed how every now and again the deer would stop and look behind to see if he followed. At last the deer stopped altogether, and entering a circle of stones at the foot of the mountain, it sprang into the air, striking the earth again with all four feet. And three times it did this, and the third time Prince Assad, who had approached, heard a great rumbling; and suddenly a great crack appeared where the deer had struck with its feet, and Prince Assad beheld before him a flight of steps going deep into the bowels of the earth. And being of a bold disposition and ever ready for some new adventure, Prince Assad forgot all about the Princess Meliha, and forthwith descended the stairway, at the foot of which he espied an iron door. And as he laid his hand upon the door he again heard a greaat rumbling, and looking upwards he beheld the earth close over the stairway by which he had descended. And this time when he laid his hand upon the iron door it opened of its own accord, and Prince Assad beheld the entrance to the most wonderful palace he had ever seen.

Without any hesitation Prince Assad passed from one

empty room to another; for there were always the sweetest voices to lure him onward. And at length he came to yet another palace. And this also he entered—drawn on by the same sweet song. And in one of the largest and most beautiful rooms of the second palace he came upon a lady of most wondrous beauty, surrounded by her court. And she beckoned Prince Assad to approach; and he fell upon his knees before her. But the lady raised him up and bade him be seated near her. And after he had complied she spake as follows:

"Know Prince Assad that I have long awaited your coming; for I am not mortal, but a fairy and the daughter of one of the good genies that inhabit the underground regions. I am Fairy Nashara; and because I knew what happiness awaited you here, and deeming you worthier of a better fate than to wed the Princess Meliha, I caused your deer to bring you hither to me. By means of a clever trick your brother, Prince Kadi, succeeded in returning with his deer first to the palace of your father the Sultan, and the wedding preparations are already in progress. But be not angry; for all is fair where love is the reward. If you desire to return to the upper world, there are none here to prevent you. But if you choose to remain beside me as the partner of my life, I will command that the nuptial feast be prepared; and O! My Prince, what happiness shall be ours. Then choose!"

But before Fairy Nashara had concluded her words, Prince Assad, who had listened with a quickly beating heart, had fallen once more upon his knees before the lovely lady;

for by this time he was lost to all sense of the outer world. And the fairy rose and drew him towards her and embraced him; and afterwards they passed from one chamber to another—each one more exquisite than the last, the walls of which were encrusted with the rarest and richest of jewels, such as Prince Assad had never seen before in all his days. And at last they came to the banqueting hall where viands and wines from every clime were in readiness, and where the guests already awaited their coming. And genies and fairies danced and sang throughout the feast; and what with the sparkling eyes of his lady, and the sparkling wine in his cup, Prince Assad attained a bliss to which he had hitherto been a stranger. And as soon as the feast was over Prince Assad and Fairy Nashara rose from the table and passed into their chamber. And months passed away in such revelry and enchantment as surely is never experienced anywhere upon earth.

But at the end of six months Prince Assad one day bethought him of his father, and at the grief which he must surely feel at the prolonged absence of his son. And Prince Assad requested permission of Fairy Nashara to return for a brief space to his father's kingdom. And knowing the strength of the bonds she had woven around him, she consented, knowing well that he would return to her quickly. And she caused a retinue of exceeding splendour to be prepared for him, and after she had made him promise neither to reveal to his father the fact of their marriage, or of her quality, nor of their place of residence, she embraced him and sent him away; and Prince Assad journeyed happily towards his father's kingdom, at which he arrived before many days were over.

Now for long the Sultan had grieved for his favourite son Assad, believing him to have died. But at length he sent for his Vizier and took counsel with him respecting Assad. And the Vizier sent to the other side of the Sultan's domain for a sorceress, whose skill was far famed. But the sorceress could tell them nothing save that Prince Assad still lived. So great was the rejoicing when Prince Assad and his splendid retinue arrived at the palace of the Sultan; and the Sultan embraced Prince Assad with great joy, as also did Prince Kadi and his bride. And Prince Assad laughed at the trick that Prince Kadi had played upon him, and commended him for his ready wit. And he described to his father how the deer which he had followed had outstripped both of the others; and how it had led him to the greatest happiness he had ever thought to know. And he expressed himself as well content with his fate, concluding as follows:

"And I know well, Sire, that it was fate to which the deer straightway led me, and well content am I with my lot. But of your love and patience I pray that you will not seek to know more than this. For more I cannot tell you, and am only come hither in order to relieve your anxiety and to embrace you once again."

And the Sultan expressed himself as well satisfied; for at first he could think of nothing but that his beloved son was once again beside him. And for two days Prince Assad dwelt at his father's Court, after which he again embraced him and returned with his retinue the way he had come. And so great was the joy of Fairy Nashara at beholding him again, and so great her satisfaction at his return, that she suggested that he should forthwith visit his father once in every month. And this Prince Assad consented to do.

But O! great is the wickedness of the human heart; and after several months had passed, during which Prince Assad had visited his father's Court many times, the counsellors of the Sultan sought to make him jealous of his son's magnificence, which was greater with every visit. They counselled him to have Prince Assad followed; but Fairy Nashara provided the horses of Prince Assad with fairy wings, so that no mortal horse could keep up with them. And again the Vizier sent for the sorceress to beseech her aid. "For," said he to the Sultan, "who knows but that some day your son will come with a great force to drive you from your kingdom."

And the Sultan listened to his evil counsellor; for by this time he also greatly feared the mysterious power of Prince Assad.

But because of the secret power of Fairy Nashara, the sorceress was again unable to discover the place of sojourn of Prince Assad. But, owing to the fresh condition of the horses upon each arrival at the Sultan's Court, she judged that it could not be very far distant, and decided to find out by guile that which she had failed to discover otherwise. So the next time Prince Assad visited the Court of his father, the sorceress changed herself into a flea, and hid herself in the shining coat of the steed which Prince Assad rode. And in this guise she penetrated into the innermost precincts of the palace wherein dwelt Fairy Nashara; for as Prince Assad descended from his horse she sprang from the coat of the horse into the bosom of Prince Assad's robe. And great was the astonishment of the wicked sorceress to behold so magnificent a domain, and still greater was the envy. But as her power was far less than that of the Fairy Perie Nashara, she wreaked her spite by occasioning discomfort, not only to Prince Assad and Fairy Nashara, but to all their genies that formed their retinue.

Then Fairy Nashara knew that some mischievous power had by some means penetrated into her domain. And to Prince Assad she said: "And greatly do I fear that this wicked flea is none other than one of your father's spies." For by this time Prince Assad was fully aware of his father's fears concerning himself.

And the Prince was greatly concerned, and suggested to Fairy Nashara that no more should he return to the Sultan's kingdom. But Fairy Nashara would have none of it. "It is far better that you should return," she replied, "else will this wicked flea sojourn with us always. For if it in reality be one of your father's spies, it will surely follow you back to his kingdom again. Fear not; for I will let no harm befall you."

So Prince Assad returned again to his father's kingdom, and in the coat of his steed once again rode the wicked sorceress. But upon looking back she failed to discover the aperture from which they had issued.

And as soon as they arrived at the Sultan's palace the

sorceress resumed her own form, and hurried to the Sultan where he sat in council with his counsellors. And she told of all the wonders that she had seen, and of the power and might of the Fairy Nashara. But again she could not tell the Sultan where was Prince Assad's place of sojourn. And the counsellors made a great outcry that not only Prince Assad, but all his retinue, should be put to death. But the sorceress counselled otherwise.

"How shall mere mortals put to death a retinue composed of genies?" she cried. "And if you should kill Prince Assad, how will you prevent the retinue of genies from returning to Fairy Nashara with the news? Great then would be the fall of this kingdom and of its Sultan. Rather than court such certain disaster let the Sultan speak fairly to his son, bidding him perform such tasks as will bring credit to this kingdom, or in the event of failure provide the Sultan with an excuse to put Prince Assad to death."

And the Sultan and all his counsellors commended the sorceress for her excellent advice; and they loaded her with rich gifts.

And when the time came for Prince Assad to depart, the Sultan, after embracing him warmly, said: "Greatly do I rejoice at your prosperity, O my son; and that you have found such great happiness in the kingdom of your fairy wife, from whom I crave a slight boon. It has long been my wish that my palace were set in the midst of the forest which lies two leagues away. It will be a small task for your fairy wife to bring the forest up to my palace gates, and greatly would I rejoice thereat."

THE STORY OF PRINCE ASSAD

Now Prince Assad was greatly downcast at these words; for the gift of a fairy is a precious thing and not to be lightly employed. And he answered his father, saying: "Greatly as I desire to please you, I can promise nothing." For he feared to displease his fairy wife, whom he so greatly loved.

But as soon as Fairy Nashara embraced Prince Assad upon his return, she observed his downcast mien, and she made him tell her all that had passed, saying: "Never fear, beloved, but that I shall always rejoice over anything in which I can assist you. It is indeed a slight task for me to bring the forests up to the gates of your father's palace." And she called her treasurer and bade him bring her a magic twig which he would find in her treasury. And when he had brought it she called one of her genies, bidding him hasten and touch with the twig the foremost trees of the forest, after which the forest would follow him, so long as he carried the twig, right up to the gates of the Sultan's palace. And this was done, so that upon the next visit of Prince Assad to his father's kingdom, it was only with the greatest difficulty that he discovered the palace at all.

And the Sultan and his counsellors, who with fear had observed the approach of the forest, feared Prince Assad all the more. And after the Sultan had embraced Prince Assad, and had bidden him convey his thanks, to Fairy Nashara, he once again sought counsel with the sorceress. And the sorceress, intent on the ruin of Prince Assad, advised the Sultan to set him a task even more difficult than the first. And the thing that she advised was that the Sultan should now request Prince Assad to procure for him a flagon of the magical and healing water from the Fountain of Lions. "For surely," she said, "will Prince Assad be torn to pieces by the four lions that guard the fountain, should he attempt to draw water from it."

And the Sultan at once sent for Prince Assad; and so great was the anger of Prince Assad at this second request, that he forthwith left the palace of his father without having promised any performance of the matter.

And once again Fairy Nashara noted the downcast mien of Prince Assad. And again she comforted him, saying: "Ask whatsoever you will of me, my beloved. For surely will I grant yet further boons to the Sultan, and thereby foil the wicked arts of that vile sorceress." And Prince Assad told her everything, and how his father had requested a flagon of water from the Fountain of Lions.

Now at this moment Fairy Nashara was seated at her broidery. "This is a very difficult task for you to perform," she said; "for the fountain is guarded by four fierce lions. But fear not for I will avert all danger from you, and instruct you how you shall proceed. Take this bobbin and, having first provided yourself with a sheep cut into four quarters and with a horse upon which to load them, cast it upon the ground so soon as you shall have passed through the iron door, and it will roll before your horse until you come to the seventh palace from here. And you shall then enter in at the gate before which the bobbin shall stop, and in the middle of the palace courtyard you shall find the fountain guarded by four lions—two asleep and two awake. But be sure that so soon as you shall enter the courtyard the two lions that are awake will with their roaring awaken the two lions that sleep. Then shall you hurriedly cast to each of them a quarter of the sheep, and while they are devouring it you will have ample time to fill your flagon at the Fountain of Lions and depart."

And the next morning Prince Assad did as Fairy Nashara had directed. And he entered in at the gate of the seventh palace, before which the bobbin had ceased to roll; and there, in the middle of the courtyard of the palace, was the Fountain of Lions guarded by four lions. And the two lions that wakened aroused with their roaring the two lions that slept. But as they sprang towards him Prince Assad distributed the four quarters of the sheep amongst them, and whilst they were yet devouring the meat he hastily filled his flagon and hurried away. But great was his surprise upon looking back to see the lions following him two by two, and thus guarded did he proceed to the kingdom of the Sultan of the Indies, carrying the flagon of water from the Fountain of Lions.

And great was the dismay of the Sultan's Court at observing the Prince so accompanied. But even yet was the Sultan dissatisfied, and once again he sent for the sorceress, who this time advised the Sultan to demand of Fairy Nashara that she should send to the Sultan's Court the smallest man that mortal eye had ever seen. And this time Prince Assad, after his father's further demand, returned to his fairy wife in a great rage. But as before Fairy Nashara said: "It shall be done."

And she took a handful of magic powder, and cast it upon

an open fire, calling loudly: "Shiratz! Shiratz!" And a great smoke enveloped the fire, and out of it suddenly sprang the tiniest man upon which mortal eye had ever rested.

Now Shiratz was the brother of Fairy Nashara, notwithstanding which his face was very evil to look upon. And he demanded angrily of his sister what she required of him. And Fairy Nashara introduced him to her beloved husband, and told him of the constant demands of the Sultan and of the spite of the sorceress. And the dwarf bade Prince Assad place a pin in his right hand, and after Prince Assad had done so he placed Shiratz in his pocket and journeyed again to the Court of his father.

And again he found his father in consultation with his counsellors and, being bidden to enter the Council Chamber, Prince Assad placed Shiratz upon the table. And the Sultan and all his advisers were horrified at the ugliness of the dwarf.

But nevertheless the Sultan expressed himself as delighted with this further proof of the power of Fairy Nashara. But as he bent over the dwarf to examine him more closely, the hands of Shiratz grew larger and larger, and the pin which he still held in his right hand changed into a heavy bar of iron. And Shiratz brought down the bar of iron on to the head of the Sultan and all his counsellors as they bent over the table, and he cracked all their skulls as one cracks an eggshell, before that Prince Assad could do aught to prevent him.

And after he had made an end of the counsellors the dwarf demanded that the wicked sorceress should be brought before

him. And her skull likewise he cracked with the iron bar,
after which he demanded that Prince Assad should be proclaimed Sultan of all the Indies.

And this was done with great rejoicing, after which Prince
Assad returned with Shiratz to the kingdom of Fairy
Nashara, who returning with Prince Assad was proclaimed
with him, amid great acclamation, as joint ruler over all
the Indies.

The Story of Baba Abdalla

WANDERING one night disguised among his subjects, accompanied by his faithful Grand Vizier Ja'far, the Khalifeh Harun-er-Rashid was arrested by the cries of a blind beggar to whom he gave alms. Great, however, was the surprise of the Khalifeh when the beggar still continued to cry, importuning the Khalifeh to strike him a blow on the head with the stick which the beggar carried for that purpose. And so persistent was the beggar that the Khalifeh did as he was desired, first stipulating, however, that the beggar should tell them the reason for this strange conduct.

Know then, said the blind man, that I was born in Baghdad, and after my parents had died I found myself with sufficient property to enable me to live in comfort all my days. But I was not content, and spent not only my days, but many of my nights also, in thought how I might increase my wealth.

Allah rewarded my efforts, and I became so rich that at length I owned four score camels of my own. These I would sometimes let out to merchants, but more frequently I would load them with my own merchandise. But never at the hour of prayer, did I forget to give thanks to Allah for all that he had done to me.

One day returning from Balsora, whither I had gone with

my four score camels laden with all manner of merchandise, which I had sold for a good price, I met a Dervish, and as we were both tired we divided our provisions and sat and talked together. After we had discussed all manner of things the Dervish informed me that he knew of a place, not far distant, which contained treasure of immense value, and he expressed his willingness to lead me thither. Great was my joy, the more so that I saw no reason why the Dervish should wish to participate in the treasure. So embracing him warmly I said:

"If you will but lead me to the treasure and assist me to lade my four score camels therewith, I will not only give you one of my laden camels, but will remember you in my prayers to Allah all the days of my life."

Now I, of course, knew that this was not a fair offer; but the Dervish seemed a good-natured fellow, and it has always been my way to endeavour to secure the utmost in my power. For a moment the Dervish was thoughtful, after which he answered:

"What you propose, O my brother, is not just; for unless I take you to the place where the treasure lies, you will have no means of securing it. What I propose is this: In return for my kindness in leading you to the treasure, you shall give me half of your camels; and after we shall have loaded them with the treasure, we will separate and go our several ways."

As I now saw that the Dervish was a shrewder man than I had at first judged, I expressed my happiness to fall in with his plan, and after we had separated the camels—he taking forty and I a similar number—we proceeded together, and after travelling some time arrived at a valley, the entrance to which was very narrow. The mountains which bounded this valley were of a circular formation, and so high, and so close together that it was impossible that any one should see us, and it was necessary for the camels to pass through singly. Suddenly the Dervish halted us saying: "Go no farther. Stop your camels, and I will go on; for the place of the treasure cannot be far distant." But in my greed and anxiety I doubted his good faith; and as soon as he had disappeared round the bend of the valley, with his forty camels following behind, I beat my camels and hurried after him, and soon discovered him—in a widening of the valley—bending over a little fire of twigs, which he had gathered and placed before the face of the mountain. Taking a flint and steel he lit the twigs, and so soon as a thick coil of smoke arose from them he muttered some strange words and cut the smoke lengthways with his hand. And behind the aperture, which he had thus made, I observed the opening to a vast chamber; for the face of the cliff had rolled away, revealing such treasure as surely mortal eyes had never before gazed upon. Heaps of gold and precious jewels were piled upon the floor of the cave, and thrusting the Dervish aside I rushed towards one of the largest stacks of gold, and began frantically to fill one of the sacks with which I had provided myself.

When I had placed upon my camels almost as much gold as they could carry, I noticed that the Dervish had touched nothing save the jewels; and when he had explained that not only were the jewels lighter, but they were of infinitely more value, I at once began to pour out the gold from the sacks I had already filled, and replaced it with the jewels.

When we had both got nearly as much treasure as we could carry on our camels, I observed the Dervish go to a part of the cave where there were numerous rich vases of gold in every shape and size, all of them richly encrusted with precious stones. And from one of them the Dervish took a small box of wood, which he placed in the bosom of his gown. And though I pretended not to have observed the incident, I nevertheless remembered it.

And when the last camel was laden to the utmost, the Dervish again went through the same ceremony, and the treasure chamber vanished from our sight as though it had never been.

The time had now come for us to part, and after I had embraced the Dervish and had thanked him again and again we turned and went our several ways. But I had not gone a hundred yards when I was overcome with anguish at the loss of my forty camels, now laden with priceless treasure. "What earthly use," said I to myself, "can such loads of treasure be to a Dervish, who if he be a good Dervish should live in poverty and humility?" And without willing it I ran back to where the Dervish was disappearing round the bend in the valley, calling after him. And he returned immediately to where I stood, asking what further I would of him.

"As soon as we had separated," I replied, "I was overcome with remorse at the temptation I had thrust in your path.

For if I had not given you my camels, you could not possibly have carried the treasure away. Wealth is an accursed thing to those who would live in humility. Would it not then be a righteous act if I were to relieve you of still further ten camels, together with their loads?"

"I had not thought of it in that light," replied the Dervish. "No doubt you are right. The loads on the remaining thirty camels will suffice me for distribution to the poor." And after I had driven off ten of the camels he thanked me, and again we embraced and separated.

But even while turning away I was overcome with a species of terror at losing the remaining camels and their treasure. "Stay, O Dervish!" I cried. "What dreadful thing is this that I would do to you. Many a man has lost his soul through the wealth which is laden on one of those camels alone. The temptation is too great for one so holy as you. Let me relieve you of yet another ten camels." And again the Dervish agreed with me; and after that I had driven off yet another ten camels, he embraced me again, and after thanking me turned away. But this thing was now beyond my control; and I cried out even as he turned away. "Never shall it be said that through any act of mine perished the soul of one as holy as thou. Let me I pray you relieve you of yet another ten camels." And without this time awaiting his agreement, I drove them off with my stick. Then, as he would have moved off with the remaining ten I barred his way: "Think of the evil you would do should you distribute any of this wealth to the poor who are unused to such riches. Rather give them good words; and let me, who am used to responsibility, relieve you of this task." And the Dervish replied: "It is good. Take the remaining ten camels and use the treasure for the glory of Allah."

But my cupidity now knew no bounds; and suddenly I remembered the box which I had seen him take from a niche in the cave, and place in the bosom of his robe. Perhaps by means of this box I might yet attain the greatest wealth of all. So I cried out once again:

"Tell me, O Dervish, I pray you, what is in the box which I saw you take from the niche in the cave? Show it to me."

And the Dervish removed the box from the bosom of his gown and opened it.

"This," he said, seeing that I was determined, "is an ointment which, if spread around the left eye of any man, will reveal to him the situation of any hidden riches." And I implored him to give me the box; for I hated to see it in the hands of any other than myself. And this he did; expressing his happiness at being able to serve me in any way. And I asked him, since he knew more of the matter than myself, to smear some of the ointment around my left eye; determined to know, before we separated, whether he had told me the truth concerning the powers contained in the box. And he took some of the ointment and smeared it around my left eye, warning me, however, not to touch the right eye with the ointment, or surely I would go utterly blind. And as he smeared my left eye, as a light illumines the darkness, I suddenly saw all the hidden treasures of the earth. Only how to attain them was not revealed to me. And suddenly

I knew that the Dervish had lied, and that if I did but smear the right eye also with the ointment, my way to all the treasures of the earth would be opened. And I cried out: "Smear me the right eye also; then shall I know how to secure the treasure!" But the Dervish refused, saying: "Why should I do this evil thing to you? For so surely as you apply any of the ointment to your right eye, you shall surely be blind with both eyes."

And again I demanded this thing; and again he refused; so that at last losing all patience I seized the box from his hand, and digging my fingers into the ointment, myself applied it to my right eye. Would to Heaven that I had believed the Dervish; for the light was suddenly struck from both my eyes, and in turn I began to abuse the Dervish, and bemoan my wretched lot, beseeching the Dervish, again and again, to restore my sight; for of what use to me were all my camels and treasure, if I were to be deprived of my sight—the greatest boon of all. But the Dervish replied: "O wretched man! Not greater than the blindness of your heart is the blindness of your eyes. Justly is your greed punished; for though I possess many secrets, there is not one that shall restore your sight to you. Allah alone can now assist your unhappy lot. Cry to him unceasingly."

And despite all my tears and importunities he turned away, driving the treasure-laden camels before him. And in my despair I cast myself upon the ground, and should have died of grief and hunger if a caravan returning from Belsora had not picked me up and carried me into Baghdad. Thus did I fall from a princely condition to an abject state of beggary; but though the blindness of my eyes continueth, Allah has heard my prayers, so that no longer am I blind in my heart. But as a token of enduring repentance I carry this stick, with which I drove off the camels of the Dervish; and whosoever presents me with alms, I demand also that they give me also a blow from the stick.

So greatly was the Khalifeh Harun-er-Rashid touched with this story that he demanded that henceforth the Vizier should see to it that the blind beggar should be supplied daily with a pension of four drachms; for said he, "You have suffered enough, and though your sin was great, Allah has heard your prayers."

And at these words Baba Abdalla threw himself prostrate upon the ground; for by this time he was aware that it was the Khalifeh to whom he had told his story.

The Story of Ganem the Slave of Love

THERE once lived in Damascus a wealthy merchant named Abou Ayoub, who frequently journeyed to Baghdad, in order to sell his merchandise. But, death suddenly overtaking him, his son Ganem became the possessor of immense wealth in the form of a hundred loads of brocade, silks, and other precious materials.

Now Ganem, who lived with his mother and sister, the radiant Alcouza, Winner of all Hearts, being of an earnest disposition, decided to carry on his father's trade in Baghdad, over which ruled the passionate but just Khalifeh Harun-er-Rashid, Commander of the Faithful. So, despite the tearful importunities of his mother, he departed from Damascus, believing that no possible harm could happen to Alcouza and his mother; for peace reigned in Syria under the rule of Krashna, tributary ruler to his cousin the Khalifeh Harun-er-Rashid.

The journey was safely accomplished; for, in addition to his own slaves and one hundred camels, six other merchants had joined the caravan, it being the custom in those days, when Bedouin Arabs attacked and plundered the caravans, for merchants to travel together in large bodies whenever possible.

From the outset of his stay in Baghdad the young mer-

Adapted from "The History of Ganem, Son of Abou Ayoub, and known by the Surname of Love's Slave."—(Warne and Co., *The Chandos Classics*.)

chant was so successful that he hired a spacious house, with beautiful gardens, his merchandise being stored in some of the empty rooms. Thence every day, preceded by his slaves carrying his silks and brocades, he repaired to the market-place, where the merchants met to transact business. These men, together with their Syndic, or chief, in memory of the dead merchant Abou Ayoub, received Ganem with much courtesy, rendering him every possible assistance, with the result that Ganem sold whatsoever goods he offered, at the price demanded.

Upon one occasion when Ganem proceeded to the street of the merchants, he found all the shops closed, and upon demanding the reason was informed of the sudden demise of a wealthy Mahommedan merchant, whose funeral was even then taking place. So inquiring the way to the mosque, Ganem, who desired to pay all respect to the dead merchant, departed for the nearby village, which lay beyond the city gates. The obsequies, which would last many days, were already in progress when Ganem arrived at the mosque, around which the tents of the mourners were pitched. Ganem had not anticipated such a lengthy ceremony, and with the oncoming of night he began to feel anxious lest the city gates should have been closed, and his house and goods be left unguarded. So as soon as the day's rites were ended he made all possible speed towards Baghdad; but alas! he went astray in the darkness and arrived at the city gates after they had been closed. This was the more unfortunate since, the village being full of mourners, there was not even a tent to be had. So he repaired to a large cemetery and, for greater safety, lay down behind one of the tombs.

Being fatigued he soon fell into a sound slumber, from which he was awakened by the sound of approaching footsteps. Judge of his horror when, by the light of a lantern carried by a slave, he observed a long casket, borne upon the shoulders of three other slaves. Unaware of the intention of the intruders, Ganem watched them from his place of concealment and was amazed to see them, after that they had placed the casket upon the ground, begin to dig quite close to where he lay concealed. His curiosity was great, and he hoped by lying quietly to overhear the conversation of the slaves. His disappointment was keen and his curiosity none the less when the work proceeded in complete silence; and he concluded rightly that all four slaves were mutes, whose tongues had been taken out either as punishment, or in order that they might be employed upon matters of extreme secrecy.

After the men had buried the casket at no great depth, and had replaced the sod above it, they gathered up their tools and crept away as silently as they had come. By this time Ganem was convinced that evil work was afoot; else why had the slaves so obviously found the casket heavy to lift. Perhaps some murdered slave lay within. He determined to see what the chest contained, and waited but for the slaves to leave the cemetery before he crept out of his hiding place, and commenced quickly to scoop the soil out of the trench with both hands, and it was not long before the casket lay exposed to view. Working in haste, and with anything that came to hand, and not waiting to raise the casket from the trench, Ganem soon loosened the cover, which he cast hastily aside. A great cry broke from him as, lying within, he observed a maiden of incomparable beauty. And it was well that Ganem had worked so quickly; for the soft rose of life still lingered in her cheek, while her tender young breasts rose and fell with her gentle breath ing. From the jewels—pearls, rubies, and diamonds—that adorned her, as well as from the richness of her habit, Ganem judged the lovely creature to be one of the ladies of the Court. Trembling mightily Ganem lifted the maiden from the casket, and for an intoxicating moment she lay in his arms with her head against his breast. Suddenly she sneezed violently and sat up, calling aloud the names of her maidens, "Matoufa! Zouhara! Come to me!" And she clapped her hands three times, as is done in the East to summon the attendants. For all around her was dark, and she had of course no idea that she was in the cemetery. As for Ganem, who had sprung aside at the moment of her awakening, what between the violent beating of his heart and the fear to still further alarm the lovely lady, he knew not what to do.

But as she continued to cry for her attendants with in-creasing alarm in her tones, he fell upon his knees beside her, addressing her in the gentlest manner: "Dear lady, be not alarmed." And then he proceeded to tell her how the slaves had carried her hither in the casket, and how he had observed everything from his place of concealment. "And, dear lady, he concluded, "my heart cannot express its utter thankfulness at having been near to assist you in your great need; for surely if I had not been your sweet life would have been forfeit to the wickedness of your enemies." Then the lady, who had drawn her veil across her face as soon as she had realised that she was in the presence of a strange man, let fall the veil before one to whom she so obviously owed her life.

"Indeed, Sir," she said, "Allah be praised for sending so worthy a person to my assistance. And, since you have been so kind, extend, I pray you, your aid still further in carrying me from this place and concealing me from those who seek my life."

And straightway Ganem offered to take her into his own house in Baghdad, which offer she gladly accepted, promising to disclose everything when she should have arrived there. And as the night was fast waning, Ganem hastened to replace the cover of the casket, after which he filled in the trench again with the soil, carefully replacing the sod so that none might observe that it had been disturbed. And after he had bidden her draw her veil and follow close behind him, they made their way swiftly to the nearest cemetery gate. And by the grace of Allah a muleteer lay asleep outside the cemetery wall, and beside him stood his mule dozing on four legs. And bidding the lady tread softly, Ganem mounted her upon the mule; and after that he had placed three golden dinars beside the muleteer, Ganem softly led the mule toward the Baghdad gate which, Allah still being gracious, was now open. And as soon as they had passed through it they made all possible speed towards the house of Ganem. And after he had conducted the lady to a chamber he expressed his great joy at her presence there; and he bade her rest until that he should come again. And immediately he set forth again, nor returned until he had found suitable attendants for the lady, and fruit and meat for her entertainment, and such raiment and other requirements as he deemed necessary for one at once so delicate and so forlorn. And, as had been arranged, Ganem informed the women slaves that they were required for the service of his sister; and so great was the gratification of the lady for all Ganem's thought that not only did she demand that he should be seated beside her during the repast; but she laid her veil aside out of respect to one to whom she owed everything.

And after they had made an end of eating, and the slaves had withdrawn, the lady bade Ganem to be seated beside her on the sofa: "For," said she, "it is full time that I made all confidence to one who has not only saved my life, but who has treated me with all possible courtesy and kindness. Know then my lord, that I am Senabra, that favourite slave of the Khalifeh Harun-er-Rashid, and here is the proof of what I state." And she withdrew from her finger a band of gold bearing the name of the Khalifeh, and upon the inside of which were engraved the words, "The lips that the Khalifeh has kissed are sacred."

As he read this inscription Ganem uttered a bitter cry and, falling at the feet of the lady, he prostrated himself before her; and even though she raised him to his feet and once again seated him beside her, Ganem refused to be comforted, but continued to cry, whilst wringing his hands. . . . "Alack-a-day! Alack-a-day, how deep a wound is this, that I should have dared to love one already dedicated to His Majesty the Khalifeh. O woe! Bitter, bitter woe!"

Senabra's heart was deeply touched at this evidence of his regard. "My lord," she said, but, with renewed distress, Ganem interrupted:

"Call me not 'lord,' dear Madam; for I am none other than a merchant—respected it is true, but of no uncommon birth. Ah, Madam, how I could have served you—how loved you had you not been reserved for one so great and noble!" And tears dripped anew from between the hands with which Ganem had covered his face from the tender glances of this lady.

"And have you not served me; and do you not, then, love me, dear lord of my heart," whispered Senabra softly, bending towards Ganem who, after the first great amaze of rapture, lost no time in flinging his arms around his beloved; whilst it is greatly to be feared that he utterly forgot the inscription which the Khalifeh had caused to be inscribed within the gold band.

But it was otherwise with Senabra. "Nay, nay, dear heart," she remonstrated, whilst gently withdrawing from Ganem's arms; "have you then quite forgotten the relationship in which we stand to our sovereign lord, the Khalifeh, or that"—and her dimples played distractingly—"I am your sister?"

"No sister of mine!" cried the badgered Ganem, stretching out his arms again. But, frowning, Senabra eluded them.

"What is this! Must I then leave this house!" she cried angrily.

THE STORY OF GANEM THE SLAVE

"I am your slave," stammered the abashed Ganem.

"Will you not hear my story?" demanded the angry Senabra.

"Tell on!" replied Ganem sulkily, and, in order that he might not be again distracted, he prepared to listen with downbent eyes, despite all Senabra's efforts to draw them to her own again.

"Know then," continued Senabra, "that her most high Majesty, Queen Zobeida—that proud lady of Baghdad, in whose hands rests the power of life and death over her slaves —has deigned to be jealous of the favours extended by the Khalifeh to his humble slave, Senabra. Greatly did I fear the anger of this lady upon hearing of the intended absence of the Khalifeh—my sacred master—from Baghdad; and by some means—I know not how—upon the departure of the Commander of the Faithful, the Queen must have provided that a drug should be administered to me, and that I should then be prepared for burial and carried out of the palace as dead. Without doubt, if I may but rest here until the return of the Khalifeh three months hence, he will greatly reward you for the great service you have rendered me. For I will then discover myself to him. But before then I dare not return to the palace; nor must it be known that I am in the city; for surely will your life also be forfeit if it should be discovered that you have succoured me."

"As you have spoken, so shall it be, dear Madam"; cried Ganem, whose gaze now dwelt fondly upon his sweet lady. "In very essence shall you be cherished as my dear sister, until such time as it is safe for you to return to the palace of our Master the Khalifeh. And if my heart should throb the swifter at your footfall, or my cheek mantle at your touch, still will I not forget that I am your slave, and that you are the favourite of our sovereign the Khalifeh." And having spoken Ganem caused her attendants to be summoned, after which Senabra retired to her chamber.

Now while these things had been happening to Senabra, the heart of Queen Zobeide was sore dismayed. For, no sooner had her wicked will been accomplished upon Senabra, than she began to wonder how she should account to her husband, the Khalifeh, for the absence of his favourite slave.

All that night she lay awake, puzzling how she might best conceal her crime from the Khalifeh; but being by morning no nearer a solution, she sent in haste for a prudent old lady who dwelt in the palace, and who upon more than one occasion, by her good advice, had assisted Queen Zobeide to escape the consequences of her cruel and hasty acts.

But, after Zobeide had related to her how she had conducted herself towards her consort's favourite slave, the old lady was sore perplexed how best to advise the Queen; for there were none within the circle of the Court but knew in how great esteem Senabra was held by the Khalifeh. Nor was this the first time that Zobeide had evinced jealousy towards a slave whom the Khalifeh had delighted to honour; and even though the Queen had great influence over her husband, even a queen may fall before the anger of her thwarted lord.

"This matter, my dear mistress," said the old lady at length, "is one of the most difficult upon which I have yet

advised you; and I would with all my heart that you had not
acted so hastily. But the danger is greatly decreased owing
to the fact that Senabra is already secretly buried; and it
now only remains to hit upon some plan whereby we may
reasonably account for her demise and conduct the necessary
rites."

"But how shall we provide a funeral, lacking a body?"
cried the distracted Zobeide. "Alack! but my heart fails
me sorely."

"Have no fear, sweet mistress, all shall yet be well. But
go you hastily before the palace is astir to the chamber
where sleep Senabra's attendants. Them you shall inform
that Senabra is sick of an infectious fever, after which you
shall command Matoufa to accompany you to her bedside.
This woman must be the accomplice of our designs, her
tongue to be the price of her betrayal. Meanwhile I will
procure a wooden statue, which shall be secretly carried into
the palace and laid in Senabra's bed. And after some days
shall have elapsed it shall be known that Senabra has died
of the fever, and that because of the infection none may be
admitted to her chamber. I myself, aided by Matoufa, will
attend to the last sad rites."

And everything occurred just as advised by the old lady;
the dummy was hidden in the bed, and so great was the
fear of Matoufa lest her tongue should be torn out, that not
one word of the truth reached the ears of any in the palace.

And after the wooden statue had been interred, Zobeide
caused a magnificent monument to be erected over the grave;
fearing otherwise that her lord, the Khalifeh, might express

the desire once again to gaze upon the features of his beloved slave Senabra.   And the entire Court put on mourning, and the report of Senabra's death was spread throughout the city.

In due time the report reached the ears of Ganem, who hurried straightly to his house and informed Senabra of her supposed demise, adding: "And without doubt Queen Zobeide believes this to be the very truth.   So rest here in peace until such time as your lord shall return.   But O, that it were not forbidden to the slave to express his love for his master's favourite.   For then might we secretly forsake Baghdad, and enjoy our love in peace."

But as always Senabra did not encourage Ganem's wooing, though secretly much moved by it.   Instead, fearing for his life more than her own, she cautioned him again to employ the utmost discretion that none might know that she was concealed in his house, until the return of the Khalifeh.

And at the end of three months, having vanquished all his enemies, the Khalifeh returned to Baghdad amid great acclamation.   But upon approaching the palace he was greatly dismayed to observe all the outward signs of mourning, which dismay was in nowise abated upon being greeted by Zobeide and her attendants, all of whom were in deep mourning.

Great was the grief of Harun-er-Rashid, upon hearing of the demise of the lovely Senabra from an infectious fever; and he instantly demanded that he should be taken to her tomb.   His grief was increased owing to the fact that he might not look again upon the face of his beloved slave:

but none the less he commanded the weeping Zobeide for her thought in erecting so splendid a memorial to Senabra.

Upon re-entering the palace, the Khalifeh summoned his beloved Grand Vizier, Ja'far—whom none the less he later so cruelly caused to be executed. To him he gave orders that for the next month suitable portions of the Koran should be read morning and evening beside the tomb of Senabra, by the readers of the Koran. And this was done as commanded, in the presence of the Khalifeh himself, who never failed to bedew the tomb anew with his tears.

By the end of the month Queen Zobeide, who was weary of the protracted grief of her consort, had come to the conclusion that the dead Senabra was a far greater rival in the affections of the Khalifeh than when in life, and her conscience by this time being calmed, her active brain began to scheme anew how she might best tear the memory of her rival out of the heart of her lord.

Suddenly conceiving of an admirable plan, she hurried to the Khalifeh, whom she found sunk in deep melancholy.

"Sire," she said, upon being bidden to approach, "only the strongest considerations for your health compel me to disclose that which I am come to tell you. But it is not seemly that one so highly placed as the Commander of the Believers should continue to mourn one who has no merit in her."

"Speak you of Senabra?" demanded the Khalifeh, rising angrily.

Now mark well how sometimes those, intending to deceive with a lie, do but unconsciously reveal the truth!

"Of Senabra. O my lord!" cried the Queen, falling upon her knees before Harun-er-Rashid, "I did but cause the report of her death to be spread in order to save you from shame. Senabra—that ungrateful slave—has taken to herself a lover, a young merchant of the city."

So deep was the mortification of Harun-er-Rashid at these words, that waiting to hear no more he demanded that Ja'far should immediately be brought to him. Him he informed of what had occurred, instructing him that every house in Baghdad should be searched, and that Senabra and her young lover should be brought before him for punishment.

Seeing the rage of the Khalifeh, and in order to save time, the Vizier himself straightway repaired to the street of the merchants There he inquired of the name of any young merchant lately arrived in Baghdad, and upon the name of Ganem being pronounced, along with those of other young merchants, Ja'far commanded that these houses should be among the first to be searched.

The time was evening, and Senabra and Ganem, having just concluded dinner, were gazing out over the roofs of the city when the Khalifeh's guards, with their naked scimitars, and the Grand Vizier with the chief cadi, or magistrate, at their head, approached the house.

Senabra, who was the first to observe them, cried out in alarm. "Alas, Ganem, we are undone! Disguise yourself quickly and leave the house whilst yet there is time; for though the Khalifeh will pardon his favourite, most surely will he exact your life!" For too late, in this moment of peril, did Senabra regret her delay in seeking out the Khalifeh; nor could she deny the chains that had held her.

Though greatly reluctant, Ganem consented to do as Senabra suggested, fully realising that should trouble come to her by reason of this matter, he could render her more assistance alive than dead.

So, assisted by Senabra, Ganem donned the habit of one of his slaves, and after smearing his face and hands with soot, passed out of the house before the King's soldiers, bearing upon his head a pile of dirty dishes. And not only did none of the soldiers suspect the ruse, but they made way for the pushing fellow.

And after that the house had been surrounded by the soldiers, Ja'far himself entered it.

Great was his grief upon entering one of the empty rooms to discover Senabra seated upon a large crate; for with the quick wits of love Senabra had remembered that upon each bale of goods was impressed the name and station of Ganem. So does the dove beat helplessly around the hawk that steals her young, and already were all facts concerning Ganem known to the Grand Vizier.

"Unhappy lady!" cried Ja'far, prostrating himself before her, "would that some other than I have fulfilled this sad mission. Tell me—where is the young merchant Ganem? think not to save your lover from the just wrath of our sovereign lord, the Khalifeh!"

Greatly disturbed that the name of Ganem was already known to Ja'far, Senabra likewise prostrated herself upon the floor.

THE ARABIAN NIGHTS

"No lover of mine is the young merchant, good Ja'far," cried Senabra, "but one to whom I owe life itself. Let me have the audience of the Khalifeh and I am assured of this —not only will he not punish the merchant Ganem, but will reward him as his merits deserve. Then let us arise, good Ja'far, and go hence."

And this they did, and after Ja'far had caused the bales of merchandise to be removed to the palace of the Khalifeh, he followed after with Senabra.

But alas! for the hopes of the devoted Senabra; for whilst yet Zobeide lingered with her consort, word was brought of the arrival of Ja'far and Senabra—whom Zobeide had every reason to believe was dead—at the palace. Filled with horror and dismay, and greatly fearing what revelations Senabra might make, Zobeide simulated a fit of so grave an appearance, that none might approach Harun-er-Rashid that night upon whatsoever business. And by morning— between pity and weariness—the Khalifeh had consented to Zobeide's importunities to refuse audience to one who had so evilly betrayed him, and to have Senabra put to death.

Greatly he regretted this latter promise, the fulfilment of which he delayed from day to day; but the accomplishment of which had been fully recited to Zobeide, by the lips of none other than the Executioner, Mesrur himself.

But instead of executing Senabra, the Khalifeh had contented himself with keeping her imprisoned in the Dark Tower, whither she had been conveyed by the tender-hearted Mesrur, who continued to do everything he could for her solace and comfort. For indeed it grieved him to see his fair mistress in so sorry a plight.

But to the Vizier Harun-er-Rashid gave orders that not only should Ganem's house in Baghdad be razed to the ground; but that it should be lawful for the common people to strip Ganem, after which they should clothe him in a coarse shirt and stone him through the streets, if he should be discovered in any part of the Khalifeh's domain. And this same thing he wrote in a letter, which he sent by carrier pigeon, to his royal cousin, Krashna, ruler of Damascus, only adding: "And it is my will, if there shall be in Damascus, any relations, whosoever they may be, of Ganem the son of Abou Ayoub, that they likewise shall be likewise clad. And during the period of three days they shall be whipped through the streets of Damascus with strokes from the bastinado, whilst before them a crier shall go announcing: 'Behold the punishment inflicted by the Commander of the Faithful, upon such as offended him.' And none shall succour them or give them relief of whatsoever nature. And their house or houses shall be razed to the ground."

And because the family of Abou Ayoub was greatly respected in Damascus, Krashna, Ruler of Damascus, was greatly grieved upon receipt of this letter. But none the less he straightway himself went to the house of Ganem's mother; fearing, should he neglect to obey the commands of his cousin and overlord, to lose the sovereignty over Damascus.

He found the mother and her daughter, the radiant Alcouza, seated at their broidery, surrounded by evidences of the greatest wealth—Persian and Indian carpets, cushions covered with cloth-of-gold and silver, fine Chinese ware, and ornaments of gold. As soon as they recognised their royal master, they fell prostrate upon their faces.

"Nay, rise good ladies," said Krashna. "I was but wishing to learn if your son Ganem is here." And after they had denied all knowledge of him he informed them of the Khalifeh's will concerning them all. And as he witnessed their bitter grief, the soul of the tender Krashna cried out against Harun-er-Rashid for the task he had put upon him for performance. For it was now the duty of Krashna to bid the widow and her daughter gather together such articles of clothing as they would require; and after he had bidden them follow him, he commanded the masons, that had accompanied him thither, to hasten with the destruction of the house. , And so weeping behind their veils, and wondering greatly at what sin Ganem might have committed against the Khalifeh, the widow and beautiful Alcouza followed King Krashna through the narrow streets that led to the palace. For greater far than the fear of losing his kingdom was the King's chivalry towards the unprotected, and a plan had already sprung fully formed into his head.

Within the tower were two women under sentence of death. In order to escape with their lives these women would gladly undergo the punishment proscribed for the relations of Ganem. So after enjoining the utmost secrecy upon Alcouza and her mother, the King of Damascus placed them in the care of the queen's ladies-in-waiting. He then sent for the Vizier, who gladly entered into the plot, and the conditions being gratefully accepted by the condemned women, these were clad in coarse shirts, and after their hair had been combed over their faces, so that none might recognise them, they were whipped through the streets of Damascus for the three days as decreed by Harun-er-Rashid. And upon the fourth day they were set outside the city gates, to find refuge wheresoever they might.

Now for many days past there had been in the heart of Harun-er-Rashid a doubt concerning the guilt of Senabra; but seeing that Zobeide believed her already dead, the matter perforce rested where it was. Yet, though his heart was sore within him, yet was he none the less furious to hear that that very Ganem, whom he had given over to the populace, was demanding audience of him. In a great rage he commanded that Ganem should be driven away, and that his identity should be proclaimed throughout the streets by orders.

This was done, and sorely was Ganem beset by the mob that day, until at nightfall, broken and bruised, he staggered into a place of concealment.

But fearing for the fate of his beloved Senabra, Ganem was not to be turned from his purpose of gaining the ear of the Khalifeh; and whilst yet the night darkened in the streets he crept again towards the palace, standing without which he unceasingly continued to cry: "Hear me, thou great Commander of the Faithful. What a reward is this to those who virtuously serve you? Senabra is in the Dark Tower, whilst Ganem, who rescued her from the wicked toils of those most near to you, is stoned through the streets of Baghdad. Awaken! thou Commander of the Faithful."

Fearfully came this cry from out the darkness into the royal chamber, where Zobeide lay beside her royal consort. In vain she endeavoured to control the trembling of her limbs; for was she not in very truth at that moment most near to the Khalifeh? In very truth she believed it to be the voice of vengeance itself.

As for the Khalifeh his amaze was beyond all reckoning. His doubts increased, and for the first time they turned towards her who in very deed was most near to his person. And always he pondered deeply in his heart.

And thenceforth, for many nights, was heard this voice of accusation by the occupants of the royal chamber. And as he bent his gaze upon his Queen, the countenance of the Khalifeh grew darker and darker, while that of Queen Zobeide grew paler and paler. And every day Ganem braved the fury of the mob, in his attempt to gain the ear of the Khalifeh; and every evening he crept to his place of concealment.

And be very sure that the report of these strange happenings in Baghdad was not long in arriving at Damascus, where they soon reached the ears of Ganem's devoted mother and sister. Great was their grief.

"My son! my son!" cried the widow, "what terrible obsession of love possesses you that for sake of it you die a thousand deaths daily in the streets of Baghdad. My son! my son, whom I never more shall see!"

Indeed the widow was long past consolation; but though great her grief it was far other with the beautiful Alcouza, whose wits were already planning how she might best serve her beloved Ganem. And before very long a plan to gain the ear of the Khalifeh of Baghdad had formed itself in her brain.

In those days it was the custom of tributary sovereigns to send rich gifts to their overlords; and seeing that the anniversary of Harun-er-Rashid was approaching, the King of Damascus had gathered together six slaves of surpassing loveliness. Yet none of them, be it said, was so fair, nor so radiant as was Alcouza—Winner of all Hearts.

Among these maidens chosen for the delight of the Khalifeh was Nantouka, the foster-sister and one-time handmaiden of Alcouza, to whom she was deeply attached. The gratitude of her heart alone induced Nantouka to fall in with Alcouza's plan, whereby, upon the first night of sojourn, upon the road to Baghdad, Alcouza should creep into the chamber where Nantouka lay, and change garments with her. And though it was with many misgivings that Nantouka observed Alcouza depart with the other slaves, she tarried not but hastened back to the palace, whilst it was yet dark.

Sad was the outcry of the widow upon hearing Nantouka's news. "Great Allah! Is then the cup of my affliction not yet full? Must I also lose my daughter—my radiant Alcouza!"

But being at last persuaded that by now, whatsoever the outcome, the thing was past all mending, the widow placed Nantouka in Alcouza's chamber, and when full morning came, informed the household that Alcouza was sick of a nervous disorder.

Before many days were past the women slaves and their escort arrived at Baghdad; and if anything could have lightened the dark mood of Harun-er-Rashid, it would surely have been the sight of these lovely damsels. He bade chambers to be allotted to them, and feasting and music to be prepared. And that night there was great revelry. A rich dinner was served, during which Queen Zobeide sat at the right hand of the Khalifeh. But Harun-er-Rashid had only eyes for Alcouza, as she sang and danced before the royal guests. And she danced the bitter memory of the pale queen from out his weary brain; and the memory of the long-mourned Senabra, who languished in the Dark Tower, from out his heart. Alcouza! Alcouza! Winner of all Hearts! Radiant as the morning; fragrant as the dawn— who shall withstand you!

So great was the fascination which Alcouza exercised over Harun-er-Rashid that he suddenly terminated the revels. And he commanded that every one, including Queen Zobeide, should retire—all save Alcouza. Thus does retribution surely follow. For if Zobeide had feared the rival charms of Senabra, how much greater were those of Alcouza!

And when they were alone the Khalifeh demanded that Alcouza should ask of him whatsoever she would. But she feared yet to put her charms to the test by craving the pardon of Ganem.

"Let me delight my lord in whatsoever manner he desires," she replied. And what with singing and dancing, and something of love, the night was far spent before they retired to the royal chamber.

THE STORY OF GANEM THE SLAVE

Yet in the first hours of her slumber was Alcouza aroused by the voice of Ganem without the palace, crying as before: "Hear me, thou Commander of the Faithful! What a reward is this to those who faithfully serve you. Senabra is in the Dark Tower, whilst Ganem, who rescued her from the wicked toils of those most near to you, is stoned through the streets of Baghdad. Awaken! thou Commander of the Faithful!"

"It is indeed the very voice of Ganem!" said Alcouza within her heart. But not until the cry had been repeated three times did she feign to awaken from slumber.

"What strange thing is this, my lord!" she cried, starting up in well-simulated affright.

"It is nothing save the watchmen calling the hours," replied the Khalifeh. "Fear nothing. You did but dream."

But even as he replied the cry came again. "Hear me, thou great Commander of the Faithful! What a reward is this to those who faithfully serve you? Senabra is in the Dark Tower, whilst Ganem, who rescued her from those most near to you, is stoned through the streets of Baghdad. Awaken! thou Commander of the Faithful!"

"Nay, but that is the cry of no watchman," cried Alcouza; "and greatly do I fear for the safety of your sacred person. With your most august leave I will bid the man go hence." And flinging the casement wide she cried: "Get you gone, rascal, nor dare to disturb the slumber of your most sovereign lord the Khalifeh, the most sacred Commander of all Believers! Begone! I tell you!"

Judge of Ganem's amazement to hear the voice of his

[293]

beloved sister issue from the royal chamber at the midnight hour. But aware of her mettle he made no demur, but raising the missive which she had dropped, arranging a meeting-place, he disappeared into the darkness.

And the next even, after the hour of sunset, they met at the place appointed. And after Alcouza had fed Ganem, and had bathed his wounds, weeping bitterly the while, he told her of all that had passed, of his love for Senabra, and of the evil part that Queen Zobeide had played against her.

And hot was the faithful heart of Alcouza against Zobeide; but fearing her undoubted power over the Khalifeh, she bided her opportunity, even requesting from time to time that she might replace the queen's tirewoman. And it being her first desire to weaken the influence of Zobeide over the Khalifeh, it so happened that one day, whilst darkening the queen's eyebrows, she let fall several drops of the stain over the fair neck and face of Zobeide. Nor did Zobeide dare to wreak her spite for this against the latest favourite of Harun-er-Rashid, but feigning illness kept to her own apartments until the stain should have disappeared.

And be very sure that Alcouza made the most of this opportunity to ingratiate herself into the affections of Harun-er-Rashid, with the result that he soon could deny her nothing—had it even been the head of Zobeide itself. So the next time that the Khalifeh asked wherein he might serve one who had grown so dear to his heart, Alcouza replied:

"Make me a great feast, and this very night will I make my request of you—O most honoured and royal master!"

THE STORY OF GANEM THE SLAVE

And never within the memory of any within the palace had a feast of such magnificence been prepared; and in the place of Zobeide, Alcouza sat at the right hand of Harun-er-Rashid. And this marked all the great nobles assembled.

And whilst the feast was yet at its height Alcouza arose from her place. And she danced before her lord as the trees sway in the wind, and as the lilies dance in the breeze, until the Khalifeh's heart melted within him for very joy of her. And as upon the first occasion the Khalifeh suddenly commanded the music to cease, and the guests to depart.

And after that they had all gone he dismissed the slaves, and would have drawn Alcouza down beside him upon the couch saying: "Now ask of me that which you have hidden from me so long. For surely can I deny you nothing, O source of all my delight!"

But refusing to be seated Alcouza fell upon her knees before Harun-er-Rashid. And with tears streaming from her eyes, she admitted her relationship to Ganem, after which she told the Khalifeh all that she had learned from Ganem concerning the treachery of Queen Zobeide towards the Khalifeh's favourite slave. And she prayed that Ganem's great sufferings might be remitted, offering her own life in exchange, if in very truth he had been false to the Khalifeh's most sacred person.

"For O, most beloved Sire, if this thing could be, the desire of life would utterly depart from your Alcouza. Send then, I pray you, for that slave Senabra and let her tell us the truth of this matter."

And Harun-er-Rashid, who was greatly distressed at all

that he had just heard, summoned a slave and commanded that Mesrur, the Executioner, should bring Senabra before him.

And when Senabra entered the presence of Harun-er-Rashid, she prostrated herself before him in all humility. And, looking down upon her, the Khalifeh commanded that she should tell him everything that had happened since he had departed from Baghdad. And this she did, word for word, tallying with that which Alcouza had already related to him; for she even knew—Mesrur having kept her fully informed—of the dreadful persecution which had been endured by Ganem for her sake. And when she had made an end of speaking the Khalifeh replied:

"I fully believe all that you have told me; but why did you delay in informing me of all you had suffered after my return to Baghdad? This is your greatest fault, and much suffering would thereby have been averted."

But Senabra replied that, desiring to keep the fact of her presence secret, Ganem had seldom left the house; and so he had not heard of the Khalifeh's return to Baghdad. "For this I know, Commander of all Believers, this Ganem, who rescued me from a living death and kept me in all honourable respect until your Majesty's return, had but one object—to cherish the honour of your Majesty even as his own. You, Commander of the Faithful, are well aware in what manner he has been rewarded. Pardon him then, restore unto him his possessions, and let him depart to his own city in peace."

Then the Khalifeh bade Senabra rise. "I own my fault,"

he said, "and not only will I conduct myself towards Ganem as you have requested, but I will grant unto him whatsoever he may require at my hands."

And after having been informed by Alcouza of Ganem's hiding-place, he commanded that Ganem should be brought before him.

And great as was the Khalifeh's sorrow at beholding the results of his anger—so terrible was Ganem's appearance—the sorrow of Senabra was so far greater that she swooned away, and forgetful of all else Ganem fell upon his knees beside her in an ecstasy of grief.

And after so regarding them for a moment in silence, the Khalifeh bent down and gently withdrew from Senabra's finger the band of gold wherein was engraved "The lips that the Khalifeh has kissed are sacred."

He then departed from the room, first having instructed Alcouza to impart his good will towards them.

And the following night was another great feast prepared and, as before, Alcouza sat at the right hand of Harun-er-Rashid. And upon her finger was a broad band of gold.

THE END